TRAVELLERS

A Novel

HELON HABILA

PENGUIN BOOKS

PENGUIN BOOKS

UK | USA | Canada | Ireland | Australia
India | New Zealand | South Africa

Penguin Books is part of the Penguin Random House group of companies
whose addresses can be found at global.penguinrandomhouse.com.

First published in the United States of America by
W. W. Norton and Company 2019
First published in Great Britain by Hamish Hamilton 2019
Published in Penguin Books 2020
001

Permission granted by Ayebia for Helon Habila's quote from his poem 'Three
Seasons' from *Fathers & Daughters: An Anthology of Exploration* Ed. Ato Quayson
(2008): © Ayebia Clarke Publishing Limited, Banbury, Oxfordshire, UK.

Printed and bound in Great Britain by Clays Ltd, Elcograf S.p.A.

A CIP catalogue record for this book is available from the British Library

ISBN: 978-0-241-98629-5

www.greenpenguin.co.uk

For Sharon, Adam and Edna

And for Sue

I cannot rest from travel . . .

ALFRED, LORD TENNYSON, 'ULYSSES'

It is part of morality not to be at home in
one's home.

THEODORE ADORNO, *MINIMA MORALIA:*
REFLECTIONS FROM DAMAGED LIFE

Acknowledgements

My gratitude, first and foremost, to the voices whose stories animate this book – thanks for trusting me with your stories. In your travels, may you find the home you look for.

Thanks to my friends who made the time to read various versions of these stories and made suggestions, especially with the German language: Pascale Rondez, Branwen Okpako, Funmi Kogbe, Zainabu Jallo, Panashe Chigumadzi and Kai Hammer.

Johanna Meier, thanks for being my guide in Berlin.

Thanks to my agents, David Godwin and Ayesha Pande, for your undying support and encouragement, and for taking care x Acknowledgements

of business. To my editors, Simon Prosser and Alane Mason, it's been a long journey over the years; thanks for making me a better writer.

The excellent *Tears of Salt: A Doctor's Story* by Pietro Bartolo and Lidia Tilotta was quite helpful in making me understand other dimensions of the refugee crisis in Europe.

The video installation referenced in Book 1 is by Branwen Okpako.

Thanks to the DAAD Fellowship for that magical year in Berlin. This book wouldn't have been possible without your support. To Flora Veit-Wild and Susanne Gherrmann at the Institute for Asian and African Studies, Humboldt University, Berlin, thanks for your friendship and support.

Finally, to those not mentioned here, you are always in my heart. Knowing you has changed me for ever.

TRAVELLERS

Book 1

ONE YEAR IN BERLIN

We came to Berlin in the fall of 2012, and at first everything was fine. We lived on Vogelstrasse, next to a park. Across the road was an *Apotheke*, and next to that a retirement home, and next to that a residential school for orphans. The school was once a home for single mothers, but eventually the mothers moved on and only the children were left. The school is made up of two cheerless structures – one noticeably newer than the other – behind waist-high cinder-block walls and giant fir trees. In the evenings the children ran in the park, jumping on trampolines and kicking around balls, their voices cutting through the frigid air clear as the bell ringing. In the mornings they sat in the courtyard behind the short fence to craft wooden animals and osier baskets under the watchful eyes of their minders. Once, out early with Gina, one of the boys, anywhere between the ages of eight and ten, sighted us and rushed to the low wall, he leaned over the top, almost vaulting over, his face lit up with smiles, all the while waving to us and shouting, '*Schokolade! Schokolade!*' I turned away, ignoring him. Gina stopped and waved back to him. 'Hello!' How his eyes grew and grew in his tiny face! Surprise mingled with pleasure as he ran back to his mates. He repeated this whenever he saw us, and Gina always indulged him, but I never got used to it. I never got used to the thin, eager voice, and how the other children, about a dozen or so, stopped and raised their eerily identical blond heads and blue eyes to watch him waving and calling '*Schocolade!*' as if his life depended on it.

•

I first met Mark when he came to the house with one of Gina's flyers in his hand. 'I am here for this,' he said, waving the yellow flyer. It said Gina was working on a series of portraits she called *Travellers*, and she was looking for real migrants to sit for her. Fifty euros a session, to be paid for by the fellowship. I pointed him to the guest room she had converted into a studio. Soon their voices carried to the living room, hers polite but firm, his questioning, arguing. He was being turned down, and I could have told him not to press, Gina would never change her mind. Later, when I asked her why, she said he wasn't right and didn't elaborate, but I guessed he looked too young, his face was too smooth and lacking the character only time and experience brings. Last week she had drawn a lady and her four-year-old daughter. I met the lady in the living room waiting for Gina to set up her easel, still wearing her outdoor coat, an old woollen affair, and when I asked her if she wanted me to take the coat she shook her head; I turned to the daughter, did she want a drink, she pulled the child closer to her. The week before that it was a man, Manu, who told me he was a doctor in his former life, now he worked as a bouncer in a nightclub, waiting for the result of his asylum application. His face was lined, prematurely old, and I knew Gina would love those lines, each one of them an eloquent testimony to what he had left behind, to the borders and rivers and deserts he had crossed to get to Berlin. She would also love the woman's hands that tightly clutched her daughter's arm, they were dry and scaly, the nails chipped, no doubt ruined while working in some hotel laundry room, or as a scullery maid.

Mark came out of the studio and stood by the living-room door, a wry smile on his face, his red jacket in one hand, still holding the yellow flyer in the other hand. Behind him Gina, in her paint-spattered overalls, was already back at her painting, dabbing away at the easel, her face scrunched up.

'I'll walk you to the bus stop,' I offered. I had been indoor all day reading, I needed to stretch my legs, or perhaps I felt sorry for him, coming all the way for nothing, or I might have sensed something intriguing about him, something unusual that maybe Gina had sensed as well, and for that reason had turned him away. That same thing that made her send him away had the opposite effect on me, it drew my attention. Right now he looked dejected, as if he had already made a budget for those fifty euros, which he was now realizing he would never see. I asked him if he had ever sat for a painter before. He hadn't. Who had, apart from professional models, but he thought what she needed were ordinary people, real people, and wasn't he real enough?

I walked ahead of Mark, down the stairs to the ground floor and out the door. My intention was to leave him at the bus stop and continue on across the road to the little lake where I sometimes went for a walk, but the bus was pulling away as we arrived and I decided to wait for the next bus with him, and when the bus failed to come on time he said he'd go by foot and on a whim I said, 'Let's walk.' It was spring and the sun lingered in the west, unwilling to set, its slanted rays falling unseasonably warm and bright. Perfect weather. We joined the flow of after-train crowd past the wurst stand, past the strawberry-coloured strawberry stand. Berliners sat alfresco eating ice cream beneath beach umbrellas, *Eis*, the sign said. Ahead of us a chubby diminutive lady in a red jacket was shouting into her phone, *Nein! Nein!* as she paced back and forth on the sidewalk, staring down passers-by. And the more people stared the higher her voice rose; for a moment she was famous. '*Nein! Ich weiss es nicht!*' she shouted, basking in the sunrays of her notoriety.

We passed a Roma couple on a bench next to a Kaiser's store, their dull, beady eyes focused on their daughter, who stood by the sidewalk with a pan in her hand. Mark walked with his head bowed, muttering to himself.

'It is a lovely day,' I said. He nodded. I'd walk with him, but it wasn't my duty to cheer him up. Two ladies walked just ahead of us, at the same pace as us, always a few steps ahead, and it was a pleasure to watch their slim and shapely bodies beneath their identical jean jackets, and their blonde hair bouncing with each step, hand in hand. They belonged to this day. One was older, in her forties perhaps, the other looked to be in her twenties; mother and daughter, or sisters, or friends, or lovers; there was a gentleness to their clasped hands, especially next to the rude screeching of tyres and the blaring of horns from the motor road.

On both sides of the road neon signs on storefronts blared out: *McFit, McPaper, McDonald's* – a very American top layer over the more traditional back streets and side streets and sleepy quarters that still throbbed on, timeless, like the tram tracks buried beneath the concrete and tarmac. In our first couple of months in Berlin, Gina and I had walked these back streets that led away from Kurfürstendamm and on and on and narrower and narrower to the front windows of artisans' workshops and soup kitchens and *Blumen* stores and family homes with children and parents seated at the table eating dinner. Just a few months ago these streets were empty and snow-covered, with garish Christmas lights strung from every leafless tree and storefront like charms to ward away winter's malevolent spirits. At George-Grosz-Platz the two women disappeared into a beauty store. Mark and I sat in the square and watched the yellow double-decker buses stop and start, and stop again, the people coming off and on. We sat, not talking, just enjoying the last sunrays of the day. Mark looked round at the people seated in front of the roadside cafés drinking coffee and smoking cigarettes and said, 'This could be Paris.' After about thirty minutes he sighed and stood up, waved and walked away with slow steps toward Adenauerplatz station. I wondered what his story was, if I'd see him again.

I continued to sit in the dying sunlight, wrapped up in my thoughts. A fat-jowled man ran awkwardly after a M29 bus, but he was too late. He stopped and waved his arms in frustration as the bus pulled away, his open trench coat flapping about him, but when he turned I saw it wasn't a man but a woman, her thick, porcine jowls clenched in annoyance. A young lady in high heels came off the M19 and sat on a bench next to me. She took out a lipstick and a mirror. When she returned the lipstick and mirror to her bag, she looked up and our eyes met, she smiled, and then she was gone, walking at that surprisingly fast clip people here have. I could have started a conversation, I could have said 'Hi', and we might have sat, and talked, elegant like Parisians. We might talk of George Grosz, after whom the square was named, painter, intellectual, rebel, who survived the First World War, and defied the Nazis in the Second, and fled to America only to be driven back to Berlin by nostalgia; he fell down a flight of stairs after an all-night bout of drinking.

'A beautiful death,' she might have said. But as I watched her go, I felt the already unbridgeable gap between me and this city widen. Even if I spoke her language, the language the city spoke, would she understand me? A month ago I had gone to the post office to post a letter, and the lady behind the counter, a flaxen-haired battleaxe, had stared at me, refusing to speak English, and we had stood glaring at each other as the line behind me grew and grew, she kept shouting German words at me, and I kept answering back in English, I wanted to buy stamps, I wanted to post my letter, till finally a lady from the back of the line stepped forward and interpreted. It was a tense standoff while it lasted, and I was sweating when I came out. A week later I started taking German classes.

2

'**Y**ou must come, darling,' Gina said to me a year ago in our home in Arlington, 'I can't do it without you.' She had been offered the prestigious Berlin Zimmer Fellowship for the Arts. One year in Berlin. Perhaps this was what we needed, a break from our stagnating life and routine. Every year the Zimmer selected ten artists – writers and painters and movie directors and composers – from around the world, and this year Gina was one of two artists from the USA. She was an assistant professor at a local university, while I was teaching ESL to Korean immigrants in a back room in the local library. I was also a TA in my school, it paid for my tuition, but teaching was something I did with circumspection. Whenever I stood in front of the expectant young faces I felt like a fraud. Would they take everything I told them as the gospel truth, and what right did I have, what knowledge, what experience, to place myself before them as an authority? I was only thirty-five; perhaps if I were fifty, if I had travelled a little more, lived a little more . . .

'It is only a job, darling,' Gina, always pragmatic, told me. 'You are being overconscientious.'

Or maybe it was my fear of commitment – Gina mentioned this, referring not just to my uncompleted PhD dissertation, but also to the fact that we had promised to get married after graduating. She had graduated, I hadn't. We had lived together for three years in her tiny student apartment overlooking a parking lot. But no, I told her, it was only my immigrant's temperament, hoping for home and permanence in this new world, at the same time fearful of long-term entanglements and always hatching an exit plan.

But we did get married, and it was a good marriage, stable, we had our routines, like most married people, we woke up together, we went to work, in the evenings we sat on our narrow balcony overlooking the parking lot sharing a bottle of wine, sometimes we went to the movies, or to dinner, and perhaps that was why I hesitated to say yes to Berlin: What if we went and things changed between us? What if Berlin transformed us beyond where we wanted to go? It was obvious to me that part of the reason she applied for the Zimmer, apart from its prestige and its importance to her career, was because my dissertation was on nineteenth-century African history, on the 1884 Berlin Conference specifically, and what better way to encourage me to resume my research than by spending a year in Berlin? Still I hesitated because I knew every departure is a death, every return a rebirth. Most changes happen unplanned, and they always leave a scar.

Two months after our marriage Gina got pregnant. We hadn't planned on that, and we certainly hadn't foreseen losing the pregnancy after just seven months. Devastating for both of us, but something shifted in Gina. She stopped going out; she cried all day; she stopped eating. There wasn't much I could do; I sat by her side, held her hand, I reminded her we were still young and there'd be opportunities to try again. I read her poems, something I used to do a lot before we got married. Her middle name was Margaret, and I would recite Hopkins's 'Spring and Fall' to her: *Margaret, are you grieving / Over Goldengrove unleaving* . . . It always cheered her up, and she'd smile and shake her head; but not this time. She turned her face to the wall and curled into a ball, making herself smaller, like a tiny foetus. Gina had always been strong, maybe stronger than I was, certainly more resourceful than me, and this was the first time I was seeing her so helpless. How suddenly and unexpectedly everything had changed, one moment we were a normal married couple, young, with our future before us, the next moment we were stricken by misfortune, prone and helpless.

One day she went to visit her parents in Takoma Park and didn't come back; the next day her mother came and threw Gina's things into a bag and said Gina needed to rest, to recover, she added, her demeanour hinting that I was to blame for her daughter's breakdown. I got along better with the father, a retired professor who had spent a year in Nigeria on a Fulbright scholarship in the 1980s, and who always looked back to that year with great fondness. Alone in our two-room apartment, every morning I put in a call to Gina to see how she was doing, and to find out when she was coming back, and after that, with nothing more to do but sit and twiddle my thumbs in front of the TV, I began to drink. I drank in the nights at first, then in the afternoons, then in the mornings. I was sliding down a precipice, but I was unable to stop.

Gina stayed at her parents' for six months, and it was while she was there that she applied for the Zimmer. Exactly six months to the day she left, she walked into our tiny apartment, her eyes shining with hope and excitement as she showed me the Zimmer fellowship email. That night she didn't go back to her parents'. We lay in one another's arms all night long. Berlin. Maybe this was what we needed. A break from our breaking-apart life.

3

Even in Berlin I miss Berlin, Mark loved to say. He lived in Kreuzberg with his three friends, Stan, Eric and Uta, in an abandoned church building next to the river Spree. The church was tilted, as if a fingertip push could topple it, one of those crumbling buildings you occasionally saw around Berlin, spared by the war, and overlooked by the demolition ball, looking odd next to the newer structures. A baroque façade with a twisted spire faced the street behind a thick wire fence that cut off the building from the neighbouring houses and the passing cars. Most of the doors and windows were gone. In the courtyard the wind, like a restless spirit, drove pieces of paper and beer cans over the unruly grass in the driveway.

Mark and his friends had inherited the dwelling from another group of 'alternatives' who had moved on to Stockholm in search of stiffer anti-establishment challenges when Berlin grew too tame for them.

'I had to deconsecrate it when we moved in,' he said. 'There was a spirit living in the walls. I have a sense for these things.' It was one of his outlandish yet casually uttered comments that would have sounded crazy coming from another person, but from Mark it sounded normal, even reasonable. I met him again toward the end of spring, in a gallery. Gina was sleeping all day after working through the night – she wouldn't wake up till late afternoon when she'd emerge looking drawn and ethereal only to grab a sandwich from the fridge and go straight back to work – and I was left alone to stumble from place to place, mostly art galleries and libraries. I had learned about this particular exhibition from the emails sent to Gina by the Zimmer people. The gallery was exhibiting apartheid-era portraits by South African photographers. A young lady at the entrance handed me a pamphlet which proclaimed in bold Helvetica the bombastic title of the exhibition: *Apartheid, Exile and Proletarian Internationalism*. There were also photographs and video installations from local black artists. I drifted from room to room, reading the texts below the portraits – the photographs were mostly of South African exiles in East and West Berlin in the 1970s and 1980s. I looked at the unsmiling faces, thinking how ironic history was, that they'd come for succour here, escaping persecution and apartheid, this place that a few decades earlier had been roiling with its own brand of persecution under the Nazis. How did they cope with the food, the new language, with being visibly different, with the bone-chilling winter of exile? Most of them had returned to South Africa, those who had survived exile's bitterness, and were now their country's new leaders, replacing their white oppressors, most of whom had in turn been relegated to exile in the dark and dusty chapters of history.

I soon tired of viewing the identically grey and cheerless faces on the first floor and moved to the video installations in the basement. Apparently, I had the whole room to myself, and it felt a bit eerie, standing in the centre of the room, surrounded by multiple flickering TV monitors showing people opening and closing their mouths wordlessly. I sat in a booth nearby and put on the headphone and suddenly the mute faces became vocal. They were speaking German. I almost jumped when a hand touched mine. I turned. A figure had crystallized out of the dark space next to me. In the gloom his red jacket had coalesced with the red couch we were seated on and I had failed to see him. Now he was offering me his hand. The hand was slim and soft, and for a moment I thought it was a girl. He noticed my momentary disorientation and smiled, as if he was used to being mistaken for something he wasn't. His hand still in mine, he said, 'I am Mark.'

It was him, the would-be portrait sitter, turned down by Gina. He recognized me at about the same time. The silence lingered for a while, then I pointed at the TV monitors. 'What's this about?'

The TV monitors formed a triptych, one on our left with a woman on it, one on our right with a man on it, and one in front showing an old movie. The two faces on the left and right appeared to be discussing the movie in real time as it played. But it was all in German. 'The movie is *Whity*, by Rainer Werner Fassbinder. And these two are commenting on its handling of race.' I knew of Fassbinder, but I had not seen *Whity* before.

'The lady,' Mark said, pointing to the curly-haired woman, 'she made this installation. She is half-Nigerian.' Mark, I discovered later, was a film student, or used to be a film student – with Mark nothing was straightforward. We sat in the dark booth for a while, staring at the movie, the German words from the headphones bouncing around meaninglessly in my skull. Mark took off his headphone and offered to recap the movie plotline for me, I listened, impressed by his intensity. When he finished I thanked him and asked if he'd like a beer at the bar. He put down his headphone and put on his baseball cap. The bar was in the basement, next to the viewing room, and at the moment it was empty except for a couple seated by themselves on a couch in a corner. We ordered beers.

'Where are you from?' he asked.

'Originally, Nigeria.'

'Your wife is also Nigerian?'

'No, American.'

He was Malawian but had lived in Germany for over five years.

'Well, cheers,' I said, raising my glass.

'To Africa,' he said.

'To Africa.'

I tried to guess his age. He looked between twenty-five and thirty. The baseball cap covered the upper part of his face, and since he was shorter than me, I had to constantly lean down to make eye contact. He had lived a rather peripatetic life, moving from Stockholm, to Stuttgart, to Potsdam, and now Berlin. He loved Berlin most of all.

'Even in Berlin I miss Berlin,' he told me that day. He was only technically speaking a student, his registration had expired – something to do with school fees, and this had, or soon would, also affect his visa status – which was why he was squatting with friends in the old church in Kreuzberg. For pocket money he freelanced for crew.com, an organization for out-of-work actors and film technicians. But it had been a while since he had done anything for crew.com. He didn't tell me all this that day at the gallery, of course, but afterward, over several meetings. He looked a bit of a mess, almost feral, his black Converse sneakers were dirty and worn out, but there was an ease about him that I responded to.

'Come and meet my friends,' he said, after my second beer, his third, when I told him I had to go, 'we live close by.'

I followed him out of the bar and into the night. He walked with a swagger, at one point he casually stepped into the road and crossed to the other side, weaving between cars, raising his hand like a matador to halt a car that came close to hitting him, ignoring loud curses from incensed drivers. He stood at the other side, unperturbed, waving me over impatiently. I waited for the light to turn before crossing, not sure if I was impressed or alarmed by his reckless self-assurance.

'This is a church,' I said when he pushed open the little gate and waved me in. My comment was half question, half statement.

'We live here for the moment, yes. Temporarily.'

His three housemates were all there, Eric, Stan and Uta. I

nodded and sat down next to Mark. When Mark told them I
was a 'fellow African', Uta immediately told me her mother
was Cameroonian, her father German. She was lying on
the couch, her legs in Stan's lap – he was half-seated, half-
reclining next to her, his long dreadlocks falling over the back
of the couch and over his shoulders. We were in what they
called the living room, in the basement, which used to be
a Sunday school classroom. There was a blackboard on one
wall, and a wooden lectern in front of it. There were bottles
of beer on a redwood table with scratched and grime-dulled
wood grain. Mark opened a beer for me. Eric was holding
a joint in one hand and browsing through a laptop with the
other hand.

'So, what do you do?' Uta asked in her tentative English.

'I teach, back in the States. And here as well.' I gave English
classes to some of the non-English-speaking Zimmer fellows,
once a week. Uta was a student at the Free University and was
currently working on a novel.

'A novel?'

'The novel is dead,' Mark declared. 'Cinema is the present
and the future.'

'You think so?'

'The cinema does everything the novel does, but without
being boring.'

I took a pull on the joint that had made its way into my
hand. I felt light-headed.

The conversation drifted from subject to subject, lulling
into a contemplative silence that never felt awkward, and then
resuming, veering off in a totally new direction. Now Eric
was talking about the last protest march they had participated

in. They had been to Davos, and several G20 meetings all over the world.

'What are you protesting?' I asked.

They all stared at me, their faces showing their surprise at my question.

'Everything, man,' Stan said.

'Everything?'

'We believe there should be an alternative to the way the world is being run now,' Eric said.

'Too much money in too few hands,' Uta said.

'Millions exploited in sweatshops in Asia. Wars in Africa,' Stan said.

'This is the twenty-first century, no child should be dying from hunger or disease,' Uta said.

I nodded. I had met others like them here in Berlin, at readings, on the train, young men and women, in thread-bare sweaters and tattered jeans, mostly living in communes in abandoned buildings, purveyors of an alternative way of life, often not agreeing on what exactly that alternative should be, just an alternative to the status quo, otherwise what was the point? I drank, and smoked, and listened. At one point Mark stood behind the altar and read from a passage from the Bible; his father was a preacher and he was mocking his father's preaching style. He stood with hands raised, eyes roll-ing, voice thundering: *The summer is ended, the harvest gathered, and still we are not saved . . .*

The others clapped. I looked on, uncertain if it wasn't self-mockery and even real pain in Mark's voice and face as he bowed to the applause before returning to his chair. They told me he had deconsecrated the church when he first moved in a month ago. 'The place was haunted. I could feel the spirits lurking all over.'

'How do you deconsecrate a church?' I asked.

'With alcohol. Pour alcohol in the corners and read secret passages from the Bible.'

Even in my tipsy, sedated state, I sensed how ephemeral this moment was. How long before they saw the world as it is, vile and cruel and indifferent, and there is really no changing it; how long before they moved out of their crumbling ivory tower and joined the rest of humanity swimming in what Flaubert described as a river of shit relentlessly washing away at the foundation of every ivory tower ever built? One day they'd start shaving and become bankers or middle managers and drive BMWs and Mercedes-Benzes; they'd start a family and surround themselves with the empty accoutrements of position and power, the same things they now derided. But now, right now, they were free and pure as morning dew on a petal, and something in me wanted to lean in and sniff the fragrance from that bud.

So I kept returning to that slanted, run-down church building in Kreuzberg. I kept returning even when I discovered they were a far cry from the downtrodden proletariats they so identified with: Uta's parents were both doctors from the former East Berlin; Stan was a PhD student at Humboldt, he grew up in Senegal where his father worked for a multinational food company, his mother was a painter. Nor were they as young as they appeared. None of them was under thirty – Mark was the youngest at exactly thirty, Uta was thirty-one even though she looked twenty-five, Stan was thirty-two, and Eric was thirty-five and married, though currently separated from his wife, who lived with their daughter in Mannheim.

4

Then it was May. Mark and his friends invited me to the May Day demonstrations. 'You'll like it,' Mark said. The first of May protests were a tradition I had to experience, they told me, young men and women breaking down store doors and government buildings and flipping over cars on the high streets, sometimes setting them ablaze, denouncing the status quo.

That day in Kreuzberg, from Hermannplatz to Moritzplatz, the police began their patrol early. They came in riot gear and bulletproof vests, they cordoned off streets with their trucks and wagons, and only documented residents were allowed in or out. I arrived earlier at the church to avoid the cordon.

I found them by the door, all dressed up in boots and jeans and ready to go. Mark was talking to a girl I had never seen before. His girlfriend, Lorelle. I stopped myself from staring openly at the pins and rings in her lips and nostrils and cheeks and eyebrows, the stud in her tongue, making her face look like a pincushion. It must hurt. I imagined more piercings in hidden places beneath her lumpy sweatshirt. There was a mandala tattoo on her left cheek, in pink and blue colours, bringing her face alive like a neon light. Her hair, one side shaved off completely, was a mix of blue and pink over blonde roots. I shook her hand.

'Well, nice to meet you,' she said, 'I have heard so much about you from Mark.'

Her handshake was firm. Her voice was nothing like her appearance, it was warm, and soft, with a strong American accent. She was American, but born in Heidelberg. Her parents were military, now back in the US; but she had remained, preferring life here. She, like Mark, was a student at the film school.

We passed through parks and back streets, avoiding the cruising police vans and large congregations. Our destination was the Berlin-Turkish café, whose owner had been turning away black people, claiming they were all illegal immigrants and drug dealers. A surprisingly large crowd had already gathered in front of the café; young men and women in jeans and boots and sneakers, some with raised placards, others with raised phones recording the protest even as they chanted along to the songs. We joined them. We threw stones at the police who stood in front of the café to protect the owner, who was cowering inside. We marched in circles up and down the block, stopping traffic. By noon I was tired, and hungry, and beginning to feel bored. I could see Mark and Uta, she beautiful in her cutoff jeans and fiery red bandanna, side by side waving their placards like baits at the police. I decided to take a break. I crossed the road to a *Bäckerei* and ordered a sandwich and a coffee. I had two missed calls from Gina. When I left home at 6 a.m. she was still in her studio painting, and I hadn't told her where I was going. I called her back but there was no answer – she would be sleeping by now. Outside, the demonstration had almost doubled in size in the short time I had been in the *Bäckerei* and I could feel the tension rising all around. Time to go home. I edged into the crowd looking for Mark to let him know I was leaving, but soon I was carried by a tide of bodies making straight for the line of policemen standing behind their shields, their sticks raised. Stones and bottles and cans whizzed over our heads to crash against the policemen's shields. A shoulder knocked into me and I fell, knees hit my face as I tried to get up, shoes marched on my hands. Everyone was running, chased by the police. I kept trying to stagger up, but I kept falling back down under the ceaseless wave of knees and legs crashing into me. I stayed on the ground, mesmerized by a dully glowing square of brass embedded in the sidewalk – I had seen them before, *Stolpersteine*, they were called, meaning to stumble. There were names on them, entire histories, birthdays, transportation days, and the names of their final, terminal destinations. Four names, the Hartmanns: Elisabeth, Marcus, Lydia and Eduard. All ended up at Sobibór, all died the same day, 5 December 1944. I was blinded by the rusted glow of the brass, shocked by the brutal indifference of history, teary with tear gas, too winded to move. A hand was pulling me up, and for a moment I resisted, thinking it was the police, but it was Mark. He was smiling, an exhilarated look on his face. 'Are you okay?' he asked. I stood up. My palms were grazed and burning, my pants torn at the knees.

'I am fine.'

But he was already gone, hurling a stone toward the line of policemen. A tear gas canister landed next to me and I saw a wild-haired youth snatch it up and throw it back at the police, its arc of smoke hanging in the air like a dying thunderhead. To my right Lorelle was running straight at a row of policemen, using her ample bulk as battering ram against their shields. They knocked her down finally and hauled her away, screaming and kicking, to a police van. I stood there, disoriented by the tear gas, my eyes and nostrils streaming freely. I was alone on a tiny island, and all around me the sea was roiling and crashing with nameless rage.

'I have to go,' I said to Mark.

'No. Not yet. This is it. This is our moment,' Mark said. He was waving his arms as he talked. 'This is our Sharpeville, our Agincourt.'

I felt like laughing at his hyperbole. What moment, I wanted to ask, will this really change the minds of the so-called capitalists and racists and bring harmony and everlasting love to the world? And yet I couldn't help being impressed by it. I said, 'You don't want to get arrested, not with your expired visa. Come now.'

'Where are the others?' he asked.

'I don't know. I saw Lorelle being taken away. Come on.'

We walked away, taking random turns, till the sirens and

chants were a distant susurration on the wind. We sat in a bar and ordered two beers. My phone rang, it was Gina. I was too tired and too rattled to answer. We finished our beer, but Mark wasn't ready to go yet. He called for another.

'That's the way,' he said. He slammed his hand on the table. 'Resist the system.' We drank and ordered another round. I felt the edge coming off gradually. Outside, the smoky yellow streetlights were coming on as the sky darkened. The day had gone by already. A patrol car wailed past, its flashing blue lights mingling with the streetlight yellow.

'I should be going home.'

'Come on,' Mark said. 'Another drink, on me.' He looked drunk already. He called for a double shot of whisky.

'Not for me. Hurry up, I'll walk you home, then I am off.'

On the way Mark stopped at a currywurst stand to buy a sausage. A boy, his face red with drink, his girlfriend tugging at his arm, flopped into the bench next to us. He bent forward, his face in his hands. '*Scheisse*,' he kept muttering. The girl was dressed in a manga comic outfit, her face heavily made up, eyes slanted with kohl. Across the street a man in a hooded sweater stood in a dark doorway, whispering to passers-by, '*Alles gut?*', never fully making eye contact.

'Let's go, Mark.'

He couldn't walk straight, so I hefted his arm over my shoulder, bending awkwardly sideways since he was much shorter than me, and together we staggered toward the train station. At the abandoned church we found the door kicked off its hinges and lying on the floor just inside the threshold. The lights were on. The chairs were overturned, papers lay across tables and chairs.

'Fucking shit.'

'What happened?'

'I don't know. Looks like we've been raided.'

Mark went from room to room, picking up chairs and books from the floor. His room was at the end of a hall, next to the kitchen. His flimsy mattress was torn and almost cut in half. His backpack, which contained all his worldly possessions, lay open in the centre of the room.

'Motherfucking pigs. It's the police, they've been targeting us for a while.'

'Where are your friends?' I asked.

He looked at me and shrugged. 'I have no idea.'

'Well, what are you going to do, where are you going to sleep?'

He said, 'I'll be fine.' He didn't sound very convincing.

'Why don't you go over to your girlfriend's place?'

'Lorelle? Won't work. She has a flatmate. But hey, don't worry. I have places I can go to. I'll be fine.'

I left him standing there with his empty backpack in hand, swaying on his feet, assuring me he was going to be okay, and then I remembered that he couldn't have gone to Lorelle's anyway even if she didn't have a flatmate; Lorelle had been taken away by the police. I was tired, I was sore, and all I wanted was to get home, take a shower, and crawl into bed.

5

I didn't hear about Mark's arrest till a week later, when I stopped by the church. There was something different about the place, the door was back on its hinges, and the yard looked like someone had run a rake through it. A pile of trash was neatly packed under a tree, waiting to be bagged. I knocked, but there was no answer. I pushed the door and went in. The ratty couches and lamps were gone. The lectern was still there, and I remembered Mark standing behind it to read from the Bible, mocking his preacher father. I felt a bit sad, and a bit hurt – they had left without telling me. They had my phone number, at least Mark did, he could have called. But then, they lived an improvised and makeshift life, they had probably been chased out by the police and were even now holed up in another squat; they might get in touch after a week or so, after they had settled down. At least Mark might. I realized I missed them; I missed stopping by the church in the evenings when Gina was working and listening to them talk about everything, from global warming to despicable politicians to refugees, even when I secretly, arrogantly considered them naïve and hopelessly idealistic. Now I had to admit they were at least able to think of something, and others, apart from themselves, they were willing to throw stones at the police and even go to jail for their ideals – how many people could do that? Certainly not my self-centred, overambitious classmates back in graduate school, and definitely not Gina's oversensitive, even narcissistic fellow Zimmer artists we met regularly at dinners and openings and readings. Throughout the week I waited for Mark to call. Did he even have a phone? I couldn't remember. In the end it was Lorelle who called. She had been released from the police lockup a day after the demonstration. I said, 'Where's everyone? I went to the church and there was nobody.'

Mark's little group had disbanded, she told me. Stan had moved back to Mannheim, Eric to France, and Uta was back with her parents. The gap year from life has ended, the search for alternatives is over, I thought, the revolution lost. I felt a twinge of disappointment.

'And Mark?' I asked. Mark had been arrested, and that was why she was calling. She wanted to meet. She was waiting for me outside Neukölln U-Bahnhof, in a café across the street from the station. She called for a chai and I asked for a coffee.

She looked a bit different, more subdued, as if she hadn't been sleeping. Even the mandala on her cheek looked less fluorescent, the colours in her hair less celebratory.

'The last time I saw you,' I told her, raising my voice over the street noise, 'you were being hauled away by the police, kicking and screaming.'

'Oh God, I was so high that day. They released me the next morning. It is routine. One of the thrills of the struggle, you might say.'

'But what of Mark?'

A young man with hair falling to his shoulders and a long, mournful face loomed over our table and meekly whispered some words to Lorelle. He smelled of urine and faeces and old sweat. He smelled acidic. His thick battered boots were crusted with layers of dirt and grime. She shook her head. '*Ich habe keine.*' He turned to me. I looked away. He shuffled off to the next table.

It seemed after I left Mark that day at the church, he had gone out to get still more drunk, then he had returned to the church and started playing loud music, and that had attracted a cruising police car. They asked him why he was staying there, and if he had a place, and when he began to rail at them, they took him away. Things got more complicated when they discovered his visa was expired. Now it was a case for the immigration service.

'Well, where is he now?'

'In detention, at one of their centres. I was there yesterday and he told me to call you. He has no one. He needs help. They are going to send him back to Malawi – it is the worst thing that can happen to him. He cannot go back.'

How definitive she sounded: He *cannot go back* to Malawi. What did she mean by that?

'Well . . . what can I do?' I asked.

'He needs a lawyer.'

'What of those humanitarian NGOs – Amnesty International, can they help?'

'I have already talked to them, but this is not exactly their province. They gave me an address though, a lawyer. He belongs to another organization, they specialize in cases like this, and they work pro bono.'

'Have you called him?'

'Yes, he is happy to help, but he needs to pay for access to documents and for making copies, et cetera.'

'How much?'

'About two hundred euros. I don't have enough, I am afraid . . .'

'Of course, that is no problem.' I was relieved it was only two hundred. I'd hate to have to ask Gina for the money. The lawyer's office was somewhere in Mitte, a twenty-minute train ride from where Mark was being held. It was a small office, with two desks, one for the lawyer, one for his assistant, a prim and sour-faced lady. Her black skirt was well below the knees; her sky-blue blouse was buttoned up to the collar, with lacy ruffs fanning round her neck and holding up her head like a neck brace; on her chest was a name tag, *Frau Grosse*. There was only one chair for visitors, so I stood. The lawyer's name was Julius Maier, but just call me Julius, he said, rising out of his chair to shake hands. He was slight of frame, almost insubstantial next to the grave and heavily present Frau Grosse. His father was from Burkina Faso, he added, as if to establish his credentials, and his mother was German. Lorelle handed him the two hundred euros in an envelope. He counted it and gave it to Frau Grosse, who counted it again before returning it to the envelope and sliding the envelope into a drawer. I almost expected her to lock the drawer with a key attached to a chain hanging from her waist. She caught me looking at her and frowned; I turned away.

'First, your friend needs to prove he is not an illegal, and to do that, he needs to establish he is still a student.'

'He came here as a student, it is on record. Why don't they believe him?' I said.

'It is on record, yes. But it is not that simple. He is now out of status, so he has broken his visa conditions.'

'Is that very serious?'

'Very. He can be deported, or detained.' He waited for me to comment, and when I didn't, he went on, 'The best way to help is if he can show that he has applied for a visa extension. I have spoken to him, and he told me that he has not applied for an extension.'

'Well, can he do that now?'

'To do that, he will need a letter from the school, saying he is still a student – but that will not be easy. He told me he hasn't been in school for the past year. He was in another school in Potsdam before coming here. His scholarship has been stopped. He has almost graduated, all he needs is to finish his final project.'

It was a bureaucratic conundrum straight out of Kafka – to get a hearing he must prove he had applied for a visa extension (which he hadn't), but to apply for the visa extension he must prove he was still a student (which he was, technically, even though his tuition had lapsed and he had not set foot on campus in a year, and because he had changed schools a few times his paperwork trail was as tangled as Bob Marley's hair). Still, the lawyer looked optimistic. Lorelle looked sceptical. I must have looked puzzled.

'But really,' he said, 'it is simpler if he asks for asylum.'

'You mean like a refugee?'

'Yes.'

'He won't,' Lorelle said.

'Why not, if it will make it easier . . .'

'Well, he is not a refugee. He is a student.'

We took a train to the detention centre, a Brutalist edifice straight out of the Nazi architecture catalogue, where we were asked to fill out multiple forms. Julius filled them out and handed them to a lady, who looked like Frau Grosse's twin. She went over them line by line, running a thick finger over each line, before bringing out a rubber stamp and smashing it to the bottom of each page, making the table shake each time. She then looked at us and pointed – her hand rising with infinite slowness to hang in the air – to a row of chairs in a corner. We sat. I felt exhausted already. I felt like I was on trial for a crime and I would definitely be found guilty and hanged. I avoided the lady's glare and ran my eyes over the long, rectangular room. A row of square windows opened high up in one wall, with parallel iron bars blocking any hope of egress – if one were inclined to seek egress that way. A metal door to the side had a sign across it, *VERBOTEN.* A man came in and talked to Julius in German, and then turning to us he switched to English and asked us to follow him. We passed through many doors, each of which he opened with a key from a bundle of

keys in his hand, each door a different key, before finally asking us to sit in a sort of anteroom facing another door. A while
later, the door opened and Mark joined us, accompanied by a
guard who stood discreetly but visibly by the door. After the
fortress-like entrance, and the multiple doors, and the bureau-
cracy, I expected to see Mark in chains. He was dressed in his
usual red jacket and T-shirt. He looked subdued, and a bit lost
and vulnerable without his hat.

'Thanks,' Mark said to me.

'You'll be fine,' I said to him.

Lorelle sat tense and straight in her chair, her eyes fixed
on Mark, as if she wanted to cross over to him and hold him,
but she remained seated, smiling whenever their eyes met. As
it turned out, Julius's optimism was well founded. Mark was
released two days later. I got a call from the lawyer and we
met in his office. Mark was there, cap low over his head as
usual, his red jacket over his layers of shirt and T-shirt, in the
same Converse shoes and high-flying jeans. He was free, for
the time being. The school had issued a letter acknowledging he was a student, the visa application had been submitted;
Mark had been released into the supervision of the lawyer.

I shook Julius's hand, impressed.

'He has to be readily available if he is needed. He must not
travel outside Berlin. They needed an address, just for formal-
ity, you know. We gave your address, is that okay?'

'Of course,' I said. I did not ask him how he got my address.
'But where is he going to stay?'

'At the Heim,' Julius said, and when I looked blank he
added, 'The *Flüchtlingsheim*.'

Refugee camp. Where asylum seekers were kept pending

the result of their asylum application. I turned to Mark to see what he thought. He was looking out of the window at a tree branch.

'But he is not an asylum seeker,' I said.

Julius shrugged. 'It is a temporary arrangement.'

I said to Mark, 'You know what, come to my place, you can crash there for a day or two before moving on.'

Mark shrugged, wordless. Thank you would be nice, but then, he had been through a lot. Before we left, Julius took me aside. 'How well do you know him?'

'About two months now. Why?'

He shrugged. 'Well, I think you need to talk to him.' He looked as if he wanted to say more but wasn't sure if he should. He looked over at Mark, then back to me. 'Just talk to him. You know, to find out more . . . about himself.'

'Okay,' I said, puzzled. Was there something Mark was hiding from me? Surely he'd let me know if there was any danger to putting him up? We stopped at a bar and I bought Mark a beer to celebrate his freedom. 'My first in days,' he said. He was quiet most of the time. I wanted to bring up Julius's comment, but how did one broach such a subject? I decided I'd bring it up as tactfully as I could at an appropriate time. When we finished our drinks he looked up and said, 'I hope your wife won't be upset with you bringing home a foundling.'

'She'll be fine,' I said. I knew that by taking him home I was crossing a line after which it would be hard to turn back. He was now my responsibility. Whatever he did, whatever happened to him, would have a direct bearing on me and Gina.

6

I heard the voices as I unlocked the front door, and I remembered we were hosting today. Gina had completed her *Travellers* paintings and was having her sitters and a few people from the Zimmer over for drinks and a viewing, and I was supposed to get the drinks on my way back. 'Damn,' I muttered, thinking of a reasonable explanation.

'All good?' Mark asked, eyebrows raised. I smiled and waved him in.

Gina was standing in the middle of the room, a glass in one hand, talking to a man in a Ralph Lauren shirt, half-unbuttoned to show his hairy chest. She opened her mouth to speak, then stopped when she saw Mark. Her eyebrows arched, forming a question mark on her face. I went and kissed her on the cheek. 'Hi darling,' I said. There were two women out on the balcony, smoking, wineglass in hand. I waved to them and shook the man's hand.

'You are Gina's husband,' he said. 'I am Dante.' He sounded French, or Italian, or Spanish. I wondered if he was comfortable exposing his chest like that. I nodded and turned to Mark. 'This is Mark – a friend.' I waited to see if Gina would remember him, but she gave no sign she did.

'Mark, my wife, Gina.'

Gina looked from Mark to me, the question mark still evident, then she gave him her hand. Mark, in his baseball cap and jeans stopping at his ankles and backpack slung over one shoulder and the stench of detention on him, looked so out of place next to the elegantly bare-chested Dante that I felt embarrassed for him.

'Come,' I said to him. I took his backpack and led him to the bathroom to wash his hands; I also needed a minute to compose myself. But what I needed more than anything else was a drink. In the kitchen there were two bottles of wine on the counter, white and red, both open. As I looked in the drawer for a glass, Gina entered. She closed the door and stood with her back against the door, not coming in.

'I have been trying to reach you.'

I filled my glass with wine and drank it all in one go. Gina came and took the empty glass from my hand and placed it carefully in the sink. I picked it up and refilled it. A week after we got married two friends of hers had come to town on their way to Baltimore, and Gina had wanted to introduce me. She had cooked and I was supposed to grab the wine on my way home from the library, teaching my ESL students, but I had totally forgotten. The annoying thing was that I wasn't doing anything, I had just sat in the library, browsing through a novel, and by the time I remembered I was three hours late. She was in bed when I came home and she wouldn't talk to me the next day.

'I forgot we were hosting tonight. I am sorry.'

She looked radiant in her red dress, I told her.

'I kept calling. I left messages.'

'I can still get more wine, if it is not too late . . .'

'Of course it is too late. Dante brought a few bottles. And who is the kid? He looks familiar.'

'His name is Mark. He was here a while back.'

'What is he doing here?'

'He needs a place to crash.'

'To crash?'

'Yes. I'll explain later.'

'You can explain now.'

'Too complicated. Later.'

'Don't drink too much, please,' she said before she left. I finished a second glass, slowly this time. Facing the guests in the living room was the last thing I wanted to do; for that I needed some artificial cheer – and a change of shirt. As I walked down the corridor to the bedroom I saw the door to the studio was open. There were people in there, a man and a woman, talking in low voices. I stood at the door and cleared my voice. In the dim light I saw it was Manu, and the woman, the daughter was also there, standing in the shadows next to a canvas.

'Hi,' I said. They all turned and stared at me, silent, as if waiting for me to make an accusation. The woman moved a step closer to her daughter.

'I didn't know you were here,' I said, keeping my eyes on Manu. They continued to stare at me in silence, and as the awkwardness mounted I went on, 'I just came in. I was out to see a friend.' Still they said nothing, and after a while the woman took her daughter's hand and, keeping as far from me as possible, squeezed past me through the door to the living room. I looked again at Manu, and after the woman. 'I never got her name.'

'Bernita.'

'She doesn't talk much.'

'She is shy,' he said.

I stepped into the room and stood next to him, before one of the canvases. There were six in all, arranged in order of size, the biggest, a 60-by-50-inch, on the left, and the smallest, a 24-by-20-inch to the right. They were placed so that a single light from a lamp fell on them. Manu's portrait, the 60-by-50-inch stared back at us, thoughtful, a little tired, but filled with gravitas, like a defeated king amidst the ruins of his palace.

'A good likeness,' I said.

On the next canvas was the woman and her child. I was seeing the finished paintings for the first time. Gina hated to show her work in progress, even to me. The woman was seated with the child asleep in her lap.

'Like the Pietà,' Manu said. A woman holding her broken child, grieving as only a woman can. She was wearing the bulky winter jacket, her face staring down at the figure in her arms, the light falling on her covered head like a halo. Three small canvases carried sketches of the child alone – I moved closer. No, they were not the child – not the woman's child. It was a white child, the boy from the motherless children's home, standing over the fence, shouting *Schokolade!* And yet, it wasn't him in the next canvas. It was a more generic child, an everychild. Anyone's child. And the next one was even more generic, genderless, neither white nor black; what was clear, though, was the almost accusatory pain in its liquid eyes. I pulled back and turned to Manu. I wondered what he thought of it. He was bending forward, his face close to the canvas.

'There is so much sadness here,' he said. When I remained quiet, he went on, 'But perhaps it is only my interpretation.'

'Do you want a beer? I'll change my shirt and join you in a minute.'

Manu had a daughter, he told me. They lived in a Heim.

'Why didn't you bring her?'

'She has her German lesson today.'

I tried to guess his accent. 'Senegal?'

'No. Libya. My father came from Nigeria, originally.'

'Oh,' I said.

Mark was on the couch, a glass of wine in hand, flanked by the two women who had been smoking on the balcony. One was Ilse, the PR person for the Zimmer, the other one I had never met before. Mark was describing his ordeal at the hands of the immigration officials to the women. Dante and Gina drew closer, and now there was a little group around Mark, who seemed to be enjoying the attention. He spoke with his trademark braggadocio, making it all sound funny. As I listened I felt like I was also hearing it for the first time, as if I hadn't been there with him, and I couldn't help but admire his resiliency. The other lady, a brunette, in a blue dress that stopped mid-thigh, leaned toward Mark and asked, 'Are you going to seek asylum then? It will be easier for you, no?'

'Mark is a student,' I said, joining them.

'Oh, I see,' she said, looking up at me. She looked to be in her forties. A journalist, from Frankfurt, I found out later. Her name was Anna. I wondered where Gina found her, most likely through Ilse. The fellowship was tireless in promoting its fellows.

'Why,' Mark said, turning to me, a mischievous twinkle in his eye, 'do white people always assume every black person travelling is a refugee?'

'They don't,' Anna said. 'I don't,' she corrected herself. 'I cannot speak for every white person in this world, can I?'

I left the group and went to the kitchen to pour myself a glass of wine, by the time I came back the woman and child had left. I saw Manu standing a little apart from the group, near the door, a glass in his hand. He was staring at the group, and when I followed his eyes I saw he was looking at Gina, who was talking to Dante. 'Your wife is very talented,' he said.

'Come and join us,' I said, 'don't stand here by yourself.'

'I am afraid I have to go now. It is getting late.'

I gave him his coat, and when I rejoined the group Anna was asking Mark if he had experienced any racism in Berlin, surely Berlin was the most liberal and welcoming of all European cities, no? Mark, unfazed, smiled and said, 'I like it here. Even in Berlin I miss Berlin.'

'Ha ha ha,' Anna laughed, delighted. She had a rather unexpectedly loud laugh. 'I like that. Can I quote you?'

Mark raised a hand, his face flushed with wine. 'Before you

quote me, let me add . . . I have also noticed this, the women always hug their bags when I am in the vicinity, without fail. Like this.' He demonstrated. 'With both hands. I didn't notice it at first, but then it became so obvious I couldn't ignore it.'

Anna laughed, looking more guarded now. Gina threw me a look – Mark was my responsibility. He was making her guests uncomfortable. Dante, trying to salvage the situation, said, 'But the race situation in Europe is good, no? Better than America? I go there often, for exhibitions. And they disrespect Obama, is true, is because he is black.'

Gina said, 'Well, it is not perfect, but it is not that bad either. We have come a long way since the 1960s and the civil rights struggles.' She looked at me, but I had nothing to add.

'What is your experience, as an African in America?' Dante persisted, turning to me. I looked at his distressed jeans, his blue Polo shirt with his chest hairs springing out of the unbuttoned top, and I decided I didn't like him, but I smiled and told them about the first time I went to New York. I had approached a policeman at Penn Station to ask for directions, which is the logical thing to do anywhere in the world, and as I got closer to him I noticed his hand inching toward the gun at his waist. I had stopped and looked behind me, thinking surely it was someone else he was reaching his gun for, not me. Now he was gripping his gun tightly, but still I asked him for directions, my voice wavering, and he looked at me, unsmiling, and said, 'Keep moving.' When I told Gina that story a long time ago, she had been angered. She had called the police pigs and racists. She was fiery then, recently she had grown more tolerant, more oblivious of what was happening around her, her gaze focused only on her painting.

7

That night, after the guests had left, and Mark lay snoring on the couch in the living room, Gina said to me, 'How long is he staying?'

'A day or two.'

'How could you invite him without asking me first? If anything goes wrong . . .'

'What could go wrong?' I asked, and even as I said it I remembered the lawyer's worried expression as he asked me if I knew Mark well enough. I pushed the thought aside. 'Is he going to set the house on fire, rob the neighbours? Come on. He may look a bit . . . disjointed, but he is okay. He just needs a place for a day or two to get his act together.'

'What kind of trouble is he in?'

'You heard him earlier. He needs to sort out his papers. He is a student. A lawyer is working on it.'

I lay awake most of that night, listening to Gina's soft breathing. I wanted to ask her about the baby in the painting, and what it meant, but she was already asleep. She slept with her face to the wall, far away from me. I lay sleepless all night long till the morning birds started chirping outside. I opened the window and poked my head outside and gulped in the morning air. I was never fully awake till I smelled the fresh morning air and heard the cry of birds in the trees, even in winter. The leaves were turning reddish on the trees. Already, summer was ending. When we came last October the leaves were already variegated and falling. Late in October I had stood at the window and watched a single leaf still clinging to a twig, thinking that must be the last leaf left on a tree in the whole street, in the whole city, in the whole world, and it was there, outside my window. Fall was my favourite season; an in-between moment, neither winter nor summer, and so brief. I loved to watch the leaves swirl and circle and rise and fall, driven by the wind and the passing cars to pile up against the fence by the sidewalk. I loved to watch the children from across the road play with them, picking up armfuls and raining them down over each other's heads. They'd hold hands and scream and jump up and down on the red and brown and dry leaves, soothed and excited by the crunching and breaking sound they made under their feet, their pellucid laughter rising through the street, up into the leafless trees to startle the birds, up into the upstairs balconies and windows still open as if in defiance of the coming winter.

8

Mark was already awake, seated on the couch, looking at the open door leading to the balcony and the top of the poplar trees lining the street. He was wrapped to the neck in a blanket, and seated like this, not in constant motion, he looked vulnerable, almost childlike. He had been out on the balcony for a smoke, and the smell had trickled into the room. I told him Gina had to go out for an event.

'Yes, I saw her,' he said.

She hadn't said where she was going. Recently she seemed to be always coming in when I was going out the door, or going out when I was coming in; she was waking up when I was getting into bed. Yesterday in the morning we stood in the bathroom side by side, but we couldn't speak because our mouths were full of toothpaste, we only stared at each other in the mirror over the sink, a brief eye contact before she bent down to spit into the swirl of scummy water spiralling into the drain. I often thought of Gina in her studio, alone all day, battling with colours and lines and fear and hope, coaxing the brushstrokes into shapes, a limb, a face, hair, eyes, and some-times despairing, as Plato once said, of ever capturing that ideal form she saw in her mind. When we first came to Berlin everything seemed to be working out fine, but now I knew she sometimes stayed in the studio just to get out of my way, just as I went out to visit Mark and his friends to avoid her. Sometimes, when she came out of the studio and found me in the living room reading or watching TV, she looked taken aback that I was there, that I was me, and she was her, hus-band and wife, in a house, together, and I couldn't tell when this awkwardness had started. I wanted to hold her and just sit quietly, like we used to do a long time ago, but it required so much energy to do that, more energy than I possessed. Instead I would put on my jacket and walk the lonely Berlin back streets, and there is no loneliness like the loneliness of a stranger in a strange city.

Mark asked, 'How did you two meet?'

'Let me get some tea first,' I said. 'Do you want some?'

'Coffee is better if you have it.'

'No problem.'

He was out of the blanket and already dressed when I returned with the beverages. I had met Gina at an Obama rally at the American University in Washington in March 2007. Obama had just declared for the presidency and Gina was a campaign volunteer. I noticed her standing next to me, with her friends, all of them volunteers, wearing campaign buttons, and she was simply the most beautiful thing I had ever seen. Twice our eyes met, and I could see she was conscious of me too – I hardly heard a word the candidate was saying, I was busy plotting how to talk to her, but they left to be introduced to the candidate before I could summon the courage to approach her.

'What were you doing in America?'

'I went there on a scholarship, in 2006 – I was doing my PhD in history. As fate would have it, she was also a student, in the same department. A week later I met her in the library and this time I did not hesitate. When I mentioned I was from Nigeria she told me her father had been a Fulbright scholar in Nigeria. That is how it started. Your turn,' I said.

'What do you want to know?'

'Tell me about Malawi. Do you have brothers and sisters?'

'Yes,' Mark said. 'Two of each, I am the middle child.' His voice was serious, the frivolous and evasive Mark had momentarily disappeared.

'Tell me about them, your family.'

'I . . . my father and I, we didn't see eye to eye. Did I mention he was a pastor?'

'Yes. What denomination?'

'It is a Pentecostal ministry, one of the few in Lilongwe. When I was a child he encouraged me to join the church drama group. I loved it. I had the flair, I guess, from very early. We'd dramatize stories from the Bible, mainly. I loved the performance, the power to make the congregation laugh with my goofiness, to bring them to tears sometimes, with only words and gestures. I was always the lead. One day I'd be the Prodigal Son, cast out, eating with the swine, and then returning home to be welcomed home by my father, another day I'd be Joseph, dumped in a well by my brothers. I can understand why actors sometimes become schizophrenic. It is easy to get carried away, and then coming back is a problem. I really believed I was those characters. Even then I guess I was trying to escape something, I don't know what. That was my childhood, in the church, no outside interests. While my friends were out there discovering sports and other interests, I was in the church, always under my father's watchful eyes. That's the sum of my childhood. When I finished secondary school, I naturally wanted to study theatre at the university, but my father would have none of that.'

'Why?' I asked.

He brought out a pack of cigarettes from his jacket pocket. We stood side by side out on the balcony, smoking. 'Well, it was okay to be an actor in church, but not outside the church. It was living a lie, he said. Making believe for a living. Ungodly, he called it. But with my mother's support, I was able to get in. I invited the whole family to my first performance. I had the lead role in *Sizwe Banzi Is Dead*, by Athol Fugard. I was nineteen. I had worked hard to master my role, you know, the lines, the movements. But still, even there onstage, I could see the disappointment on my father's face.'

'What exactly didn't he like?' I asked.

He dragged deeply on his cigarette, then he leaned over the balcony and flicked away the stub. 'He said it would bring disgrace to the church. He said it was too worldly. You have to understand, my father lived in the church, in the Bible, for him there was nothing else. Well, I was so disappointed, I stopped going home. During the holidays I'd stay with my friends and we'd perform in small theatres and nightclubs and in the streets. We made enough money to live on. I had fun. My mother came to see me, and she begged me to come home. But I didn't go back. When I graduated I moved to South Africa to stay with my uncle Stanley. He is my father's youngest brother. He is a lecturer at a university, and he is the direct opposite of my father. I never went back home again. It was he who suggested I should look into going abroad to study further. He linked me up with his friend at the Goethe Institute in Johannesburg. I registered for German-language classes, and applied for a scholarship to come here to study. Just like that, everything came together.'

'Have you ever thought of returning?' I asked. He shook his head and shrugged. 'Sometimes. I miss my mother. And my uncle, and his wife and kids, and my brothers and sisters. But I don't see myself going back. Not soon anyway.'

I wanted to bring up what the lawyer said, but Mark took me by surprise when he said he had to leave.

'Leave?'

'Listen, I am not sure your wife is happy with me being here. I could see it last night. And this morning she didn't reply when I said good morning.'

I said, 'I am sorry. But you really don't have to go. Gina's just preoccupied at the moment . . .'

'It's okay,' he said. 'Really. I appreciate all you have done for me.'

I felt like Judas walking Mark to the bus stop, at the same time I felt a relief, which I tried to suppress. He said he had friends who'd put him up, and if that didn't work out there was always the Heim. I reached out and gave him a hug, the Judas hug, and watched him run through a gap in the traffic, the wind lifting his ridiculous jacket behind him. He had lost some weight in the last few weeks. He caught the M400 bus and as it pulled away I saw him through a top-deck window, waving. I waved back, my hand leaden.

My chest was heavy and my legs dragged as I walked back. Everything was changing. The leaves in the trees, the display clothes in the shop windows. There was an almost impercept-ible chill in the air. I thought of home and the harmattan in November, and how it always made me sick, my mother said it was my body adjusting to the change in seasons. Our bodies always want to continue with what they know, pulled along by inertia. I hadn't spoken to my mother in a while. When I first got to America I used to call her every Sunday, talking through five-dollar call cards, the phone being passed from her to my father, to my sister and my two brothers. The plan was for me to return after my PhD, but then I met Gina, and the days turned into months, and the months into years, and then I just stopped calling home. The last time I called, over a year ago, my mother's voice had sounded so distant she could be talking about the weather to a stranger. I had handed the phone to Gina, but my mother always found it hard to under-stand Gina's American accent, and the call had lasted only a few minutes. I thought of Gina before the pregnancy. We used to sit by the window in the evenings, drinking white wine, watching the empty parking lot across the street, kids step-pushing their skateboards on the concrete, roaring down the pavement, jumping high in the air with skates glued to their soles, falling, jumping up again, high-fiving after each success. I was so lost in thought I bumped into a woman looking into a display window, then immediately after into a man. I was on a strange street, I couldn't recognize the landmarks and the store names. The man was tall and fashionably dressed in a leather jacket. He held my arm by the elbow and shook it, jolting me out of my sleepwalk. 'Hey. Watch it.' I nodded and walked on.

9

As it turned out, my questions were answered
one week after the day I walked Mark to the bus stop. It
was the day of Gina's exhibition at the Zimmer Gallery,
somewhere on Karl-Marx-Strasse. Gina hadn't commented
that day when she came back and Mark was gone. Our life
had reverted to its normal rhythm. We went out to dinners, and openings, and readings and performances by Gina's
fellow artists. Today she looked happy as she guided visitors from painting to painting, answering questions about
colour, technique, concept. There was a solemn instrumen-
tal music playing in the background, her fellow artists from
the Zimmer were all there. It was going to be an all-day

affair. I stood in a corner, trying to be helpful, chatting with Julia, the Zimmer director, a thin, tall, unassuming woman, with her partner, Klaus, a tall beefy man who kept downing glasses of Riesling like it was water. I had been there for three hours, and I was tired, and hungry, and I was thinking of where to go for a bite – I wanted something more substantial than the finger food on offer, I wanted to ask Gina if she'd come with me, and at that moment a man walked in. He looked familiar. He was with a group of three, and he saw me at the same time.

He left the group and came over. It took me a while to recognize him. It was the lawyer, Julius. He looked different in jeans and T-shirt. I told him it was my wife's exhibition. 'Oh,' he said, looking impressed. 'I heard about the exhibition from my girlfriend.' He pointed to one of the girls in jeans and bombardier jacket. 'You know, I was going to call you tomorrow. I need to get in touch with Mark. Is he still staying at your place?'

'Actually no. Is everything okay?'

'Well, I need to get in touch with him. It is regarding the visa renewal application.'

'He left my place a while back, but I can pass on a message . . . I am sure I can locate him if necessary.'

The lawyer hesitated, then making up his mind he said, 'Well, it is urgent . . . I just found out today that his application for visa renewal was declined. I am sorry.'

'Oh,' I said, 'I am sorry to hear that.'

'Can you let him know, please?'

'Of course.'

As he turned to go, he said, 'This is none of my business,

but . . . you know, his real name is Mary. But I guess you knew this already? After all you are very close.'

I looked blankly at him. Mary?

'He is a girl, or rather she is a girl. Mary Chinomba.'

Mark, a girl? 'Are you sure?' was all I could manage.

'Yes, of course I am sure. I saw the official documents. I see, you look surprised. You didn't know.'

10

My phone calls to Mark went straight to a voice who told me, in clipped German, to leave a message, *bitte*, and after a while it stopped taking messages. I called Lorelle. She also hadn't seen him in a while, but she had heard he was putting up at a Heim close to the Görlitzer Bahnhof. We met at the station and walked together to the Heim. We passed empty and decaying buildings with graffiti in blue and green and black running down the walls, and shops with their pull-down doors permanently shut; we passed seedy corner shops with drunk men coming out of the narrow doorway with six-packs of beer under their arms and their beer guts spilling out of untucked shirtfronts, and moustachioed Turkish men smoking from hookahs under beach umbrellas. We came out on a completely deserted street with a fence blocking the far end and long grass growing beneath the fence.

'Have you been here before?' I asked Lorelle. She shook her head.

We took a corner and entered another street, also deserted except for two men sitting on the pavement with their backs against the wall and their legs sticking out in front of them, still captive to whatever chemical was coursing in their bloodstream. They stared at us, their faces red and grimy, sucking greedily on their cans of beer, until we turned another corner. The Heim was an abandoned school building, most of its windows had no panes, and its yard was overgrown with grass and trash. The front gate opened into a driveway that led to the big grey building. On one side of the driveway was a smaller structure, which must have originally been the security post or an office building, now its windows were boarded up with plywood turned black and peeling from rain and sun. Four men, three black, one Asian, stood at the doorway, talking in whispers. They stared long at Lorelle's hair and piercings, before turning to me. One of the men, with a red, yellow, green and black Rasta man's beanie over his dreadlocks, nodded at me and I nodded back. At the main building's entrance, a huddle of men, dirty, unshaven, and visibly drunk, stood haggling over something. They looked up when they saw us, and one of them, the lone black man in the group, walked away. The smell hit us even before we entered the building: fetid and moist and revolting. Heim. Home. This was the most un-homely place I had ever seen.

'This is it?' I asked Lorelle. It was a four-storey building and from here I could hear voices and muted music coming from upstairs windows.

'This is it.'

By the first landing was a bathroom, its entrance faced the staircase, half-blocked by a pile of trash falling out of and partially burying a trash can. A man came out of the bathroom, stepping carefully over the trash, a towel around his waist, his scrawny chest bare, his hair still wet.

'Hi,' I said. 'We are looking for a friend. Mark Chinomba.'

His glance switched from Lorelle to me. He shook his head. 'Where he come from?'

'Malawi,' Lorelle said. '*Sprechen sie Deutsch?*' she switched to German, sensing the man's wavering English. He shrugged his scrawny shoulders. 'Check upstairs.'

Stuck to the walls by the stairs were handbills screaming slogans, *No to Borders! No to Illegal Detention! Asylum Is a Right!* They ran all the way along the staircase, some announcing events, in English and French, but mostly in German: drama group meetings, church group meetings, social worker schedules. We met no one on the second-floor landing, so we turned right into a double doorway that led into a long and dark corridor littered with old bicycles and broken tables and chairs and more trash. A row of doors faced us, most of them half-open, showing bunk beds with tattered mattresses on them in which men slept with their legs hanging over the sides.

I knocked on one of the doors and entered. A man stood in front of a small stove with a pot on it, in his hand was half a chicken, in the other hand a knife. The sight of Lorelle behind me seemed to startle him – obviously women didn't frequent this part of the Heim. He put down the chicken on the table next to a pile of freshly cut peppers and onions and, wiping his hands on his pants, turned fully to us. No, he had never heard of Mark Chinomba. 'From Malawi? No, he cannot be here. This room is Senegal.'

Another man sat on his bed, watching a TV screen on a table next to the bed – it was an old TV, with the convex protrusion behind it. He didn't look up as we conversed with the man with the chicken; he continued to stare fixedly at the screen whose light illuminated his face, his expression swiftly changing with the images. There were shoes and more mattresses on the floor, cluttering the passage between the beds. A rancid smell hung over the room, rising from the cooking and the shoes and the unwashed bodies.

'Where are the Nigerians?' I asked, curious.

He pointed up, shaking his head. 'You can't find Nigeria now. If you want Nigeria you come back in nighttime. Most of them sleep now.'

I stopped at the foot of the stairs. I felt tired, depleted. I said to Lorelle, 'I think I've seen enough.'

She looked at me. 'Don't you want to find Mark?'

On the next floor the door opened into a room much larger than the last one, a small hall, with all the mattresses on the floor. Most of the men appeared to be Asian, most likely Syrians, or Pakistanis or Bangladeshis, or Afghans, with a few black men, all with the same furtive, calculating look, all quick to shake their heads when we asked after Mark Chinomba. A few lay on their mattresses, fiddling with their cell phones, some sat around a table in the centre of the room, playing a card game, their voices raised in dispute. As we passed in front of more open doorways and stepped over more piles of trash – almost fainting from the stink – nodding at the men congregated in groups on the balcony or standing idly by the windows, I seemed to be passing through some region of Dante's *Inferno*. None of them had heard of Mark. The topmost floor was the women's floor, and from the stairs we could hear a voice trying to calm down a screaming child. Its shrill, piercing cries brought me to a stop.

'Do you think he'd be there, with the women?'

She shook her head. 'No. Never.'

We left.

The next day Lorelle called. 'There's a film showing this evening, at the Neue Kino, it is a documentary about Mumia Abu-Jamal. A friend mentioned it. Mark is a big fan of Abu-Jamal,' she said.

I had no idea who Mumia Abu-Jamal was, but I took down the directions she gave me. After the movie we sat in a little café next to the tiny cinema house. There were people seated at neighbouring tables, still talking about the searing documentary we had just seen. Mark and Lorelle sat on a couch, holding hands, Lorelle gazing at Mark with a tenderness that looked alien on her hard, pierced face. She hadn't seen Mark in almost a month. Earlier, when we came in and saw him by the concession stand talking to the barman, they had thrown themselves at each other and locked lips, and the people nearby had cheered while I stood and watched them, absently thinking it must be painful for Lorelle to kiss with all the rings on her lips, but touched like everyone else by the performance.

'I had never heard of Abu-Jamal before.'

'But how could you have?' Mark said, laughing. He looked

upbeat. 'You live in a big house, with a beautiful wife. You live in America where everybody is a movie star and drives a big car.'

'You make it sound like it is a sin or a disease to live in a big house.'

'Well, I wouldn't go to see movies about men in big houses. I wouldn't make movies about them either.'

'Quite a manifesto. What kind of movies would you make?' I said.

'Let me tell you the kind of movie I'd make. It is about a man in a tunnel. A long and endless tunnel, at the end there is his lover waiting for him, but he begins to realize that also, next to his lover, there is death waiting. But we never see him reach the lover, or death, just a single continuous shot of him in the tunnel, nothing more. The journey is the thing, the monsters that leap at him from the dark are all in his mind.'

I nodded. 'Nice allegory about the human condition. Beauty and death, side by side. We are all in a tunnel, pulled forward by love, but love is actually death in disguise. To desire is to die.'

'Yes, and not to love is also to die,' he said. He let go of Lorelle's hand and leaned toward me. 'When I make my movie, it will be edgy. It will be Marechera. Dostoevsky. Caravaggio. Knut Hamsun. So edgy it will cut your heart to watch it. What is the point of art if it is not to resist?'

'To resist what?'

'Just to resist, period. On principle.'

'That's the kind of films you want to make?'

'That's the life I want to live. Where art and life become one.'

'Wait till you are older, and married with kids, with bills to pay.'

He laughed and shrugged. 'Maybe that will never happen.'

Lorelle listened, her head on his shoulder, smoking a cigarette. She leaned forward and said, 'Mark's made a short, it won an award.'

Mark made a movie? My surprise must have shown on my face. Mark laughed and waved her away. 'A short short. Thirty minutes long. Something I did for a school project two years ago.'

'But it won a directing award, here in Berlin.'

'Nice,' I said. 'About a man in a tunnel?'

'You have to see it. I have a copy I can lend you,' she said.

I wanted to talk to him about his options now that his visa application had been rejected, but he didn't appear to be interested in talking about it, and perhaps this wasn't the place.

'Try and call that lawyer. Today if possible. Julius. He has been trying to reach you.' He nodded, and immediately changed the subject. 'Hey, are you free next week? There's a vinyl record store you have to see. It is humongous, the biggest in Berlin, maybe in all of Europe.'

'I am free.'

'Good. We'll go, the three of us. We can have lunch afterward. Hang out.'

'Great idea, but you must promise not to disappear again,' I said.

Mark raised his beer and, laughing, quoted from Shakespeare, '*When shall we three meet again, in thunder, lightning, or in rain . . .*'

He looked happy, and that was how I'd always remember him, leaning forward to clink glasses, with Lorelle beside him, because as it turned out that was the last time the three of us were ever together again.

'*When the hurly-burly is done / When the battle's lost and won,*' I completed automatically.

A day after our meeting at the Kino, the refugee riots, as the papers later dubbed it, happened. The inmates at the Heim woke up to find the building surrounded by policemen, their vans and cars blocking all the exits to the streets. Next to the police vans were buses provided by the local council, long double-decker buses. A police spokesman, talking through a megaphone, told the inmates to pack their belongings and vacate the building – they had six hours. The neighbours, it appeared, had complained to the council, they felt threatened, their daughters and sons were not safe on the streets where refugees sold drugs, and got drunk and fought; the aliens had turned the entire street into a dumpster, trash everywhere. Six hours to move out. The buses were there to take them to another Heim outside the city, meanwhile no one was allowed to go in or out. To hurry them along, the lights and water were cut off. But soon activists in the city heard of the blockade and descended upon the street, forming a human chain around the block, chanting in solidarity with the inmates, shouting at the police to leave.

'Mark texted me about it. Tension was high when I got there. Already the police were throwing tear gas at the activists, warning them to keep away. They wouldn't let us go beyond their perimeter,' Lorelle said.

'Where exactly were they being taken?'

'Nowhere. It is a trick they like to play. They pile migrants into buses, promising to resettle them, and then dump them outside the city, in the middle of nowhere.' She sipped her tea, as if to wash the bitter taste away. 'It is a cruel thing to do to helpless people. You know what is written on the buses?'

'What?'

'*Fahren macht Spass.*'

'Riding is fun?'

'That, accompanied by images of happy families holding hands – children and parents and even dogs. It is cruel.'

'What happened to Mark?' I asked.

'I kept trying his number, but he never answered, and I began to hope that maybe he had managed to slip out.'

She laughed and shook her head. 'It was wishful thinking. Mark wouldn't do that. He loved such standoffs with authority. "This is our moment", he would say, "this is our Sharpeville, our Agincourt." He was in there, barricaded with the rest. They had locked the doors from inside, blocking them with iron beds and tables so the police couldn't break in. We could see them at the doors and windows, waving their shirts and holding hands. The police said they were ready to wait for as long as it took. It took three days.'

'But, it wasn't even in the news . . .'

'The news covers what it wants to cover,' she said, her voice flat. 'I was there. Go online, look for alternative news sources, you'll read all about it. On the third day, when the police got tired of the standoff and threatened to break in and drag them out, the migrants soaked their mattresses, bedding and floors in kerosene, they promised to set the building and themselves aflame. Some went to the roof and threatened to jump. Mark was there, on the roof. I recognized his jacket.'

'What happened?'

'I saw his red jacket. I saw him fall, from the roof to the concrete pavement.'

'He . . . he jumped?' I asked, waiting for a twist in the story. But there was no twist.

She said, 'Afterward, I saw his body in the police car head-lights before they took him away.'

I said nothing. I continued to stare at her. We were seated outside a café we had often visited with Mark and Uta and Stan and Eric. Across the road was the church, looking more abandoned than ever. Mark was dead.

'They say he jumped.'

'Well?'

'He wouldn't. He loved life too much. Others say he was pushed. I believe them.' She lowered her head, her face was filled with the heaviest agony.

'Pushed? Why?'

'Because he was different, and even in that moment, that desperate moment, they couldn't forget that. Anyway, what does it matter now? He is dead.'

Mary Chinomba. A preacher's daughter who loved to dress in drag, who loved to perform male roles onstage, who wasn't interested in the nice boys nudged in her direction by her parents. Who ran away from home to stay with her uncle, the only one who must have known and sympathized with what or who Mary was. The scholarship to Germany must have been the perfect solution for everyone involved, a godsend, literally.

'Once, you told me that Mark could not go back to Malawi. What did you mean?' I asked.

'A year after her arrival in Germany, Mary wrote her uncle a letter, pretending it was from her friend. The letter said Mary had died in an accident, and that the body had been cremated because nobody came to claim it. She signed the letter "Mark". That was the day Mary died.'

'Did the uncle believe him . . . her?' I asked.

'The letter wasn't for the uncle, really, it was for the father, the family. She figured it was best for everyone concerned. Mark dropped out of her first university in Hamburg and became a nomad. He didn't want to be traced by accident. I asked him if he would go back home someday, and he always said, Maybe.'

We sat down, watching our food go cold. None of us had the will to stand up and say goodbye.

'Tell me,' I said, 'how did you meet her?'

'Him,' she said.

'Him. How did you meet him?'

Lorelle got married at twenty-two, against her parents'

will. The parents had been redeployed back to the US and wanted her to go with them, but she refused. After a few years, her husband, a DJ she had met at a party in a converted bunker, had turned abusive. 'He beat me. I tried to leave him a few times but he threatened to harm me if I did. I eventually ran away to Berlin; I enrolled at the university. I met Mark, on the very first day. We became friends, much later we became lovers. A weird couple around campus, the cross-dresser from Africa and the freak from the US. Mark gave me the courage to ask Thomas, my husband, for a divorce. I grew up. Because of Mark.'

I took her hand. 'I am so sorry.'

She nodded.

'So, you are going back to America?'

'I've been thinking about it for a while, now this . . . I feel as if things have lost their focus for me here. I want to see my parents, get to know them again. What about you?'

'I am not sure yet.'

'Well, good luck. And when you come back to the States, give me a call.'

•

I got off the bus at the stop next to the *Apotheke*. I walked past the retirement home, my head bowed in thought, and as I passed the school for the homeless children I saw him running to the fence, waving, chased by his eagerness, his face alight just as in Gina's painting. '*Schokolade!*' I averted my face and walked faster, but then I stopped and turned to him. I had to admire his persistence. I raised my hand and waved back. He stood with both hands on the top of the wall, just like in the painting, his shock turning to delight as I called back, 'Hello.'

Slowly his hands dropped and he turned and walked back to his friends. I walked on beneath the poplar trees, my mind still churning.

The summer is ended, the harvest gathered, and still we are not saved. The line ran in my mind. I could see Mark standing behind the lectern, thumping his fist on the baize surface, his eyes flicking over his imaginary congregation, imitating his father.

'I am not going back,' I said to Gina. I had not thought about it, but as soon as I said it I knew I had decided long before today. I would stay in Berlin, for a while. I could support myself for a few months teaching ESL while I decided what to do next. I could also do some work on my long-neglected dissertation. Gina was seated on the couch, a book in her hand. She didn't look surprised. I thought of our home in Arlington. The parking lot across the road, and us sitting on the balcony, watching the kids skating. That seemed like another life now; recently I couldn't find myself in that picture, next to Gina. She was sitting alone.

'We used to be so happy,' she said. And I knew she meant before the miscarriage. 'I thought if we came to Berlin, together, away from everything . . . I thought Berlin would heal us.'

She sighed. The silenced lengthened, broken occasionally by birdcalls. Perhaps that was what we needed, silence. A little time apart. She looked directly into my eyes, and nodded. Somewhere, in the trees outside, a cuckoo's unmistakable call. I went to the window and looked up. A chittering, a flash of wings, grey and white and dappled. Then it was gone.

Book 2

CHECKPOINT CHARLIE

Manu walks up the driveway, then back, flexing his fingers and stamping his feet to keep the circulation going. It is almost midnight, two more hours to the end of his shift. His thick army surplus coat and the layer of woollen sweater under it feel useless against the cold claws of Berlin winter tearing into him. He is so hungry he feels weak. Stay awake, he whispers, stay alert, that's all you have to do for two more hours. He forces himself to imagine the clients staggering out, flush with drink and dancing. Part of his job is to hold the door for them as they come out trying to orient their senses to the cold, sometimes he helps them find their car if they can't find it by themselves. In the one month he has been working here he's never had to lead a lady to her car, there is always an eager and muscular young man with the ladies as they come out, laughing and listing on their high-heeled boots. To be escorted home afterward by young men is why most of them come to the Sahara Nightclub, after all. Mostly white and older ladies, mostly black and younger men.

The Sahara sits like an island amidst the parked cars, its brash neon sign reflecting in red and green off the cars' shiny bodies. Both sides of the sidewalk are covered in snow, heaped up like sand at a construction site. He shivers again and takes another drag on his cigarette. He is not a smoker, he got this from his partner, the Turk, but neither is he a doorman, or a bouncer, or a Berliner, but here he is, holding the door, bouncing, smoking cigarettes, in Berlin. Two more hours. He curses the cold again but quickly catches himself; he is lucky to have a job at all given his status. His daughter needs new shoes now that she'll be starting school, new clothes, new underwear, including training bras – she gave him a list. She will be twelve in May. Bras. What does he know about bras, apart from how annoying they can be to take off when one is in a hurry! Ah, the cold, the blasted European winter. Perhaps, if he has some form of distraction, apart from smoking and listening to his talkative partner, the job, the bouncing, may be less tedious. Sometimes the clients come out to catch a quick cigarette, or spliff. He mostly ignores them. Keep it professional, the manager told him on his first day. Keep it professional or you are out. Gruff-looking, gruff-talking redhead, incessantly smoking. She wore jeans that were too tight at the thighs and calves, emphasizing her short, chunky legs, her hair was piled high on her head, as if to give her extra inches. She looked up at him when he stood in her narrow office and told her he had heard of an opening. The office was dark and filled with cigarette smoke; on the walls were photographs of musicians and actors, some of them in the outlandish costumes of their art, some of them posing with the manager, there were bold, ostentatious signatures across the face of each picture. Next to the pictures was an old poster from the movie *Mandingo*. 'Aren't you a bit too old for this job?' She blew smoke at him. He was only forty, he wanted to protest, and he might look a bit tired, but every muscle on him is real, earned in the strawberry and grape fields of Greece where he spent last season picking fruit, sleeping on hard floors, escaping the police and the neo-Nazis, and making sure Rachida was safe. The manager reluctantly nodded, acknowledging his lean, imposing presence, and said he could start tomorrow.

•

They come out, they smoke, they make small talk, and they go back inside to the loud dance music. Mostly young, mostly muscular, most likely West African. He wonders if they have wives back home, children, waiting to join them here in Europe, or waiting for them to come back rich and with all the right papers, the all-important papers that would open up life's cornucopia. He wonders what his wife would think if she saw him now, a bouncer at the Sahara. She'd understand, surely. Rachida needs a new jacket for the winter, new underwear. Just for the winter, in spring he'll find something somewhere, cleaning, construction, dishwashing. All temporary, till he gets his papers.

•

He recognizes the green jacket as the woman staggers out as if pushed by the loud dance music that follows her from inside the hall. He helped her with it earlier when she came. She arrived after 11 p.m., and she is leaving already. Maybe she doesn't like the music. Maybe she doesn't like the men. She staggers a little, pulling the jacket tight around her, looking around slowly. As he turns to her, mouthing 'Alles gut?' and smiling, always smiling, trying to look as harmless as possible, she casts a contemplative stare at him, up and then down. The light falls directly on her and he notices her eyes are clear, probably not that drunk, just a bit disoriented, the brash lights and the cold do that to you coming out. His partner, Ahmad the Turk, pushes him aside and starts talking to her in his overfriendly, overeager way. She hugs herself beneath her jacket and, ignoring Ahmad, looks directly at Manu and says, 'Can you help me find my car? It is somewhere out there.' She points.

He takes the keys and goes out among the cars, pressing the beeper on the fob. The cold gets worse the further away he goes from the building. Ah, a Mercedes-Benz. Tucked away between a wall and a tree at the edge of the parking lot, as if she doesn't want it to be seen. New to the Sahara, most likely. He gets in and turns the key; loud music from the radio startles him, and he almost hits his head on the roof as he pulls back, then, relieved, he laughs at himself. He turns down the volume. The car smells of vanilla and sandalwood. Basma smells like that in the mornings, fresh, dressed for work. He leans back in the plush leather, he closes his eyes and lets the music wash over him like balm. It carries him away and he is home, Rachida is two again and he is putting her to bed, she can't go to sleep without her favourite lullaby playing softly in the background. A loud knock on the passenger-side window jolts him back to the present. Where is he? Green jacket. He wipes the moistness from his eyes before leaning over and opening the door for her. She gets in.

'Hallo,' she says.

'Nice car. Scared I'd run off with it?'

She looks surprised by the question. Of course, she wouldn't expect small talk from the bouncer, only he isn't a bouncer, not really. 'Well . . .' he mutters, and begins to step out, but her leather-gloved hand on his right arm stops him.

'Stay, please,' she says. She removes her hand from his arm and begins to take off her gloves, a finger at a time. As she removes the jacket he notices for the first time the luxurious fur at the collar. She smells of perfume, rich, musky. The music comes to a stop, another tune starts.

She puts her hands over the air vent, turning them over slowly like meat on a grill.

'I have to get back to work. Will you be okay?'

She shakes her head and gives a small laugh. 'I . . .' she begins, 'I am no good when I've had more than two drinks. Can you drive me home, please? My place is not far.'

'I can drive, but I am working.'

'I asked your partner, he said it is okay. He says he will cover for you.'

He looks at her, he looks outside at the pile of snow glowing in the dark. 'Okay,' he says.

•

They drive in silence. She sits with her head uptilted, her eyes closed. He enjoys the silence, the dreamlike ride in the deserted night streets. On a narrow back street a homeless man staggers into the road, looking like something out of Dickens with his overcoat blowing in the wind behind him, his long beard, his wild, baleful eyes caught briefly in the headlights, then he is gone. Manu follows her directions, conscious of her form, her smell, her swan neck illuminated by the streetlamps and the headlights of the cars they pass, and he knows she is conscious of him too for she sits half-facing him, expecting him to say something. She lives in Grunewald. He follows her finger down a quiet and dark street and eases the car into the narrow driveway, the tyres loudly crunching the gravel on the cobblestones. He turns off the engine and they sit in the dark for a while, then she stirs, and he stirs. She points him in the direction of the U-Bahn and hands him a fifty-euro note. He hesitates, then he shakes his head. 'No.'

'Well, *gute Nacht.*'

•

They leave the Heim early as they do every Sunday. Sunday is a good day, he and Basma were married on a Sunday, and Rachida was born on a Sunday. If she is going to be there waiting for them with the boy, if a miracle is going to happen to them, it is most likely going to be on a Sunday. And so, every Sunday, for the past one year since they arrived in Berlin, he and the girl have taken the train from the station near the Heim to Kochstrasse U-Bahn, and from there they walk across Oranienstrasse to Checkpoint Charlie.

He is glad the trains are mostly empty today. He hates the

weekdays and the rush hours and having to stand face-to-face with other passengers, breathing in the smell of stale beer and sausage and cheese, listening to their loud, unrestrained chatter on their cell phones.

They sit side by side, away from the cold wind that blows in every time the doors open. At a station an official appears before him and demands to see his pass. He always maintains a month's pass for the two of them, no need to take chances. After the ticket check he feels Rachida tugging at his arm. 'Father.' He is muttering to himself again. He clasps her hand. She looks at his face, anxious. Recently it is happening more regularly. The sallow-faced young man next to them leans over to lock lips with his even sallower-faced girlfriend. His hair stands in a ridge on his head, held up by gel. The girl wears a biker jacket and knee-length boots. Manu looks out the window, willing Rachida to look away. As they get off the train they face a billboard with a completely naked man seated on a stool, leering into the camera, his crotch barely covered by his hands clasped over it. A few months ago Manu would have stepped in front of his daughter to block her view, but now he simply turns his gaze away. It is a new world, another culture. She'll get inured to it. Beside the naked man's picture is another of a starving, fly-specked black child, looking out plaintively at the passengers, asking to be saved from whatever hell the viewer imagines is lurking in the shadows behind her. What does Rachida think of it all? He looks down at her walking quietly next to him, her face set, trying to avoid the pedestrians, trying to keep up. She needs her mother.

As they come out of the U-Bahn and join a body of pedestrians waiting for the light to change, he feels a familiar mix of hope and dread. Two weeks back, as they waited right here to cross, in this very spot, he thought he saw her in the distance, holding a toddler, the same height and hair shape as Omar. He pointed and they ran, ignoring the cars, pushing through the cluster of tourists on the sidewalk, past the mock MPs, one black, one white, standing in front of the guard hut on the median, hoisting the American flag, posing for pictures with tourists at two euros per picture. A child in a blue jacket momentarily separated from its parents stood in their path, alone on the sidewalk, looking about, trying not to panic. They turned left into Zimmerstrasse and hurried past the Stasi Museum, past the ancient Lada cars parked by the sidewalk, past the giant balloon waiting to take up its passengers for a lofty view of Berlin. Then they turned back, breathless, toward Stadtmitte U-Bahn.

'Where are they?' Rachida cried. There were tears in her eyes. The woman had disappeared, her black jacket swallowed by a sea of black jackets, then she reappeared crossing the road, hand in hand with the child. She was like a swimmer dipping and surfacing in a choppy sea.

'There,' he shouted.

'Mother!' Rachida shouted.

They waited at the crossing, watching the pair receding further into the crowd. The light changed, they ran. He felt a clutch of pain in his chest, he needed to exercise. He realized he was pulling Rachida too hard, her hand almost slipping out of his moist grip. But they were catching up to the woman and the boy, who had just entered a souvenir shop. Why was she not looking around, searching for them like they were searching?

Later, he sat on a bench by the roadside, his hands shaking, trying to console Rachida as she covered her face with her hands, her shoulders shaking. The memory of the woman's surprised, then frightened face as he grabbed her hand shamed him. Her gaze went from him to Rachida, two demented faces in the middle of the souvenir store, he shouting 'Basma, darling!' and the girl shouting 'Mother!' Passers-by looked casually at them and he wondered what they saw: a tired-looking man and a crying girl by the roadside, clearly foreigners, in their old and ill-fitting winter jackets – mostly, though, they didn't see you at all.

•

The lights change and they cross, he takes Rachida's hand at a crossing, pretending to guide her through the crush of bodies, but really just wanting something to hold on to. They loiter around the souvenir shops and then they turn back and head toward Stadtmitte U-Bahn. Their legs are used to these routes by now, rising and falling and turning automatically, only the eyes are on full alert, head swivelling, searching for the beloved faces. Hours later, when the girl's legs begin to drag, he stops and they enter a McDonald's. She orders a chicken sandwich. Again, he is reminded that only last year she was ordering the Happy Meal: six chicken nuggets, fries and a drink. He tries to make small talk as she eats. He feels her eyes on him, full of questions, and he quickly smiles and touches her cornrows. 'Your hair looks different. When did you do it?'

Her eyes light up as she runs her hand over the imbricated, dovetailing rows. 'Hannah did it, last night while we were waiting for you to return.'

Last night. While he sat in the car with the lady in the

green jacket, yearning to put his hand over hers, his lips against her neck.

'It's beautiful. We must thank Hannah when we get back. Maybe we'll pick up something for her.'

They hang around till the crowd has thinned, and the doner kebab and imbiss stands by the roadside have closed and the tourists are replaced by another kind of crowd, younger, louder, walking hand in hand, and then they head back to the trains.

•

At the Heim, Hannah is waiting for them in what the inmates refer to as the garden. A barren and gravelled space at the back of the huge and charmless building. It is littered with cans and plastic bags clinging to the base of the building, vestigial rosebush stalks, and iron benches presenting a windswept and dismal tableau. The inmates, especially those with children, come out on warmer days to sit on the benches and gaze at the slate-grey skies, enjoying a moment of quiet, pretending they are somewhere else, not at a Heim in a strange city thousands of miles from home.

Hannah turns her kindly, questioning eyes on him and he smiles briefly in response, saying nothing. Is that a flicker of relief on her face? He feels a spark of anger at her. He knows what she is thinking: for another week they will remain a make-believe family, till next Sunday when he and the girl go back on their search. They met in Greece and for one year they travelled together, almost a family, he and Hannah and Rachida, in the manner he has seen many people do on the road, childless women falling in with motherless children, wifeless husbands with husbandless wives, proxy partners for as long as it lasts – then they parted when she came to Berlin ahead of them, and now they are together again. Sometimes he wonders what she wants from him. Love? Friendship? Protection? For almost two years she has never asked for anything that he wouldn't have offered without being asked. Protection, yes, friendship, certainly, but not love. She is a beautiful woman, and even in these circumstances she manages to look pretty, with long silken hair framing a face from which the joy and light are fading. She sometimes mentions a daughter and a husband back in Eritrea. She never offers more details, and he never asks for more. Details have a way of piling up, layer upon seductive layer, making you think you know the person, until one day you realize you don't. Stories are made up and traded as currency among homeless, rootless people, offered like a handshake, something to disarm you with. He has long stopped wanting to know – he knows better than to get too close. They are here for a new start, not to re-create or hold on to the past. The water they all crossed to come here has dissolved the past. But, he can't give up on Checkpoint Charlie. Because she is alive. He knows. If she isn't he'd know, and if she is alive she'd never rest until she finds them.

•

His partner, the sour-tongued, sour-tempered Ahmad, says, 'What these young men want is power. When they fuck these women they think they own the world. By fucking them in the ass or the mouth or wherever, they feel they are fucking the whole of Germany. I swear, that's what they think. Haha. What do you think, Ghaddafi?'

'I don't know, Ahmad.'

'You should know. You are educated. You must have an opinion.'

'You are right, I guess.'

'You are right I am right, Libya.' He pauses, dragging on his cigarette. 'Tell me, if you are Libyan, why are you so black?'

'My father is originally from Nigeria. He settled in Libya before I was born.'

He never considered himself different from any Libyan till after the fall of the dictator when ordinary citizens, including his neighbours, some of them his patients, began attacking whomever they thought looked different, foreign. He doesn't tell the Turk this. He shrugs. 'There are many like me.'

The Turk is an ex-boxer. Ahmad the Turk, they called him in the ring. Once, he was a contender for the heavyweight title for the region of Bavaria, but he broke a wrist in the fifth round, he didn't even know his wrist was fractured till the next round. He just couldn't feel his hand any more.

They stand side by side in the little alcove next to the entrance, sheltering from the cold, smoking furiously to keep away the cold. Ahmad is given to hyperbole, especially on nights like this when the cold is most bitter, and the women and young men that pass before them seem to be having all the fun in the world. He knew the Klitschko brothers, he claims. Once, he was a sparring partner for both brothers, three years back, when they came to Heidelberg and he got to stay with them in the Hotel Europäischer Hof Heidelberg, the most expensive hotel in town. Sometimes he gets overcome by nostalgia for his fighting days, usually when the weather dips too far below freezing, and the Sahara is deserted, then he'll smoke cigarette after cigarette while doing a little shadowboxing, his fighter's muscles rippling under his jacket, and when he gets tired of that, he'll step into the bar to refill his hip flask with vodka.

'Muammar,' he says, sipping his vodka, 'these women come for company, a little fun, and our job is to help them get it. Right?'

'Right.'

'One day, one of them asked me to walk her to her car, just like it happened to you that day. Hold my hand, she said, and we went. Beautiful. Young. Tits this big. I walk her to her car and she pulls me inside and begs me not to let her go home alone. I swear to Allah, Libya. Now we are holding each other in that car, and we go at it, giving no quarter, boom, I go at her, and she comes back, pow, she scratches my back until I bleed, I pound into her, she pushes up, I push down and now the car is rocking with our movement, and still we go at it.'

He assumes a boxer's crouch, fists forward and raised. 'Now we are locked together, like this, swaying together. She is a tigress. And all the while that woman Fairuz is playing on the car radio. Now we both fall back into the car seat, locked together, breathing heavily in each other's face. She holds me, like this, two hands around my neck, as if scared of falling off a cliff, harder, she says, harder, and then, I can't hold back any more, my body shakes, I am down. I am out.' He leans against the wall, panting in recollection. 'Ah, Ghaddafi. Those were the crazy nights . . .'

Then he straightens up, looking past Manu into the night. 'Hey, look who's here.'

For two weeks the club had been shut down. A mysterious fire had started behind the bar, some say it was a jealous husband who had followed his wife to the club. Not much damage was done.

In those two weeks, as he walked the streets of Berlin looking for casual employment, and even on Sundays at Checkpoint Charlie, he thought about her, attracted and guilty at the same time. He remembers her hand on his arm, a brief electricity, a frisson, and her mouth near his ear as she whispered, '*Gute Nacht.*'

Now he watches her approach. The cold has intensified over the last few days. As she approaches, swathed in her green jacket, he feels like turning and walking away in the other direction, into the cold night. She ducks into the tight alcove next to him and takes out a cigarette.

'How can you stand this cold?' she says. He hands her a light, saying nothing. She takes a drag and passes him the cigarette. They smoke, not talking.

'You should go in,' he says. 'It is warmer.'

'I am okay here,' she says. 'I am not a very good dancer.'

'Then why do you come here?'

'Maybe I need the company,' she says. She turns and looks at him directly. The Turk slips into the bar and returns with a bottle of vodka. 'I can't drink,' she says. 'I have to drive back.'

'I can drive you,' Manu says. The Turk winks at him and makes a shadowboxing motion with his fists.

'That will be nice,' she says. She takes the open bottle and sips.

Later, in the car, he asks, 'What is your name?'

'Angela.'

'Like the chancellor,' he says. At her house, they sit in the car for a while, listening to a piano concerto on the radio. The night is quiet, all the windows are dark. A cat slinks across the balcony and into a garden.

'What do you do?' She turns, facing him. 'I mean, before you came to Berlin.'

He says, 'I was a doctor. A surgeon.'

She takes his hands and looks at them, as if by so doing to divine the truth of his claim.

'I knew there was something different about you when I first saw you that night. You looked out of place standing there, helping people to their cars. What happened? Where's your family?' When he says nothing, she rubs his hand in hers. 'You have very good hands.'

'Thanks.'

'Your partner told me you are from Libya. Do you miss your country?'

'I have no country.'

'Come inside.'

He looks out the car window at the house, quiet, the darkness settled around it like a mist. 'Perhaps not,' he says gently.

'Come on, have a cup of tea before you go. I live alone.'

He follows her into a big hall. He can tell it is a big house even though she doesn't bother to turn on the lights. A baby grand piano stands near a window in the living room, which connects to the kitchen in an open plan. A silver shaft of light comes in through the kitchen window, falling on the silver refrigerator and stove. She opens the fridge and takes out a bottle of gin, then she leads him through the living room, into a corridor, and then into a bedroom. She leaves him there, standing in the middle of the room, the bottle of gin and two glasses on the table next to him, and disappears into the bathroom. Soon he hears the shower running. He looks around the dark room, feeling his way to a light switch. The overhead light comes on, transfixing him in its glare, he quickly turns it off and turns on the night lamp. He sits on an ottoman by the window, and takes off his thick boots. The boots are worn at the heels. He has been wearing them for two years now. When she comes out of the bathroom, wrapped in a flimsy robe, he continues to sit, motionless. She drops the robe.

'I have a wife,' he says. His voice is hoarse, his eyes fixed to her voluptuous body.

She sits next to him on the ottoman, the heat from her body rising toward him. 'And I have a husband. But we are separated.' She takes his hand and places it on her breast, all the time looking into his face. Slowly she helps him take off his jacket, dropping it on the floor. He stands up, conscious of the bulge in his trousers. 'I'll take a bath.'

In the bathroom, still warm, the mirrors still covered in steam, he fills the tub with hot water. The heating at the Heim has broken down and bathing for the past month is simply turning on the freezing shower over his head and standing under it for as long as he can endure before dashing out of the bathroom. He dips his leg into the very hot water, and then the other leg, then slowly lowers his body; the hot water on his skin is a benediction and he almost cries out with pleasure. He sinks in to his chin and closes his eyes.

The sun coming in through the blinds wakes him up in the morning, and he sits up momentarily disoriented. Where is he? He is in a strange room, in a strange bed, and there is something important he has forgotten. When he sees the naked woman next to him he gets out of bed and begins to dress. It is Sunday.

'Where are you going?' she asks, reaching out an arm toward him. He continues to dress, hurriedly, almost desperately. 'My daughter will be waiting for me,' he says finally.

'What is her name?' she asks.

'Rachida.'

'Bring her, one of these days. I'd love to see her. I have horses, she could ride them.'

•

Each time he goes back to Grunewald she asks him to bring Rachida, and each time he promises he will. He goes on weekdays when he isn't working, and on Saturdays before going to work at the Sahara. Occasionally he stays overnight, but never on Saturdays. He makes up excuses for that: he has to take Rachida to the park, he has German-language lessons – which he does, though not on Sundays. To Hannah and Rachida, he says he is out job hunting in Grunewald, and he tries to salve his conscience by getting them little presents, things he can afford, scarves for Hannah, sweets and trinkets for Rachida. Sometimes Angela hands him a grocery bag stuffed with packets of sugar, tea, fruit. 'For your daughter.' Hannah takes the bag each time, saying nothing, but her eyes are always filled with questions, which he avoids.

'Where are we going, Father?' Rachida asks. Her apprehension shows in the way she clutches his hand as they get off the train at Grunewald, she walks close to him, staring at the gated houses with vines running over the walls and fences. This is far from Kreuzberg and the Heim, far from the touristy bustle and noise of Checkpoint Charlie, far from anything she has experienced since they came to Berlin.

'We are going to see a friend. She has horses and she might let you ride one.'

She looks up at him, surprise and doubt on her face. How will she behave with Angela? he wonders. It will be fine. Angela is charming, easy to talk to, and surely she will be great with children. With her he can talk about the past. Lying in bed naked, post-coitus, the words come easily, gently coaxed by her attentive face, the right questions, and on each visit he tells her more. 'Tell me about Libya,' she always begins. He told her how the students at Rachida's school began to disappear, one by one. 'What happened to all my friends?' Rachida had asked him. 'They don't come to school any more.' The school population dwindled as the violence grew, the NTC rebels gradually took over town after town, those who could afford it left, till only the children of the poor remained. The worst part was when the teachers started to leave. By the end of 2010, almost all the schools in the area were closed.

'Every day I woke up, I took the kids to school, I went to work, I pretended that things would soon get back to normal. I was the only doctor left for miles around, when eventually even the sick stopped coming to the clinic for fear of the violence on the streets, I told my wife to take the children and leave. She refused, she wouldn't go without me. Then one day, I took the kids to school as usual and the gate was closed, not even the guard was there, that was when I knew it was time to go. When we came home, my wife was ready, unknown to me she had packed weeks before, and just waiting for me to come to my senses. And still I was reluctant to go. "But if we go, who will take care of the sick and the wounded?" I asked. "Let the politicians take care of them," she said.

'We decided to come to Berlin, that's where everybody was going. Also, I had an old school friend here, Abdul Gani. We had no plan, nothing. The most important plan was to get out of Tripoli alive. Also, I told her, "If anything happens on the way and we are separated, continue on to Berlin. Look for me at Checkpoint Charlie. I'll wait there, every Sunday."'

'Why Checkpoint Charlie?' Angela asked.

He shrugged. 'I had read about it in books. It seemed as good a spot as any.' Then he added, almost shyly, 'In the movies lovers always meet at a prominent landmark, like the Empire State Building, or the Eiffel Tower.'

'You must love your wife very much.'

'Yes,' he said.

'So, did you meet your friend, Abdul?'

'Unfortunately no. By the time we got here he had moved on. He now lives in America, in San Diego.'

•

He wonders if Rachida can sense his nervousness, how his steps falter as they approach the front door, how his hand takes an infinitesimally long time to rise to the doorbell. The door opens and a man stands at the door, a man with a thin, unsmiling face, his hair greying. Manu can tell he isn't that old, mid-fifties. He looks at Manu, then the girl, then back to Manu.

'Who are you looking for?' His voice is challenging, his posture, one hand on his hip, is aggressive. Manu turns to Rachida, unable to hide his confusion, he looks at the house number again, 47, then he says to the man, 'I think we have the wrong house. Sorry to disturb you.'

He pulls her hand and they turn to go. As they cross the road he hears Angela's voice calling, 'Manu! Hey, Manu. Come back.'

They take off their muddy shoes by the door. The man is seated behind the piano, running his fingers aimlessly over the keys. He doesn't look up when they enter.

'Joachim, this is Manu, a friend. And this is Rachida, his daughter,' Angela says. She comes forward and frames Rachida's face in her hands, pulling it close, running a hand through her hair. 'She is so beautiful, Manu.'

'Hello, Joachim,' Manu says.

Joachim remains bowed over the piano, his back curved over the keyboard until it seems he is going to tip forward, then he raises his hands and a tune rings out. It rises and falls, repetitive, rising and falling.

Angela leads the girl away. 'My, you are so cold, come to the kitchen, I'll make you a cocoa. And you, Manu, I'll get you a coffee.'

The man keeps playing, his head lowered, his eyes closed. Manu sits, feeling the awkwardness of the moment. Joachim is the husband. Angela has mentioned the name several times. He wonders what he is doing, why he is back. His eyes run over the familiar room, every surface is redolent of him and Angela caught in blind passion, panting and sightless and naked. The piano. She, bent over, her hair dripping into the keyboard, he behind her, his hands on her waist, together banging out a sweet and strange tune. He begins to stand up, and just then Joachim turns and says, 'Charles Mingus.'

'What?' Manu asks, smiling. He takes a deep breath to regain his poise, always smiling to show he is harmless.

' "Take the A Train", by Charles Mingus. You know it?'

'No. I am not a musical person, unfortunately. I am a doctor.' He adds the last with a squaring of his shoulders.

But the man interrupts him. 'Did Angela tell you I am a musician, jazz?'

'I believe she must have.'

He continues before Manu can answer, 'Jazz is like life. You have to trust in chance, sometimes it will work, sometimes it will not work. It is like sex. When it does work, it is magic. Tell me, does it work like that for you?'

'I am not a jazz person myself,' Manu says.

'I don't mean jazz. With my wife. The sex, is it magic, is it chemistry?' He has been playing as he talks, but now he stops. Manu turns to the kitchen, hoping Angela will appear. He can hear laughter from the yard outside, coming through the open back door. He hasn't heard Rachida laugh like this in a long time. He stands up. 'Let me see how my daughter is doing . . .'

And just then Angela enters, a cup of coffee in her hand. She hands him the cup. She looks from him to Joachim, who has gone back to picking at the piano keys.

'What are you two talking about?'

Joachim continues to play, turning fully to face Angela. Manu stands up and heads for the kitchen and the back door leading to the courtyard. Rachida is in the barn, feeding a piebald mare an apple. She turns and sees him, her face alight with wonder. She hands him the apple. 'You can feed her, Father. Isn't she pretty?'

'Yes.'

He can see into the living room from where he stands. They are shouting at each other. Joachim is trying to take her arm, but she shakes him off angrily and walks away to the kitchen. Joachim follows her, she leaves the kitchen and heads into the corridor to the bedroom.

'Come, we have to go now.'

'The horse, Father, what of the horse?' she asks. She is wearing a pair of Angela's boots. He hugs her tightly, 'I am so sorry, child. This was all a mistake. We have to go.'

'But . . .'

'Hurry, Rachida, hurry.'

As they pass through the living room, a door opens and Angela comes out. Manu whispers, 'Sorry, we have to go now. Thanks for everything.'

'You don't have to go.' She goes to Rachida and takes her hand.

'I am sorry,' he says, looking into her eyes. 'This was a mistake.'

Rachida looks with perplexity from her father to the woman.

'Come, Rachida,' he says. Their feet landing on the hard snow makes hollow crunching noises as they leave.

•

'She says she can't go today. She is not feeling well.'

Hannah stands by the door, a tense smile on her face. She is wearing a quilted housecoat that reaches below her knees.

'Well, it is Sunday. Please go in and remind her. It is Sunday.'

'What happened yesterday? She came back distraught.'

He searches her face, most of it covered by her hair falling forward like a veil. He wonders how much Rachida has told her. It is Sunday, he wants to repeat, but says instead, 'Can I see her?'

He steps forward, trying to go around her into the women's section. The women and children occupy the top floor of the Heim, and although it is not forbidden, the men consider the women's section off-limits. If they want to see a woman, they stand at the entrance and send for her. Hannah remains static.

'Come,' she says, 'let's go to the garden.'

In the deserted garden a plastic bag flies in the wind around the square space, and ends up stuck on the leg of the bench they are seated on, side by side. Hannah says, 'I heard from my lawyer today. The review board has approved my asylum application.'

He looks at her, speechless. Finally, he says, 'Well, that is great news, Hannah. I am so happy for you.'

She nods. 'I have been allocated a place, a small place. One bedroom, and a living room. A bath, a kitchen.'

'When do you leave?'

'No date yet, but soon.'

'Rachida will miss you.'

She nods again, silent. He adds softly. 'We will miss you.'

'You two can come with me.'

'But we can't,' he says.

'Why not?'

When he gives no answer she lays a hand over his. 'You don't have to answer now. Think about it. Rachida is like my daughter now. I want to know she is okay. I want to watch her grow into a woman.'

•

A light snow is falling, turning the sidewalk white. He exits the train station and walks toward Checkpoint Charlie, alone. The mock MPs are at it again, posing with tourists. The wind in his face brings tears to his eyes. The diehards brave the bone-chilling cold, drifting like windblown paper from one display to the next, their faces barely visible pink splotches under scarves and hats. He continues on Fried-richstrasse till he sees the blue *U* sign in front of Stadtmitte U-Bahn. The lighted sign sucks him forward like a fly, and soon he is on the train, not caring where he is going. He changes trains a few times, from U-Bahn to S-Bahn and back again. Once, he starts and looks around, fearing he has forgotten something. 'Rachida,' he mutters. As he gets out of a station he notices the train tracks running in multiple directions: at times they look like fault lines separating sec-tions of the city; other times they are stitches, holding the city together. Now he is walking by the Spree, alone, and where is everybody, the summer crowd sitting in the grass watching the tourists in boats gliding by. Lumps of dirty snow from the last snowfall litter the dry brown grass. He stands staring at the water.

He can hear Hannah's voice, rising from the water, 'Why don't you take a break today?' And his voice, sounding hor-rified, 'You know I can't. What if she comes today, the very day I decide not to go? I won't forgive myself . . .'

'Maybe it is time to let go, Manu.'

'What are you saying?'

'Rachida . . . She knows her mother is never coming. She is doing this just to please you.'

'What?'

'Listen . . . my husband . . . he is not coming either. He died, killed in front of my eyes.'

'But you said he was coming, you are waiting for him.' She was lying to him. Why was she doing that? But she went on, gentle yet still insistent, 'We say things sometimes to keep our sanity. Your wife, she died, didn't she? And the boy, and you blame yourself.'

'Shh. Stop. You know nothing about me.'

He left her and ran out into the street, clutching at the hot molten pain in his chest, till he got to the train station. Now his face in the Spree stares back at him – tired lines on his forehead and around his eyes, deep like a freshly ploughed field. His hair, when did it turn so white, so thin at the top? The wind blows over the water surface; ripples, waves rise, tall and towering like horses rearing up to attack, and everywhere he turns there are bodies floating, people screaming. He holds on to Rachida, he is a good swimmer, but Basma, where is she, she has the boy, he can't see them anywhere. Bobbing and sinking. Flotsam everywhere. But he won't give up. He will go to Checkpoint Charlie every Sunday. Rachida will come with him. They will walk past the souvenir shops and ice cream stalls, together. If they keep their memories alive, then nothing has to die.

Book 3

BASEL

1

A drive of twenty minutes outside the city toward Liestal and a confusion of intersections led to the tiny town where the woman lived. Katharina, that was her name. They'd left the autoroute and taken a narrower road that rose gently into the hills through little towns with cars bearing ski equipment clamped to their roofs parked in front of houses and hotels. Skiers getting ready to go off to the mountains, the taxi driver explained, he pointed ahead, French border. The border was even closer than Basel, which was still visible behind them, its tall buildings and communication masts rising into the cloudy sky. The house was tiny, separated from its neighbours by fir trees and grass hedges. Portia told the driver

to wait. She got down and stood before the door and peered
into the glass panel before ringing the bell. A woman opened
the door halfway, sticking only her head out in the crack
between door and frame.

'Katharina?' Portia asked.

'Yes.'

'I am Portia. David's sister. We spoke on the phone.'

The woman nodded and opened the door wider. Portia
paid the driver and followed the woman into the house.

'Welcome in Basel,' Katharina smiled. She ran her hands
through her hair, twisting it into a knot at the back. *To*, Portia
found herself correcting mentally. It was the same in Berlin.
Welcome in Berlin, they'd tell her. It was a direct translation
from the German, she knew, but she corrected them anyway,
mentally. Welcome *to* Basel.

'Sorry, it is a very small house,' Katharina said. Her hair
was raven black and tousled. A beauty, Portia noted grudg-
ingly, if you like the petite type – she stood just over five feet
tall. Part of the reason she was here was to see this woman
whom her brother chose, to try to understand why he chose
her. What was the attraction? She was an educated woman,
a former lecturer at a university, a PhD. Was that part of the
attraction, an intelligent person he could talk to, look up to,
or was it the beauty? That would be a good place to start,
an instant icebreaker. Why do you think my brother chose
you? Unless of course if it was she who did the choosing. The
house was a veritable dollhouse, the living room already felt
crammed with only two of them standing in the middle. Two
bedrooms at most. An open door led into a kitchen adjoin-
ing the living room. A square patch of tartan rug covered the

floor, on the edges of the rug were a couch, two armchairs, and a circular dining table by the window. A glass flower vase with a single red rose in it rested on the window ledge – it was a large window, almost taking up the whole wall, and it gave the small room an illusion of space. Next to the window was a bookshelf. Everything in its place, a tidy mind.

'It is a beautiful house,' she said.

'Thank you,' Katharina said, and, out of modesty or a stubborn determination not to concede the point about how unimpressive the house was, she pointed at the wood beams in the roof, thick and long and tubular. 'It is an old house, my aunt built it. Long ago. Maybe twenty years now.'

They sat down, the ice still unbroken. Katharina took out a picture of her aunt from the desk drawer and showed it to Portia. A large, stern-faced woman, hair tied at the back of her head, her back straight and her chest thrust out like a drill sergeant at a parade. She had died a few years back, at the age of eighty – an independent, strong-willed woman, who lived in a time when such attributes were considered unwomanly. She grew up poor, she never married, worked various jobs all her life: laundry maid, nanny, cook, bus driver, all the time saving her money, driven by one desire, to build her own place. And she did, saving every penny. She taught herself carpentry and some of the wooden furniture, like the bookshelves and dining table and chairs, she made herself. Katharina was her only niece, and they were close, and she left her the house when she died.

'Sometimes I feel sad. She didn't enjoy life, she saved and economized, and now she is dead. She should have enjoyed more, you know.' As Katharina talked her eyes kept straying to the passage leading to the door next to the kitchen, and a minute later the door opened and a man came out. Average height, about forty, leading a bull terrier on a leash. He was dressed in boots and a windbreaker, ready for the outdoors.

'This is Sven.'

He shook hands with Portia.

The dog went over to Portia and she let it sniff her hands and her feet, circling her, before returning to Sven. He pulled at the leash, heading for the door, speaking softly to the dog in German. Katharina spoke to him in German and he nodded. '*Ja, ja.*' His eyes behind his glasses blinked weakly as he smiled and said, 'I am taking Rex for a walk. It is good to see you.'

'Bye, Rex,' Portia said.

Man and dog reappeared in the path outside the window, heading for the faraway tree line. Sven leaned down and scratched Rex behind the ears before taking off its leash. Rex bounded forward and the man followed till they disappeared into the trees. On the horizon a dense black cloud swarmed up over the fir and spruce forest, it changed into a storm of birds, a murmuration of starlings, shape-shifting, now a funnel, now a wave, now a sphere, now a sickle, rising and falling, breaking up and reconfiguring, fast and evasive and then it was gone.

Katharina said, 'Sven and I grew up together. At one time we were engaged, we were going to be married.'

'Oh,' Portia said. 'And?'

'It was a long time ago. Before I met your brother.'

Portia waited, but Katharina didn't offer more, her eyes were fixed on the distant line of trees where man and dog had disappeared.

'What happened?' Portia pressed.

Katharina shrugged. 'I talk about Sven if you like. But he is not too important for this, yes? Not concerned. My father and his father, they went to university together. Sven, he is a professor.'

'So, it was expected then, that you two would marry?'

'Well, not really, not like arranged marriage. He was my first boyfriend and we like each other, and everyone thought we were going to get married. Yes. Is there anything more you want to know about him?'

Portia shook her head, surprised by the directness and abruptness of the question. So much for breaking the ice. She wasn't the one who brought up Sven − but she sensed the woman was merely circling, sniffing her up, two strange dogs meeting. Portia smiled brightly, this was going to be a chess game. 'How old is he?'

'He is forty now. Five years older than me.'

'So you were about thirty when you met my brother?'

'I was twenty-nine. Your brother was thirty.' She stood up. 'I'll get some tea. You want?'

'Yes. Any green tea will do.'

Portia went to the bookshelf and looked at the titles: Bertolt Brecht, Goethe, Kierkegaard, Spinoza, all in German. Katharina had studied philosophy or something in that line. She wondered what they discussed, she and her brother, at night. She wondered why she was here, what purpose this visit would serve, after all, her brother was dead, gone. *Lycidas*. That poem had been running on her mind all day, driving her crazy − *For Lycidas is dead, dead ere his prime*. Three years dead. This inquisition, this raising up of the past, of what good was it? But she was here, and Katharina was here, so she might as well get on with it. Outside, the fog was steaming off the grass, rising to cover the trees.

As soon as she came back with the tea, Katharina jumped into her story without further preamble. They had met at the Basler Fasnacht festival in Basel. 'You know the Fasnacht? No? It is famous ceremony here. People dance and sing, mostly folk songs and political songs. People come from many countries to watch. That night, me and my friends, we were following the singers, they walk in the streets with their lanterns, dressed in traditional clothes. I was in final year for my PhD, and I was happy and carefree.' She paused, her eyes wistful, perhaps reliving the moment of her past happiness.

'Was David there to watch as well?'

'He was there with his wife, this he told me later. They were having some argument, I think. She left and went home. And he was alone . . .'

'My brother had another wife, before you?' she asked, putting down her tea. Katharina smiled, her cup held in both hands. She nodded, amused at Portia's reaction.

'Yes, he had a wife. Her name is Brigitte. And his name it was not David. It was Moussa. When your brother first came in Switzerland he was staying in a refugee hostel outside town. It is old building near a farming village, nobody was staying in the building so they give it for refugees. It is remote, far from town, and the refugees were not allowed to go anywhere, not church, or library, or public buildings. It was a new law. The government was trying to control immigration, too many new people coming in, and all over the country people are not sure how to treat them. There was suspicion.

The government even started paying refugees to return to their countries. About a thousand francs per person, I think.

'But Moussa didn't want to go back. He applied for asylum. They were allowed to work on farms, helping the farmers and also making some pocket money. When they first met, he was working on Brigitte's father's chicken farm and she had come to visit from the city. Her father and mother liked him very much because he is very nice, and sometimes he stayed for dinner after they work on the farm and they talk about things, what he planned to do. They even wanted to get lawyer for him to help him with his asylum application. But this day the daughter, Brigitte, she came with her two-year-old daughter. Brigitte was divorced. She was surprised to see him. Her parents have already told her about him, but she didn't know what to expect. He told me at first she was very hostile to him, she thought he was trying to take advantage of her parents. They were old, in their seventies. But later they became friends. Your brother, he was easy to talk to, yes? Very charming.'

Portia caught the faint cynicism in Katharina's voice. It was understandable, for despite all that had happened, Brigitte had been the first wife and still a rival, even if only after the fact. She went on, 'Very soon she was taking him to her place in Basel for weekends, and before a few months they were talking of marriage.'

'And did you meet her, this Brigitte?' Portia prompted when Katharina paused for a long time, her eyes on the teacup, which she held before her chest in a meditative pose.

'I have met her. I don't want to sound mean, but she is a common person, not very educated, you know, she was an assistant in a store. But she was lonely and just coming out of a divorce, and I think she loved him and her daughter liked him – he was very good with children. So why not, they try to get married quickly. And I think he told her that was the best way he can get his papers, and she wanted to help. So they went to the registry, but at registry they meet more problem. Instead of getting married he was detained for many days and finally he was deported back to Mali.'

Moussa. Portia was hearing that name for the first time. She had a lot of catching up to do. David had left home fifteen years ago, she was nine then, and he was nineteen. All she remembered was a long-legged kid who played soccer with his friends in the backyard, who was protective of her, and whom she idolized. She remembered one morning, walking her to school, he had told her he was going away for a long time and she might never see him again, but he would write to her and he would always love her. He left the next day, to South Africa, she later found out, illegally. He had spent a year in prison there. He came back home, and when it appeared he had finally settled down and was ready to return to school, he left again one year later, this time on a boat to West Africa; from there he planned to cross the desert to Europe.

She imagined his deportation. In England, when she was doing her MA, a classmate from Kenya had told her about an uncle who had been deported but had somehow found his way back. He told her it always happened at night. She imagined her brother, alone or with other deportees, handcuffed, led by immigration officials through a deserted terminal, *at night*, to a waiting plane chartered specially for the purpose. It would be a long and interminable flight. Once, on a plane to

Frankfurt on her way to Zambia, an Arab family had boarded, man, woman, two children, escorted by immigration officials. 'Why?' the man kept shouting, looking into the faces of the passengers as he passed through the aisle. 'Is it because I am Muslim, because I am not white? You send me back to die? My blood on your head.' In his seat, he banged his head repeatedly against the headrest and the armrest. 'I kill myself before I go back.' The children and the wife screamed with him, loud and sorrowful, delaying takeoff, till finally the pilot came out of his cockpit and spoke to the agents and the crying screaming family was led off the plane. She remembered the man, a portly, middle-aged man, in fishnet singlet and jeans – he must have been surprised by the agents as he watched TV or ate dinner with his family – and the quiet, tearful wife holding the two children, one on each arm. Did her brother also scream and beg to remain, and when they got to Mali, was he simply dumped at the airport with nothing but the clothes on his back, and who was at the airport to receive him? What do deportees feel: relief, shame, anger? Surely, they must feel relief to be away from all that European suspicion and alienation? And yet, some of them, no sooner do they arrive than they begin to plot their return. It is as if some homing device, focused toward Europe, is implanted in their brains and it never stops humming till their feet are on European soil.

'Why was he deported to Mali, why not to Zambia?' she asked.

Katharina looked at her and shrugged. 'Because he told everyone he was from Mali. That his family is there. Even me. I didn't know his family is from Zambia till much later.'

'What happened after the deportation? How did he return to Switzerland?' Portia asked.

'Brigitte, she promised she'd get him back. She got a lawyer who told her the only way he can come back is if they get married. So, she got on a plane and went to Mali and they got married.'

Despite herself, Portia was impressed by Brigitte's tenacity. What was it about her brother that attracted these women? She took a sip of her tea – it was cold. What is it about black men that acts like a super-magnet to these white women: curiosity, the exotic factor, love, or is it pity? What is it about white women that black men can't keep away from?

'She must have really loved him,' she said.

Katharina laughed. 'Yes. Like a movie, yes? Very romantic. And also, very foolish.'

'Foolish?'

'Well, it didn't last. They got married in a court in Mali, they came back, husband and wife. He got his papers, he started working at the rail station, everything was going well, then they were fighting. They live together less than two years only. He told me she wanted too much to be in charge, all the time, and his life became hell. He said his life was better when he was living in the refugee camp.'

'And that was when he met you?'

'It was love at first sight. For both of us. After that night at the bar, it was only one month later he left her and he started to stay with me.'

'Well, if you were so in love, why did you kill him? Why did you kill my brother? Can you make me understand that?' Portia asked. Katharina put down her cup, she went to the table and pulled out a drawer and took out a cigarette packet. She opened the window and blew the smoke outside. 'So, finally you ask your real question. This is the reason why you came. I wondered when you were going to ask.'

Portia sighed. At last, the ice was truly broken.

•

In the taxi going back to her hotel, Portia watched the raindrops hitting the window and she imagined heaven and earth conjoined by pillars of rain. Rainy Basel. *He must not float upon his watery bier / Unwept, and welter to the parching wind*. It had been raining yesterday when they arrived in Basel. A wet welcome. It felt like it was raining in every town and village and hamlet all over Switzerland. It had been raining at the Hauptbahnhof in Berlin when they boarded the train, and it rained all the eight hours the train ride lasted. She closed her eyes, exhausted by the bad weather, by her session with Katharina. In her mind she played over and over again Katharina's words, her halting English, the hand gestures, the direct, combative stare, till toward the end when she ended the conversation abruptly. She was too tired, she said, the memories were too disturbing, she didn't know they would be so strong, could they continue tomorrow? She would call, she had Portia's hotel number.

•

He had insisted on taking a room with two separate beds. To give her some space, he said. Or, to give himself space. He was a married man, separated, but still married. He liked her, she could tell, otherwise he wouldn't have said yes to her invitation. Come with me, to Basel. She had surprised herself. She hadn't known she was going to make the invitation till she did it; in her defence, she had been drunk at the time. Two days ago she hadn't even known who he was, and now here they were, in Basel, together, even if in separate beds. She loved having him here, she felt excited every time she turned in her bed and saw him in the next bed, mere metres away, a book in his hand, and he'd sense her looking at him and he'd give her his easy smile and ask if she was okay. She had wanted to go to Katharina's with him, but he had advised against it. 'We don't want to spook her.' He was right. His presence would have been a distraction.

He was not in when she entered the room, perhaps out for a walk. She decided to take a bath before he got back. The room was bare, almost utilitarian. A flat-screen TV was hooked to the wall, the table was wooden, the chairs plastic, she liked the spaciousness and the austereness. The beds were firm and comfortable. She had found the hotel on the internet, attracted by its proximity to the train station, and booked it hours before they left Berlin. She loved the view of a wide, grassy fen with willow trees and the fog hanging over it. Beyond it was what looked like a river, or a lake. *Watery bier.* She imagined drowned bodies floating in the water. She shivered. This was part of the old city, nearby was the university and many excellent restaurants, according to the pamphlet given to them by the receptionist when they checked in last night.

2

She had always wanted to see Berlin and had decided to stop over for a day or two before passing on to Basel. Luckily, she met a couple online who offered her a place to stay; they were out of town, somewhere in Denmark, and she had the use of their place for two days. She spent the first day indoors, sleeping. She had had to wake up at 4 a.m. to catch her Ryanair flight from Gatwick. She was reluctant to go out, even though she had a long list of attractions to visit – the wide, cold and wet Berlin streets were intimidating, and if only she spoke some German. All morning she watched American movies and sitcoms on television. Mostly old movies. Denzel Washington in *Training Day* sounding very fluent in *Deutsch*. They reminded her of the Hong Kong kung fu films David had been so fond of, and how they'd laugh at the off-sync between the English voice-over and the actors' moving mouth. The Germans, however, were not so sloppy, the asymmetry between lip movement and voice-over lasted only a syllable, a half-syllable, and you had to be assiduously watching for it. She amused herself watching for it, giving herself one point whenever she caught one; an idle game to pass an idle rainy day. By midday she was tired of watching TV and beginning to feel like a prisoner, so she explored the flat.

There were pictures of Hans and Ina, her absent hosts, on the mantelpiece, hiking, biking, camping, in different countries, mostly tropical, maybe even Africa. She had spent the night on the couch in the living room; she felt like she was camping here. There were two bedrooms, the one next to the living room was the guest room, mostly bare, with a bed neatly made up and a table and chair by the window. She had gone there only to get the duvet and return to the couch and the TV. Everything was in place, ordered, organized, they must have cleaned before they left. In the morning she got an email from Hans, he gave her their hotel phone number and wanted to know if she was fine? He had forgotten to tell her there was food in the fridge, eggs and bread and cheese, she was free to use that.

The rain stopped by midday and the sun came out. Furniture was being moved in the next apartment, somebody was moving in, or out. She had to go out. She had no excuse, the sun was shining, she had a map, and she had only a day left in Berlin before she moved on to Basel. This, after all, was why she decided to stop in Berlin, to see the city and the historic places she had read about in books: the museums, the famous streets, the WWII memorials.

She took a shower and changed into a pair of jeans and a T-shirt; as she stepped out into the corridor she noticed the door to the next apartment was open, in the doorway was a man on a ladder, a black man, and when he turned and looked at her, she knew he was African. What are the odds, she thought, as he returned her surprised gaze. She stood in the passage before the door, staring at him; she couldn't help herself. She had been starved of human contact for two days, black human contact, apart from the German-speaking Denzel Washington, and now right in front of her was a black man, an African, looking down at her from his ladder. But what if he wasn't African, what if he was one of those rare Afro-Germans she had heard about, who had lost all memory of Africa, who spoke nothing but *Deutsch*?

He was stepping down from the ladder now, a picture frame in his hand, his head tilted, mirroring the way her head was tilted to look up at him. She straightened her head. And then they spoke at the same time. 'Excuse me . . .' she began.

'Can I help . . . ?' he asked. In English. Not German then. The accent was West African, probably Nigerian. Nigerians were everywhere. She had met many in Zambia.

'I am sorry,' she said, blushing mentally.

'Can I help?' he said again. He was good-looking, not the sweet and lyrical Denzel Washington kind, but subtler, especially when he smiled just now. He had stubble, he looked like he hadn't been sleeping well.

'I was wondering . . . I am looking for directions.'

'Okay.'

They stood side by side over her map.

She followed his directions to the Museumsinsel, and it wasn't as hard as she had feared. She wanted to see the Egyptian collection, but when she got there she couldn't get in because of the long line. It'd take hours. The line looped and curved in on itself. The Museum Island was like a fair, with determined-looking tourists coming and going – a group of red-faced young men came riding past her on a contraption that looked like a bicycle, with five or six riders facing each other in a circle, all of them pedalling on the multiple pedals, a huge barrel of beer on the flat board in their middle from which all were sucking through giant straws.

She loafed around for a while, browsing through the books and DVDs for sale, then she joined a sidewalk procession toward the Brandenburger Tor, bumping into bodies and muttering excuses, and when she finally got tired of loitering and taking pictures at the gate, she took a bus and returned home. A wasted day. She should have purchased the museum ticket online before coming, she should have bought it the day before, she remonstrated with herself as she sat on the bus. She was usually well-prepared, and to be caught this flat-footed annoyed her.

•

The neighbour's door was closed. Maybe he didn't live there, most likely a moving man hired to move things. But no, he didn't look like a moving man, something about the way he looked and spoke. She was surprised at how sharply disappointed she felt. She paused briefly before the door and listened, hoping to hear the sound of lifting, or music, or feet, but all was quiet. It was almost 4 p.m. She opened her door and turned on the TV, she couldn't wait for tomorrow to come so she'd be on her way to Basel. Berlin had been a disappointment, her fault, not the city's.

But now the TV failed to occupy her and she wandered the apartment, from room to room, opened cabinets in the kitchen, read the labels on the wine bottles in the pantry. There was half a crate of red, and a full crate of white. She picked out a Bordeaux. She'd knock herself out and wake up tomorrow. She searched in drawers and cabinets for the corkscrew, but she couldn't find one. And, not until much later, after she had gone and knocked on the neighbour's door and, flashing her best smile, asked to borrow a corkscrew, please, and laughingly invited him to join her for a drink if he wanted and he said yes, why not, give me five minutes, and they were seated at her hosts' circular, three-seater dining table, raising glasses in cheers, not till then did she admit to herself that she could have drunk the Chablis with the screw cap but she had decided to drink the corked red as a pretext to go talk to and perhaps invite the neighbour for a drink. But, she had a good excuse; she had many good excuses: she was alone in a strange city and he was a fellow African and she was going stir-crazy.

'Portia,' he said. 'Very Shakespearean.'

Her name was a cross she had borne all her life. But he wasn't making fun of her as the perplexed kids at school had done, he wasn't puzzled as the lecturers at university had been. In England, at postgraduate school, a classmate had asked her if it was a traditional African name.

'My father was a fan,' she told him.

'So, how long have you lived here?' he asked.

'I don't live, here. I am couch-surfing.'

'Couch-surfing?'

'Couchsurfing.com. Never heard of it?'

'Sounds like a porn site.'

She laughed. Nice sense of humour. But what if he was dangerous, a rapist, an opportunistic ripper? Clearly he knew about porn sites. Well, too late now. Her mother would read all about it in the Zambian papers tomorrow. Hopefully, the circular glass table between them would offer her a minute-or-two head start before he reached her.

'It is a site that connects travellers with hosts, people willing to offer their couches to perfect strangers who might someday return the favour.'

'I feel bad that you didn't get to see the museum, and you are leaving tomorrow. Do you want to go out? Grab something to eat?' he asked. A rapist wouldn't be asking her to go out, unless he was the brazen kind that gets his kick out of doing it out in public. A flasher-rapist.

'I want African food,' she said. She hadn't eaten properly in over a day.

He thought for a minute. 'The closest I can offer is Asian, but it is about twenty minutes away by train. It is good, promise.'

She was still dressed from her outing, so she freshened up in the bathroom, picked up her handbag, and they left after a glass each of the wine. Restorative, the wine proved. She wasn't aware she had been tired from her first venture into the city. They took the train and sat side by side, but they couldn't speak for the din, so they smiled silently at each other whenever their eyes met. Two musicians, one a chubby child with an accordion, the other a man-and-woman duo with a music box, vied with one another to see who'd break the noise barrier first. She watched the stoic Berliners absorbing the abuse, their faces impassively turned to the view outside the train window. A *Mots* vendor tried unsuccessfully to get her to purchase his newspaper but she had no change. He handed the vendor a euro coin and took a copy even though, he told her when they got off, he couldn't really read German. 'You looked like you needed rescuing.'

She thanked him. Was that the vibe she gave off, like she needed rescuing?

'This way,' he said. They were on a busy side street, and almost every second or third store was a secondhand bookstore displaying English and German books in the window. Sandwiched between the bookstores and record stores were Asian restaurants: Thai, Vietnamese, Indian – people sat at tables on the sidewalk, reading menus, looking bored as Roma minstrels played popular tunes on their accordions and trumpets. Another bookstore. Inside a woman in a hat sat behind a desk, facing the street. She caught Portia's eyes and smiled, waving them in. Portia grabbed his hand. 'Come, let's look at books.' The interior of the store was a thicket of books, falling out of shelves, spilling out of cartons on the floor. It was hard to find a path around the room without stepping on books and magazines. Now Portia realized it was actually a man wearing a wig under the hat and a flowery red dress. Two men, actually, one in a blue shirt, youngish, sat further inside the store, half-hidden by a bookshelf. On the table before them were two glasses of red wine and a half-empty bottle.

'He is the real deal. He is Barack Obama before the celebrity,' the man in the blue shirt was saying.

'Oh, you are a Cory Booker fan too,' the man in the red dress said. 'How good to know. I love that man. He is my mayor. I am from Newark, you know.'

Americans, rolling their *r*'s and flattening their *a*'s. Portia pulled out books at random. They were used copies, 'for rent or for sale', a sign glued to the shelf said. There was a whole section dedicated to Graham Greene. She ran her hand over the spines, reading the titles. Her father was a fan, he had sent her Greene's memoirs, *Ways of Escape* and *A Sort of Life*, on her nineteenth birthday. She found the writing a bit too macho, a bit too Hemingwayesque.

The store appeared to be an apartment doubling as a bookstore. This was the living room, she could see the kitchen through a half-open door with dishes in the sink and a packet of what looked like cat food on a shelf. A closed door next to a shelf probably led into the bedroom, half-blocking the door were more boxes of books, some opened with books spilling out of them, some not yet opened. It was like a hoarder's haven here. She felt stymied by clutter, hamstrung. She waded back to the entrance where the man in the wig and hat and his friend were still talking about Cory Booker.

'They have Achebe here,' he said to her. She joined him. A whole section dedicated to African authors of the earlier generation, Alan Paton, Mazisi Kunene, Naguib Mahfouz. He flipped through a copy of *Things Fall Apart*. It was an early edition, with a folkloric sketch of Okonkwo's face upside down on the cover, and Introduction by Aigboje Higo. Inside were more folkloric sketches at the start of each chapter.

'I'll take this,' he said to the men at the table, 'how much?'

But they were laughing so hard they didn't hear. Tears formed runnels down the face of the man in the red dress, cracking his makeup.

' . . . that is so preposterous,' the other man kept saying. He banged his hand on the table and sipped his wine, all the time laughing. 'Preposterous!'

Portia picked out a book and handed it to him. He looked at the title: *Prison Dialogues*, by James Kariku. 'I remember this book. I had to study it for my secondary school finals.'

'My father,' she said.

'Your father is James Kariku?'

She nodded. She looked defensive, she had had this conversation many times before and was weary of it.

'No way,' he said. He looked at her, then at the book, as if trying to determine if she was joking.

'I am Portia Kariku. If you want, I can show you my ID,' she said, and turned away from him.

'Of course, I believe you, it's just . . . so unexpected. Okay. I'll take it and you'll sign it for me.'

'You buy it if you want, but I can't sign it for you. I am not my father.' Her voice had grown cold. He paid for the book and they left. What a clutter. Her skin crawled retroactively at the cat hair on the carpet and the spiderwebs on the roof and the dirty plates in the kitchen sink. How incongruous it all was, with the fancy storekeeper by the entrance, drinking red wine in his wig and la-di-da hat next to all that grime.

When they came out after eating, the very last sunrays of the day glistened on the wet cobblestones. It was an Indian summer day; the golden sunrays poured on the buildings and trees and sidewalks like honey. They took a train back to Mitte. 'Let's get off here,' he said.

'This isn't our station.'

'Yes. But it is a beautiful day. Let's walk,' he said. She followed him along a line of stones marking where the Berlin Wall once stood, and soon they were in a throng of young people, all moving in the same direction. She looked at him, questioning.

'They are coming from the park over there, Mauerpark. Come.' He took her hand and pulled her away from the crowd. She liked the feel of his hand in hers.

'I'll buy you a drink,' he said.

They entered a tiny bar, its entrance almost invisible from the street. Inside was dark and empty save for the barman, who was standing behind the bar, his back turned to the empty room, staring at a TV screen over the shelf of bottles on the wall. One part of the wall was lined with cigarette and pinball machines. A door led into yet another section of the bar, perhaps the restaurant, from which they could hear loud voices and laughter. They sat down, and eventually the barman came over.

'Two shots of vodka for me,' Portia said before he could speak.

He shrugged at the barman. 'Same for me.'

They downed the vodka in one gulp and then asked for a glass of wine each, red for him, white for her. 'So,' he said, 'what do you do?'

'I teach,' she said. 'My mother has a school in Lusaka, I work for her.'

'Do you like it?'

'I didn't at first, but it grows on you. The kids are adorable.'

An old woman in a white faux-fur jacket, its collar raised up around her neck, entered, in her hand a bunch of flowers. The front-door light in her red hair was a brush fire at night. She shook the rain off her jacket as she looked around the empty room, then she limped over to them. She picked out a pink rose and held it out to Portia. The woman had a ring on every finger, including her thumbs. Portia shook her head.

'Take it,' he said. He gave the woman a few coins. Portia held the red rose to her nose, then she placed it on the table next to her glass. 'Thanks.'

The old woman shuffled over to the bar and handed the barman the coins, she sat on a stool with her bunch of flowers on the counter in front of her.

'What are you doing in Berlin?'

'I came with my wife, over a year ago.'

'Oh,' she said. She pushed the flower further away. 'Where's she now, your wife? Of course, you don't have to answer . . . forget the question.'

Of course, she had seen the ring impression on his finger, but she hadn't given it any thought. They were two strangers in a strange city, soon they'd part and perhaps never see each other again.

'My wife left for America a few months ago. We used to live in a different part of town, in Charlottenburg. I moved here when my wife left.'

'Who lives here?'

'A friend, who I met through another friend. Her name is

Lorelle. She and her roommate . . . they left for America. I am helping them take apart the furniture and get it into storage, in exchange I get to stay for a few months, rent-free.'

'What do you do afterward?'

'Move on, I guess. I have to go back to the States and finish my PhD, eventually.'

'Oh, what are you working on?'

'The Berlin Conference of 1884 . . . though I discovered that here in Berlin they call it the Congo Conference.'

'That's an interesting topic. What's the title of your dissertation?'

'You really want to know?'

'Yes, really. I just finished my MA and I am thinking of going back for a PhD, eventually.'

'You should. My title is, "The Berlin Conference: Imaginary Borders and the Scramble for Africa". What do you think?'

'I like it.'

'Good. Now, your turn.'

'Yes, my turn. Give me a minute.'

She stood up and went to the barman, they talked and the barman led her to the cigarette machine and she came back with a packet of Marlboro. She opened it and handed him one.

'I don't smoke,' he said.

'Me neither, but I feel like a cigarette right now.'

They lit up and dragged in the smoke tentatively, coughing, their eyes watering.

'So, my turn. I am going to Basel. My brother used to live there. I am going to meet his wife.'

'Basel. Switzerland. Where does he live now?'

'He died. I am going to meet his Swiss wife, Katharina. I have never met her before.'

'Why do you want to see her now?'

'My mother wants to know how he died. The papers didn't say much. And Katharina was in prison for killing him, so we couldn't reach her.'

'His wife killed him?'

'Yes.'

A laying down of the ghosts. After her father died last year her mother had started talking about David more and more. Where did she go wrong, and why did he feel he had to go away? He had been so obsessed with emigrating. A month ago, when Portia was getting ready to go back to London to submit her MA thesis, her mother said to her, 'I want you to go and see her when you finish with London. Talk to her. I want to know what happened, why he left us for her, what he was looking for.' She handed Portia a photograph. The photograph, the one on the nightstand by her mother's bed. In the picture her brother was standing next to Katharina, looking at the camera with no expression. What was he thinking? The photo had come five years ago with a letter, the only letter he ever wrote since he left home. In it, he said he was fine, he was now in Switzerland, married to the lady in the picture, and they shouldn't worry about him. The next time they heard about him, he was dead.

Portia looked at her, shaking her head. 'Mama, it will not bring him back. He had made his choices.'

'But I want to know. I was a good mother, wasn't I, and a good wife?' And because all her life all she wanted to do was to please her mother, to make her happy, Portia said yes.

Her father had also left, long before David did, but her father did come back. He came back irreparably damaged by exile, and it could be said that the return was what ultimately killed him. She didn't tell him all this, though she wanted to. She felt she could tell him even the most intimate things and he'd respond with respect and full attention. She wondered what his story was. There was something lost and dreamy about him, as if he was waiting for something, or someone. What was he doing in Berlin, all by himself, his wife thousands of miles away in America?

She picked up the rose, sniffed it again, and said, 'So, do you give every woman you meet a rose? What would your wife think?'

'That poor lady looked like she needed the money,' he said. The lady was bent over the bar now, a cigarette in one hand, her drink in the other hand, the flowers on the counter next to her. She was staring up at the TV screen, discussing what was showing with the barman.

'That's a good reason. Well, thank you. I'll put it in a vase when we get back.'

After a while she said, suddenly, 'My birthday is next week.'

'Well, happy birthday in advance. How old?'

'You first. How old are you?'

'Old,' he said. 'Thirty-five.'

'I am twenty-five.'

'You are so young.'

'You sound disappointed.'

'I am not. I just feel . . . old at the moment. Superannuated. What is your wish, for your birthday?'

She shrugged. 'Joy, happiness, wisdom. What more can

one wish for? And, talking about happiness, I must mention you do look a bit solemn.'

He shrugged. 'I guess I have been indoors and alone too long. I have forgotten how to compose my features in company.'

'Compose your features, that's an interesting way of putting it. Why are you unhappy?'

'Is happiness very important to you?'

'Well, isn't it, to everyone?'

'To some, yes. In Dostoevsky's *The Brothers Karamazov*, Father Zosima says the purpose of human existence is happiness. God Himself wants us to be happy. Creation is fulfilled when God sees us happy. We are only unhappy if our mind is not very clean, if we sin.'

'Sounds like a rather convenient argument for the church.'

'It does.'

'Dostoevsky doesn't sound like he understood very well how life works. Happiness is important, but I wouldn't say it is the main purpose of human existence.'

When they got back to the apartment they stood by her door. She wasn't ready for the night to end. She dreaded going into the empty apartment by herself, so she waited, playing with the key on the key chain. He said, 'I'd invite you for a nightcap, but my place is a mess. The dust alone will give you an infection.'

'In that case, come to mine. We still have some wine left.' She hoped she didn't sound too forward, too shameless.

'Good. Let me get my phone. I left it when we went out. Ten minutes?'

Before he came back, she changed into a skirt and a fresh T-shirt. He walked around the room, stopping to look at the record collection.

'Mahler, Beethoven, Bach. Snooty folk, huh?'

He turned to the pictures on the wall. 'Turner. Kandinsky. Prints.'

'You know painting?'

'Only by association. My wife paints.'

He joined her on the couch. She handed him a glass of red wine.

'What if your friends walked in now? How would you explain my presence?'

'Is there anything to explain? We aren't breaking the furniture. At least not yet.' She looked contemplatively at him.

He said, 'You have nothing to fear from me.'

She liked that he said that seriously, that he could tell she wanted to be reassured.

'Tell me something about yourself. Anything.'

He told her about his friends, Stan, Mark, Uta, Eric, who used to live in an abandoned church. She listened. His voice grew sad as he described Mark's death. He stood up. 'Let's play some music. I don't want to depress you.' He slotted a CD into the Bose player.

'What song?'

'David Bowie. "Heroes",' he said.

She shook her head. 'Nice, but . . .'

'But . . .'

'Too white for me. I am a lover of the blues. My father had a stack of them, records with brilliant album-cover artwork. Billie Holiday. Robert Johnson. Muddy Waters.'

She went to the kitchen, her glass of wine in her hand. He stood up and followed her. The kitchen was long and narrow, a window opened into a courtyard with a gnarled and twisted ash tree in its centre. He stood by the window. 'I have the same view from my kitchen.'

'What of love?' she asked, coming forward to stand next to him. She could feel the drink, making her light-headed, but she didn't care. She leaned into him and pressed her lips on his briefly. 'What does Dostoevsky have to say about love?'

He put one arm around her waist, saying nothing. She pulled away and began cutting a block of cheese into cubes onto a plate. She opened a tin and poured out cashew nuts and almonds beside the cheese. They faced each other, he still by the window, leaning against the sill; she resting her hips against the sink, her head tilted. She picked up the bowl and returned to the living room. He came and sat next to her, saying nothing. She wondered if they were about to cross a certain line, a certain border. She felt happy, expectant. She got up and sat on the floor before the TV, the remote in her hand, flipping through channels.

'You look beautiful, sitting there, like a TV fairy.'

She turned and looked at him, still flipping through channels. She stopped at a channel showing a western, in German. 'Do you speak German?'

'*Ein bisschen,*' he said. 'A little bit.'

She fell asleep before the movie ended. When she opened her eyes he was still seated on the couch, the light from the screen playing on his face. She smiled up at him.

'I am putting you to bed, then I am off.' He picked her up and carried her to the guest room, putting her down gently on the narrow twin bed.

'Don't go,' she said.

'It is one a.m.'

'If you go I can't sleep. I've been sleeping badly.'

'These people, the owners, what will they think?'

'They won't be back for a few more days,' she said, then added, sleepily, 'Come with me, to Basel. I don't want to go by myself.'

3

'You've been humming that word for a while now. Lycidas.'

They were in their beds, waiting for their room service meal, neither of them feeling like going out in the rain. He had her father's book of poems in his hand. He was seated, his back against the headboard, she was lying on her stomach, her face turned to him. Outside the grey cumulus clouds hung low in the sky, over the trees and roofs, and the deluge seemed to be rising from the marshy bog itself.

'It is a poem, by Milton. An elegy for a friend who died in a boating accident. All day it has been in my head and won't go away. Perhaps it is the rain. It is making me sad.' She went to the window and stared out into the night.

'Were you close to your brother?'

She shrugged, not turning. 'He left when I was very young. I was around ten when I last saw him.'

'Fifteen years ago.'

She nodded. 'Yes. My father was in Europe then, trying to be an exile.'

'Trying?'

'He could have returned home anytime he wanted, but he refused.'

'Why did he leave?'

She returned to the bed and sat down, facing him. The room was dim, only the light from the TV flickered weakly against the blue wall, the rays soaking into the walls, like water on sponge. 'He got into trouble with the government because of his writings, not just his poems, but articles as well, in the newspapers. He was something of a rising star, I guess. Some people saw him as a possible future candidate for the presidency. He was young, smart and fearless, or foolish, depending on how you look at it. He belonged to that nationalist era in African politics that produced young idealistic men by the bucketful, and then promptly threw them behind bars or killed them – the lucky ones like my father escaped into exile to spend the rest of their lives in limbo.'

'What did he write about?'

'Well, you have read his poems. His articles and essays accused the government of corruption, among many other things. He was part of a university-based group of intellectuals agitating for multiparty democracy, they wanted Kaunda to resign. And they had a good following, and also supporters in America and Europe, which made them more threatening to the government, plus, they had a case, the economy was bad, people wanted a new beginning. I heard about it mostly from my mother, the rest I learned from history books.

'My mother met my father at university, just after independence in the sixties, they became lecturers at the same university, in the seventies. She was in the history department. He was in English. He was in prison for two years, then he was released and held under house arrest. While in prison he wrote his book of poetry, it brought him international attention when it was published by the Heinemann African Writers Series. He became an international celebrity – PEN awarded him the Freedom to Write Award, Wole Soyinka and Harold Pinter held a joint reading from his book in London. He was offered fellowships and visiting lecturer positions in England and America, but he didn't want to go. He wanted to stay in Zambia. Yet, despite numerous appeals and pleas, he never got his job back. My mother persuaded him to leave the country. She had just given birth to my brother and all she wanted was to be somewhere safe. They left in 1980, with the help of my father's foreign friends. They were in exile in England for ten years. My mother said it was the best years of their marriage, but she only saw that in hindsight. It wasn't a bad life, he had a job at the University of Leeds, teaching African literature, but while he was becoming more and more settled in exile, she was pining for home. Kaunda's dictatorship was over anyway. So, when she got pregnant with me she decided to come back to Zambia. My father told her to go on ahead, he'd join her in a few months. So, she took my brother and left. She returned home and managed to make a life for herself. She started an elementary school. But my father didn't go back. By then he had developed a taste for exile.'

Her voice was flat, bitter. She lay on her back, directing her words at the ceiling.

'How long did he stay back after your mother had left?'

'Seventeen, eighteen years. I never saw my father till I was eight, for me he was always a photograph on the wall, a wedding photograph with my mother, he in a suit, my mother in a wedding dress with yards of tulle flowing behind her. I saw him for the first time when we visited him in Copenhagen, Denmark, he was doing a fellowship there. We stayed with him for a year. I remember that year. It was cold, and my mother had no friends, she was always sitting by the fireplace, waiting for my father to return from some outing with his friends. Famous authors would stop by the house, all of them exiles, Soyinka, Mahmoud Darwish, Breyten Breytenbach – of course I didn't know who they were then, till later when my mother told me – and they'd talk poetry far into the night, about their countries, and exile, and they'd read poems they were working on or had just published.

'There was a little yard in the back, with a magnolia tree in the centre, and when the weather was good I would ride my bike round the tree, round and round and round till it got dark and my mother would shout for me to come in. I think my mother hoped my father would come back to Zambia with us after the Danish fellowship, but he didn't. He had become something of a professional exile. He went from fellowship to fellowship, from asylum city to asylum city. All over Europe. And they loved him, even though he hadn't written a book in over twenty years. He gave comments after every coup in Africa, on every civil war that broke out, every uprising, every plane crash. He was the Africa expert. He wrote fiery opinion pieces in newspapers attacking the government in Zambia, even though by now the government and most of the country had forgotten who he was. But in Europe he was a hero, telling truth to power. They called him the conscience of Africa. My father ate it up.'

Her voice died down with a sigh. Their food came, they ate in silence. She ate in bed, sitting up, her plate in her lap, he moved to the chair by the window, flipping through the book of poetry as he ate. She watched, and gradually her expression darkened. Why was he keeping so far away from her? Why did he come? And why were they in separate beds? In Berlin she had kissed him, and she thought he would kiss her back, but he hadn't. Perhaps he was here because he thought she needed protection, just as he thought she needed rescue. Her sullen mood persisted and she didn't answer when he asked her if she was okay. She went to the bathroom and brushed her teeth, she got into bed and pulled the sheet over her head. He came over and pulled back the sheet. He lay down next to her.

'I can't sleep,' she said. He held her, not saying anything.

'You mustn't be bitter against your father,' he said. 'Sometimes poets have to be imperfect so their poetry can be perfect. Reading him has taken me back to my school days.'

It was the most profound thing anyone had ever said to her about her father, and she felt grateful. Her mood lightened. He kissed her head. Like a brother, she thought. She closed her eyes. 'Tell me a story.'

'What kind of story?'

'Any kind.'

He told her about a rich young man who was addicted to palm wine. One day his father dies, and many days after, his palm-wine tapster who draws his palm wine from the palm trees falls from a tall palm tree and dies. The rich young man misses his supply of palm wine, and his friends no longer come to visit. He grows despondent. So, he decides to go to the Dead's Town to find his tapster. It is a long and hazardous journey. It leads him from his town to various parts of the bush, places outside civilization, inhabited by all sorts of inhuman creatures. Thus begin his many adventures. He stays with a man who promises to give him directions to the Dead's Town, but he must first rescue his daughter, who has been attracted to a Handsome Gentleman and followed him into the bush. The Gentleman, it turns out, is not really a person but a wild creature of the bush. He had returned with his young bride to the bush, and as he entered, he gave back each bodily part that he had rented from a human being, until he was nothing but a skull; he then held the young woman captive. The rich young man searches for the host's daughter, finds her, and the two escape the bush . . .

She fell asleep listening to him, her head on his shoulder. When he stopped talking, she opened her eyes.

'I know that story. Amos Tutuola. My MA is in post-colonial literature, remember. But go on, did he get what he wanted? Did he get his tapster back?'

'He got more than that. He gained wisdom, he also got a magic egg with a never-ending supply of palm wine.'

She drifted off, half-awake, half-dreaming, half-remembering;

she saw her father getting off the plane at Lusaka International Airport. He was home, finally. She could feel her mother's nervous excitement as they watched him at the customs counter, presenting his passport to be stamped. Her mother was wearing her best dress, her best jewellery. It was the happiest Portia had seen her in a long time. He, on the other hand, looked perplexed. He was in his black suit, with a white shirt and his best Oxford shoes.

'Where are the secret police?' he whispered, he looked disappointed. He was expecting to be arrested, to be whisked away in a black car by security agents. In the car he kept asking about old friends, why weren't they there to receive him at the airport, surely they must have read in the papers he was coming back? He had written about it in the English papers. Her mother told him most of the old friends had retired, returned to the village. Many were dead.

As the days passed alarming signs began to show, he appeared disoriented, unsure where he was, or what day it was. He'd go to the window and peek outside at passing cars, expecting the house to be stormed by agents looking for him. He tried writing. He was working on a volume on exile, he intimated, but he couldn't make headway, the lines came out dull and uninspired. Soon he started talking about going back. He had been home just two months, but already he felt stifled. He couldn't work here, he complained. Once, they found him seated in the yard, under the cashew tree, in the pouring rain. Portia took him inside, even as he fought her all the way. Then one day, they came back from work at her mother's school, and he was gone. He had left a one-line note on the table: he was going back to England. When had he planned this, when did he buy the plane ticket? They rushed to the airport, and when they got there they found him seated meekly on a bench in the departure lounge. He hadn't been allowed on the plane because he had no visa.

He thought he could just walk into the plane with no documents.

A month later he tried to leave again. An official, who happened to be her mother's cousin, called to tell them he was at the airport. He had attacked the immigration official who stopped him from boarding the plane. His passport had expired, and he still had no visa for the UK. This time her mother didn't go to the airport with her. When Portia got there, she saw him through the glass door, dressed in his best suit and white shirt, his carry-on bag in his hand, ranting as he paced up and down, waving his passport, and when she entered she heard him, in his careful professorial British English, asking them if they knew who he was. 'James Kariku. You can look me up. Google my name. I am a poet. This country doesn't appreciate talent. In Europe they will roll out the red carpet for me. You think I am lying, go ahead, google my name!'

She stood at the door, too embarrassed to go in, though the three officials at whom he was ranting could see her standing there. Finally, she took a deep breath and went in. She whispered 'sorry' to the officials and led her father to the car. In the car she broke down in tears and turned to him, asking, 'Why don't you want to stay with us, Baba? Why do you want to leave?' He remained quiet, hunched against the car door, staring out at the line of jacaranda trees with their fire-red flowers looking ghostly against the night sky.

He kept to his room, and from behind the door they could hear the sound of his typewriter, banging furiously. When he died two months later, they found a pile of paper covered in gibberish, only one line was clear, repeated over and over again, 'Down with the dictatorship.' He was a resistance poet, it was all he knew, just like exile was all he knew. He had been home less than one year. Her mother said, 'I made a mistake. I shouldn't have pressed him to return. Exile was his life. The return killed him.'

·

'Think of him happy,' he said. Her father had been happy in Denmark, drinking and arguing all night long with other poets. And she remembered the time she saw him in London. She had not seen him since that trip to Denmark, when she was eight. 'I saw him in London, he had flown in from The Hague, where he had been living as a writer-in-residence. I was doing my MA at SOAS, it was my first year there, and it was a bad year. I was homesick. It was winter, wet and dark and cold, typical London winter. I couldn't read, I couldn't think, I'd spend days in my room, sleeping, only coming out to get supplies. I was diagnosed with depression due to the weather and the doctor told me to install bright fluorescent tubes in my room, to compensate for the gloom. Anyway, my father came to town. My mother called me from Zambia and gave me his hotel address and his number. I went to his hotel and they made me wait in the lobby. He was still sleeping, they said, but they would let him know I was there. I didn't tell them he was my father, I just gave my name.

'Then he came down. There were two people with him. I

hadn't seen him in a long time, but I recognized him, he still had his beard even though it was all salt-and-pepper now. I was sitting in a corner in the lobby – and he almost passed me. It seemed he had forgotten I was there. Then he saw me. "Portia. You look exactly like your mother."

'He gave me a hug. He introduced me to his friends, "My daughter." He looked happy to see me. But it was awkward. I didn't know how to be a daughter, and clearly, he had forgotten how to be a father. Plus, I didn't know what to call him, Dad, or Father, or Baba. I followed them to the reading, I even remember the title of the event: Poetry, Exile and Resistance. But the truth is that he had long ceased to be a poet, and most of the resistance was imaginary. But the people there, they loved it. They didn't care. They didn't even know where Zambia was on the map of Africa. As far as they were concerned, all of Africa was one huge Gulag archipelago, and every African poet or writer living outside Africa has to be in exile from dictatorship. My father knew his audience and their expectation, he gave them what they wanted. He was dressed for the occasion, the beard, the austere dashiki. He read. He vituperated. He narrated his prison experience that had happened decades ago as if it were just happening now. The audience, they ate it up. They clapped. They cried. They bought books. I guess I also felt a bit proud. My father was a star, a minor one, but still a star.

'I followed them to dinner and spent almost two hours listening to him hold forth about African nationalism, pan-Africanism. What did it all mean? Ideas that at sometime, long ago, meant something but are now empty as any political jargon, something to whip out and flash before the masses, or in textbooks. I hate politics, what it makes people do, what it does to people. One of the ladies with him was his translator, she was nice. She was the only one who tried to make conversation with me. Her name was May and it turned out she was a lecturer at SOAS, she had translated my father into Greek, and I could tell there was something between them. She asked me about my studies, about my mother, but all I wanted was to talk to my father, alone, for just a few minutes, I wanted to ask him when he was coming home, if he missed my mother and my brother and me. I waited, but he wouldn't stop talking. So, I left. I told them I was going to the bathroom, I didn't return. I slipped out and returned to my room.

'The next day I left for Zambia, abandoning my studies. I knew if I stayed a day more I'd lose my mind. I did go back to finish my studies, eventually, but that year was my worst, ever. When I told my mother about the meeting she said, "Something is wrong with us. Our men keep deserting us." But I told her it was not us, it was them. There was something they wanted, something just beyond the horizon, something outside their grasp, they would keep searching for it till they died. He stayed on in London for about seven months, with his translator girlfriend, then he came home and that was the end of it.'

4

'Was she upset yesterday?'

Katharina had phoned early in the morning to say she wasn't available to meet today as planned. Portia stood at the foot of the bed, her expression switching between perplexed to annoyed. She was already dressed up and ready to go out when the call came. He was also up, still in his striped pyjamas, by the window with a laptop in his hand.

'Not really. She was a bit defensive, which is normal. I mean, she just came out of prison, I expected her to be a bit reticent, and even erratic, but I thought because I am his sister she'd want to talk to me about this.'

She dropped her bag and sat down on the bed, her face

downcast. Her flight back to London was tomorrow. In London she'd catch a connecting flight to Lusaka. She imagined the disappointment on her mother's face.

He said, 'Give her a call later, to see if she changes her mind.'

They went out for a walk. The rain had stopped; the sun was out. They ate an early lunch in a roadside restaurant. When they came back to the hotel the receptionist handed Portia a note. 'Miss, you got a call.'

She took the note and read it. 'The bitch. So whimsical. She is coming. She is having dinner with us. This evening.'

•

Paintings of dinner scenes covered the restaurant walls, rising all the way to the ceiling. Corpulent gentlemen and thick-waisted women, reaching into plates piled high with all sorts of meat – huge-thighed chicken, enormous slabs of ham, gigantic shanks of lamb – their mouths bulging with food, glasses raised and dripping with blood-red wine. The rest of the wall was taken up by colourful frescoes of flowers and birds, giving a warm and cheerful ambience to the room. The painting looked like an epicurean Last Supper, a bacchanalia, with Jesus left out, perhaps hiding out of sight, horrified by the gluttony. Gormandize, Portia thought. Her secondary school principal, Mrs Joyce Bisika, used the word often in her speech at Assembly, as in, 'Girls gormandizing in the cafeteria, asking for extra portions. So unladylike,' or, 'Girls gormandizing on life with their shameless, unladylike behaviour.'

Katharina saw Portia looking at the paintings. 'I hate them. They say it has been here even before the restaurant started. This used to be some kind of school cafeteria.'

Katharina had arrived at exactly 4 p.m., alone. Portia had expected her to come with Sven, but there she was, by herself, waiting for them in the lobby, looking subdued and almost formal in a black knee-length dress. She said nothing when she saw Portia was not alone. She said she had made a reservation for them for 5 p.m. and the restaurant wasn't far from the hotel, so they walked. They walked through quaint, constricted streets, cobbled and sloping, and as they came down the hill they could see right into compounds below, most of them with open courtyards in which stood tall, leafy trees, and then they were in an open street.

'This is a shopping area, very touristy,' Katharina said. Today she was friendly, even charming, at one point she took Portia by the hand as they walked, and Portia could see how a man would easily fall for her. The streets were crisscrossed with tram rails making the walk confusing, and not knowing where to look when crossing, they had to trust Katharina as they now dashed, now waited, now strolled through the wide, winding streets. They were not far from the university, and most of the people on the streets looked like students. They took a narrow alley and came out on another wide street. She pointed across the road at an imposing red stone building. 'That is the *Rathaus*, the city council chamber.' They crossed over.

'It is beautiful,' Portia said. In the centre of the courtyard, facing the street, was a sculpture of two gargantuan men, their arms and torsos impossibly twisted around one another in a silent, frozen combat, pulling at each other in strife and opposition, and yet balanced and equally matched. There was something elemental, almost mythic about them. Katharina took them to an imposing cathedral, from the cobbled courtyard they could view the Rhine below, and across the water in the distance the city itself. They looked down into the sluggish, frigid water, and Katharina, now enjoying the role of tour guide, told them how in the summer young men and women would dive into the water and drift downstream, their clothes tied in a waterproof bag which they also used for flotation.

She looked at her watch. 'Time for dinner,' she said. The restaurant was next to the Jean Tinguely Fountain, a little basin populated by curiously shaped sculptures and wheels and scoops, all playful, all lighthearted, but now all frozen and trapped by winter's breath.

'So, you go back tomorrow,' Katharina said. They had finished their meal and were finishing off a bottle of wine. Katharina had looked amused when Portia said she didn't eat meat and ordered a fillet of sea bass. 'But your brother loved meat. In fact, all the Africans we met really liked meat. You are the first African I am meeting who doesn't like meat.'

Portia opened her mouth, then closed it again. To Katharina's credit she shook her head and immediately apologized for her comment. 'I am sorry. That sounded so silly.'

'Tell me more about him,' Portia said. But Katharina shook her head firmly. 'We make deal. Today, I am your host. I show you Basel. We eat, nothing serious. You come to my house tomorrow and we talk about your brother. I feel happy today. Nothing sad.'

•

They checked out of the hotel early in the morning. Her flight was in the evening, from Basel to London, from there to Lusaka through South Africa. He would take the train back to Berlin.

'Why?' she asked Katharina as they sat down at the circular table by the window. They were alone, the men had gone out with the dog.

Katharina nodded and smiled. 'Maybe I ask you the same: Why do you want to meet someone who killed your brother? And if you had followed the trial you know I didn't plead guilty. I said I didn't kill him.'

'But you were found guilty, and sent away for three years. Very lenient. In most countries you'd hang.'

Again, Katharina nodded and smiled. 'Okay. You are his sister. You deserve to know. I tell you everything.'

'Not everything. You can skip the sentimental stuff, the romantic meeting and "love at first sight".'

'But what if it is true, the sentiments as you call it, the romance, even the love?'

'Well, convince me. That it was all true, that you loved him, that he wasn't a victim.'

'Victim how? Of what?'

'Of your anger and jealousy. Of the whole system, of Europe.'

'No. Moussa was never a victim. He knew what he wanted, and how to get it. That night, after the dance, my friends wanted me to go, but no, I said. I stayed talking with him till the bar closed at midnight. I was in love.'

That was the day they met, at the twilight of his first marriage. After that night, after that dance, she told Sven their engagement was not going to work. 'I didn't love him. He was a good, decent guy, but I wanted more at that time.' She shrugged. 'I was not so young any more. Time was passing for me. I wanted more . . . excitement.'

She looked out the window at the distant figures in the mist, dog, men, and Portia wondered what she was thinking.

'Exactly two weeks after that meeting, he left his wife and moved in with me. I was staying in a little place near the campus, one bedroom and a kitchen. Twice Brigitte came to shout at him and beg him to go back, but he said no, he wanted divorce. She didn't give him the divorce till after one year.'

'And your family?'

'Well, that is another story. My father is a theologian, you know. I am the only child. He is a good man, he didn't object to my relationship, but he didn't say yes. Every year we used to go on a retreat, we go with my family and the people in my father's church, and I wanted to bring Moussa, but my father said no. I either come alone, or I should not come at all. It was the most painful thing. I realized also how serious all this was. I talked to my mother, I begged them to talk to Moussa, to try to understand him. We had a big fight. I told them I was sorry to be source of embarrassment for them. Everything they had taught me was a lie then. They said we should love strangers, we should never judge people by how they look. It was the most disappointing time of my life. I was very close to my father, you know. I looked up to him. I asked him, What if he turned up in your church, would you turn him away?

'We got married. Just the two of us. I did not invite my family. My mother wanted to come but I told her no, I had no family. After the wedding we went to Mali. I took some time off from my studies, and he got time off from the railway where he worked. He had told me a lot about his father in Mali, and his brothers and sisters, and I wanted to see them. He never mentioned that they are not his real family. I only knew what he told me, that he was from Mali.'

Portia bowed her head and shrugged. 'I guess he was ashamed of his real family.' She wanted to know what this other family was like, the one he chose over his real family, over his mother and his sister and his father.

'In Mali we stayed in a hotel in Bamako. It was my first time in Africa and it was different than what I expected. It was big, and noisy, and everybody was busy. I thought it would be a bit like India, I was in India once, in Goa. But it was different. The house was on the outside of the city. Our first night he left me at the hotel and went to greet the family alone. I was surprised, but he told me that was the tradition. The next morning, we went together to greet his father and his mothers, there were four wives of the father. He is an Islamic teacher and there were many children learning with him. He received us in a little room, just outside the main house, and he was seated on a mat and we sat next to him, I had to cover my head because women were not allowed into the room with open head. Moussa had warned me about that before, so it was not a problem.

'The father was old, with a white beard, but very active. Also, he spoke good French, and I also know French, so we were able to communicate. He welcomed me, and he said Moussa was a good and dutiful son and he hoped we would have a happy life. Then he begin to tell me how Moussa came to him from the sea. He said it was God who told him to go to the sea that day, and he found Moussa and two other young men at the waterfront, they had just arrived and they didn't know where to go next. He brought them home. He said from that day Moussa became his son. I listened. I was confused. This is the first time I am hearing that the man is not Moussa's real father. But I didn't say anything there. I keep quiet and I pretend as if I know. After telling me the story of how Moussa became his adopted son, the old man prayed for us. Next, we went into the house to meet the women. It was a big compound behind a mud wall, with different sections for the wives and their children. There were many children and they all came to touch my hand, my hair, my nose. They were very excited by the visit. They ran out to invite their friends to come and touch me. We sat in the senior wife's living room, this is Moussa's mother, his adoptive mother now I know, and all the other wives joined us. They giggle when I speak. They find everything I do funny because it was the first time they were seeing someone like me in their house. We gave them a little money and the presents we brought, mostly clothes for the children, and for the wives. Finally, we went back to the hotel. For me, the holiday was already spoiled because of what I learned. I ask him, Why didn't you tell me about your real family? What kind of marriage is this when I don't even know where you really come from, your real family? He said he was planning to tell me. But when? I asked him. I say to myself, What other things is he keeping from me? I think like that in my mind. I make him promise to write to his mother, his real mother, and to tell her about me, about our marriage, with a picture of us, me and him. We didn't stay long in Mali. We had planned to stay one week in the hotel but we had to leave after three days.'

'Why?'

'Why? Because now I am angry with him. I feel I don't know him any more. Also, people kept coming to see us, his friends, more family, they'd knock on the door as early as six a.m. They will bring food, and they'll sit for hours and they won't go. It was impossible. Every day. I mean, this was supposed to be our honeymoon. So, we left to spend the remaining three days in Senegal. Things were better there. We met a German couple, tourists, Ingrid and Hermann, they said they came to Senegal for bird-watching. They wanted to see the African grey owl. Moussa went with them once, but I was not interested. By that time, I was tired, I wanted to come back.'

'A very short visit then,' Portia said.

'Well, that was our honeymoon. We came back with many plans. Moussa wanted to go to university, because he didn't finish his education, you know that. He also wanted us to make peace with my parents. He talked about parents and how important they are. When he talked like that, I find it confusing, because he himself was not at peace with his real parents, and he never told me why. Now maybe you can tell me.'

'I . . . wish I could tell you. He wanted another father, I guess, another family,' Portia said, turning away to the window.

'Why, what is wrong with his real father, your father?'

'My father . . . he left us. He was a poet, a political poet. He lived in exile all his life. He died recently.'

'I didn't know that. I am sorry for your loss.'

They sat without speaking for a moment, then Katharina took a deep breath and continued, 'Anyway, my plan when we came back from Mali was to finish my PhD, and maybe one day, to have children. Well, it was not easy. Moussa didn't have many friends, and some of my friends now started to avoid us. It was interesting. I would call, and they'd be busy, or they wouldn't answer the call. At my graduation only my husband and his one friend from the railway came, everybody else have their family there, and friends, we only three of us.

'After my graduation we decided to move to Geneva. It was becoming too lonely here in Basel. We had only two friends, a Nigerian woman, Obi, and her Swiss husband, Alfred. Geneva was more international. There were more mixed families, and we became part of that community. There were also many international cultural events . . . at one point our social life revolved only around international events, at embassies, at cultural festivals, at weddings, well, this is Switzerland, after all. Very international.

'I knew what I was going into when I married an African. But, still . . . The most painful was my parents. It was over one year before we finally made peace with them. It was Moussa who said to me, Let us go and meet them. He said he felt guilty, that it was because of him that my family left me. Well, we went. We knocked on the door and my father opened the door. He looked surprised when he saw us there. He wasn't expecting us. I felt sad when we all sat there, in the living room, with my parents, as if we are strangers, and my mother asking us if she can make tea for us. I wanted to say to her, Mother, I am your daughter, I have not changed. Why do you talk to me like this? And my father . . . ah, it was so painful because I used to be so close to my father, you know. But funny enough, they started talking, my father and Moussa. My father said he had a funeral service to attend the next day. And Moussa said his father oversees so many funerals in Mali. My father was interested when he learned that his father was an imam. And so they started talking about religion. My mother and I moved to the kitchen to talk. She wanted to know if I needed anything, if he was treating me well. I said I needed nothing, that I was fine. That I just missed her and my father. So, for a while things were back to normal with my parents.

'I started work in Geneva. Teaching at a research institute affiliated to the university, as a junior faculty member. I was making some money, but we needed more. He still worked for the railway, the plan was for him to go back to school, but he always made excuses. The truth is, he couldn't afford to go back because he was sending all his money back home to Mali, I discovered that later. I had to pay for everything. Sometimes he was supposed to pay the bills, but he wouldn't, he will forget, instead he will send the money to Mali. I discovered also that he had taken credits from the bank, just to send to his father. I saw the letter from the bank, reminding him to make payment. I was disturbed. He said he sent the money because his father was dying, and I said why didn't he tell me. He had told me about his father being sick, but I didn't know it was so serious, that he was dying. He said I didn't listen to him any more anyway. Ah, it was so frustrating to talk with him. I never talked about this to anyone before, not even my mother, but you are his sister, so I am telling you everything.

'He started accusing me of not wanting to have children, and I said I couldn't take care of two children, him and our baby. And he lost his temper, he said I was calling him a child. He said I was disrespectful, and that I was racist like all my friends. He had changed. We had those fights, but we always make up. But one day, it got so bad. He was praying, on a mat . . .'

'He was very religious then?'

'He didn't use to be, but suddenly he became religious and will pray five times a day on a mat. He will fast during the fasting time. And he even said that I must change my religion, that a wife must have her husband's religion. I said religion was not very important to me, and we started to argue. But anyway, that day it got so bad. I had just come back from work and right there in the mail was another bill I thought we had paid. He was going to pay, it was water, or electricity, I can't remember. I had a bad day at the office, the students, you know, they make you angry sometimes and I was beginning to think maybe teaching was not the best thing for me. It seems every decision I have made so far have been bad decisions, and then there was this bill. I couldn't take it any more.

'He was in the living room, praying on a mat. I couldn't wait for him to finish. I started waving the letters at him, I threw them in front of him, but he ignored me. I went to the kitchen and made tea. In the kitchen drawer I saw more bills, and I saw a Western Union receipt, he had sent almost a thousand francs to his family and here we were, our light bill unpaid, and also we were already behind on rent. When he finished praying we started arguing, and I pushed him in the chest and I said I had had enough of the marriage, I said I was leaving. That was when he took a knife, a kitchen knife, and pointed it at me. He said he would kill me and then he'd kill himself. I had never seen him like that before. He was shouting and banging on the table, and he put the knife on my

154   Helon Habila

chest, right here. It was late at night and the neighbours called the police. But by the time they came he had calmed down. But I didn't sleep there that night, I ran to a friend's house. And that was it, that was the end of our marriage. Two years of marriage, three years since we first met in that bar on Basler Fasnacht, and it was over.

'I was exhausted. I called Sven and he came with me to the house to get my things. Moussa couldn't believe I was really leaving. After all, we had fought and made up before, but this time I was afraid, for my life. Maybe I was overreacting, maybe it was all in my mind, but I kept seeing him with that knife, and he had changed. I was afraid. He begged me, but Sven said he'd call the police if he interfered, so he just sat there with tears in his eyes as I took my things. I was crying too. I think I still loved him. A little bit, but I couldn't trust him any more. I left my job and moved back to Basel.

'I had a little breakdown at that time. Everything for me had ended. At this time my former friends came back. And I am shocked at all the nasty things they say. They think they are trying to make me happy. They will say, You are lucky you didn't have any children with him. Or they ask, What did you guys talk about all the time? Did he even know how to use fork and knife? I told them that's it. Leave me alone, don't ever come back. What right did they have to judge him? What have they ever stood up for in their whole life? I told them I was ashamed to be their friend. I am sorry. He is your brother, but I have to tell you the truth. Some people here are very racist. I don't want to upset you.'

'Do I look upset?' Portia asked. A woman had once screamed in her face in the Tube in London, dementedly shouting, 'Fucking foreigner!' Foreigner, for some reason, was the worst form of insult the woman could think of. She had read in the papers about people being thrown out of moving trains by skinheads for being black.

'Don't worry about upsetting me,' she said. 'Just go on with your story.'

But still, she was touched. She had misjudged Katharina. Despite everything that happened, she had been truly cour-ageous, going against her family and friends, standing up for love.

'Did you see him again, I mean, before the last time?'

'Yes. I'll tell you, but first, I go out for a cigarette.'

They went out together and stood by the door, smoking.

'I saw him. He also moved back to Basel. I couldn't stop him, he had the right to do that. But we didn't meet. We made contact only through my lawyers. I needed a lawyer because I didn't feel safe. Of course I sometimes see him at the station where he worked, at the Hauptbahnhof. And he will wave to me and I will pretend I didn't see him. And then, I don't know what happened, I came back one day and I found him waiting for me here. I don't know how he found my address, maybe through one of our old friends, maybe he followed me, I don't know. But he was waiting for me outside the door, and he waited for me until I had opened the door, then he came and said we should go in and talk. He said he was going back to Mali. I didn't believe him and I said he should leave. He left. Just like that. He just looked at me sadly and he shake his head and he left. I was surprised.

'Then the next day, I got off the train, and there he was. It was late in the evening, on a Sunday. The platform was almost empty. I think he came on the same train with me. I am not sure, but I think he followed me. I turn and he was there, coming toward me. I stood there, I was terrified. He looked so serious. You understand, I was not thinking clearly at this time. My aunt had just died, and then all the pressure from him. I stood there, paralysed. I wanted to scream for help, but I just stood there, watching him still approaching, and the place was deserted, just me and him. He said nothing, he came and hugged me. I remember a train was coming in then. It honked, very loud, and that added to my panic, and at that moment the train lights flashed into my eyes and it was as if I was released from chains. I . . . pushed him with all my might. I thought he was going to kill me. I am sorry. You know what happen next. There was the trial. At first, I didn't want to defend myself, I wanted to die, to be punished. I caused his death. I kept seeing his body, cut into pieces. But my father said, What is the use? Best to tell the truth and fight for my freedom. We got a lawyer and, you know the rest. They gave me three years, not for murder, but for what we call *Totschlag*, manslaughter.'

•

The community cemetery was located on a hillside populated by pine trees. It looked like a park, peaceful, the sort of place one would want to be buried in. They were the only people there, Sven was in the car, waiting for them.

'I have never been here before,' Katharina said, 'I was in detention when they buried him.'

It was one of the few community burial grounds in Basel that had a section for Muslims. They found his grave next

to a tree, tucked away at the back of the neat rows of head-
stones, all ritually positioned to face the east. It was raining
again. They clustered solemnly under one umbrella over the
headstone, speaking in whispers as if scared they'd disturb the
dead. Portia felt the tears fill her eyes. It was hard to believe
that under this stone lay her brother's remains. What drove
him, what did he seek, so far away from where he was born,
why so restless, and was he finally at rest, here, in this foreign
place? No wonder philosophers and poets always describe life
as a fever, a burning raging fever from which we all seek
relief. Her father had sought his in his activism and exilic
delusions. Her brother had left home and taken a boat to Mali,
and he had ended up in the home of the preacher who became
his father, but the fever had still raged, driving him to Europe,
and she wondered if it was all worth it. He had died at thirty-
three, so young. Would his soul fly back to Africa, back to
where he was born? She had started thinking more and more
about death, since her father died. And she, what did she seek,
what was her fever and how did she seek relief from it? She
wanted to make her mother happy. She wanted to find out
more about her brother – but she could hardly call that a fever.
And what was the use blaming it all on their father – he was
a shitty father, of course, but ultimately we all make our way,
driven by our own appetites and predilection.

On the way to the airport they passed people standing at
bus stops waiting for the next bus, it was wet and watery and
windy, somehow that was how she always imagined Europe
to be. Katharina sat silently in front, next to Sven, looking
at the passing landscape. Earlier, in the cemetery Portia had
asked her what her plans were. 'I am not sure,' Katharina

said with a shrug. 'For me I cannot stay in Basel again, not in Switzerland. I have lost my friends. Maybe I go to another country, maybe Germany. I have my education. Of course I come back to Basel once in a while since I have my house, but I have to find a new life somewhere.'

When they got out of the car Katharina stood in front of Portia, her eyes wet. 'I have nothing more to say, but I want you to know I am sorry and I really loved your brother. But there was so much problem between us and it was never going to work. It is life.' She rejoined Sven in the car, walking away without looking back, her shoulders heaving violently.

Now there were just the two of them, sitting on a bench, not talking much. Her mind was here, and also in Lusaka. She was walking down a tree-bordered path toward a modest brick house in front of which her mother was standing, waiting for her. She still wasn't sure what she'd tell her mother, she wasn't sure if the journey had been a success or a failure, but she was glad she came. She mentioned this to him. 'I didn't want to come, you know. I told my mother, What is the point? Plus, he is already dead. But this has been worth it. I met you.'

'I am also glad I came.'

She wrote down her number and her email. 'Call me, or write. I am also on Facebook. Will you?' He held her tight for a long time, then they parted. Walking toward her gate, she imagined him watching her until she disappeared. She refused to turn back, if she did she'd break down and run back to him and say, 'Come to Lusaka with me.' He had said yes to her once, why not a second time? But, she had no claim on him. When she asked him drunkenly that night to come to Basel

with her, she had been surprised when he said yes. Perhaps
he also needed to get away, deferring a final decision by aim-
less motion. Now he had a train to catch, he had to return to
Berlin, back to the house in Mitte, cluttered with boxes that
he had to put in storage. His mind was in between places.
Eventually, she was sure, he would make the right decision.
Maybe he would go back to his wife. She hoped he wouldn't,
she hoped he would write, she hoped they would meet again.
She came up on the escalator and there, through the glass, she
saw a plane on a runway speeding for takeoff. She watched,
impressed by the certainty, the power, every bolt, every screw,
every drop of liquid focused on that takeoff. Nothing tentative or hesitant. It was amazing, and beautiful.

Book 4

THE INTERPRETERS

It was fortuitous that I bought a ticket for the French TGV train instead of the Deutsche Bahn, which, it turned out, was on strike today. It meant I had to go through Zurich to transfer to a Berlin train. I passed through a line of disappointed Deutsche Bahn customers waiting for answers regarding their travel. As the train pulled away from the glum faces on the platform, I tried to suppress a smug feeling of false prescience we all get when things work out for us and don't work out for others in the same situation. It was three hours to Zurich, so I closed my eyes as soon as we got under way. I jerked awake as the train came to a stop at the Zurich station. I stood up and ran to my next train, I felt sluggish, slowed down by sleep, but I made it before the doors closed. I put my head down and slept off again. The next time I woke up a border policewoman was standing over me. We were at the German border, the train had come to a stop and the police were going around the train, checking documents. There were two officers in the carriage, the other, a man, was talking to another passenger a few seats away from me. I couldn't help but notice that the other passenger was also African, with the tall thin frame and curly hair common to some East Africans. A Somali, most likely; with him was a boy of about twelve.

I handed the officer my passport.

'Nigerian,' she said. She looked at the picture in the passport and then at me in that way immigration officers always do, then she asked me if I had bought any watches or jewellery in Switzerland. I wasn't worried about my documents, my German visa still had two more months on it, and I'd be long out of Europe before it expired. The other passenger seemed to be involved in a long discussion with the officer who had now taken his document, a piece of A4 paper, and was consulting with the female officer. They went back to the Somalian and asked him a few more questions before returning the document to him. Our eyes locked and he nodded at me, I nodded back. I closed my eyes, but I couldn't return to sleep. When the train stopped at the next station and I opened my eyes, I saw he was sitting opposite me. 'This seat is free, yes? You don't mind if we sit with you?' he asked. We were the only black people in the carriage, and it was natural for him to assume some solidarity, a closing of ranks, the same way some black people would carefully avoid talking to another black person in a room full of white people. Obviously he was starving for company. I nodded. 'Please.'

He looked to be in his middle to late fifties, but when he smiled he had a twinkle in his eyes and it took away five years from his face. 'I see you from there, you look sad. That's why I join you.'

'I look sad?'

'Is about a girl, maybe?' he said, leaning forward, eyes twinkling. I thought of Portia on the plane. I smiled, saying nothing. He pressed on, 'This girl, she is your wife maybe?'

'No, not my wife.'

'I see. I understand. But you love her.'

'Why do you say that?' I asked, not sure if I should be offended by his persistence or not.

'I see in your eyes. I travel a lot and I see many things. I know love when I see love. You tell this girl you love her?'

I laughed at his intensity.

'Are you travelling in Europe?' he asked. I caught the odd phrasing. Of course I was travelling in Europe, but I understood he meant something else; he wanted to know the nature of my relationship to Europe, if I was passing through or if I had a more permanent and legal claim to Europe. A black person's relationship with Europe would always need qualification – he or she couldn't simply be native European, there had to be an origin explanation. I told him I had been to Basel with a friend, and I was now going back to Berlin via Frankfurt.

He said, 'I live in Munich. Two years now in Munich. I take this train to Munich.' He had the hoarse voice of the cigarette addict, with the accompanying phlegmy cough and nicotine-stained teeth. I turned to the boy, who was staring at the passing landscape where the day was slowly evanescing into night. He had a vacant look on his face.

'What's your name?' I asked. He looked from me to his father, then he turned back to staring out at the landscape.

'His name is Mahmoud. He don't like to talk. He is shy of strangers,' the man answered. The boy looked at him, the annoyance briefly flashing in his eyes the way all kids at that age are always annoyed at their parents. He said something to the boy, and I asked him, 'Is that Somali you are speaking?'

'No, that is Turkish.'

'Ah, you are from Turkey!'

'No, Somalia. But we lived in Turkey long time. He speaks Bulgarian as well, and Arabic, and some German, and English.'

'Wow. A walking Rosetta stone,' I said.

'Stone?' He looked puzzled.

'How did he learn to speak so many languages? He is so young.'

'My son, he have very small school education. He learn everything from travel.'

'I see.'

'We have been to many countries, but now we live in Germany. This boy, he has been travelling since he is four years, now he is fifteen.'

'So, you are going back to Munich?' I asked. Clearly, he wanted to talk. I wasn't particularly in the mood for talking but I was intrigued by the boy, who sat silent, looking out at the passing landscape – rather quiet for someone who spoke so many languages. I wanted to hear him speak, I wanted to test him.

'Tell me something in Bulgarian,' I said. He didn't even turn from the window.

'We go to Munich first, then maybe we go to Bulgaria,' the father said.

'You are going to Bulgaria today?'

'Yes, maybe, but first we go to Munich. Listen, is a long journey, many hours before we come to Frankfurt. If you want, I tell you my story. To kill time. It is long story, but interesting, and is all true. I swear, by Allah, it is all true.'

The offer was made matter-of-factly, it sounded reasonable, we had a long trip ahead of us, what better way to shorten the trip? I leaned back in my seat. 'Go ahead.' I could always feign sleepiness if it got boring.

•

His name was Karim Al-Bashir and he was born in Somalia, long before the tribal wars and internecine killings started. His father was not ethnic Somali, he came from North Sudan as a young man and settled in Mogadishu, the Somali capital. The father, Al-Bashir, married into a good and moderately well-to-do family of traders, he was hardworking, and lucky, he prospered. His father-in-law gave him a loan and he started his own business, selling provisions in a corner store. His first son, Karim, was born one year after the marriage. Al-Bashir died in a car accident when Karim was only twelve years old, and suddenly the young Karim had to assume the responsibilities of an adult. With support from his uncles he was able to continue his father's business, buying and selling. He got married at twenty and had his first daughter before he turned twenty-two. And then gradually things began to change. In 1990 President Siad Barre died and overnight Somalia descended into political chaos. Time passed. Factions organized around family ties and tribal loyalty divided the country into fiefs overseen by tribal warlords. And thus began Karim's personal nightmare.

In his phlegmy voice he said, 'One day a young man come to my shop and says he wants to marry my daughter, Aisha. She is only ten. She is too young, and I want her to finish school. But I am afraid of telling him no. This is a powerful man, the son of the local warlord, even though he is young, everyone knows him. His name is Abdel-Latif. He go around with a group of bad boys, all with guns, and they can shoot you, just like that. So, I go and tell my in-laws. My mother-in-law she knows about this man Latif and she tell me, Be careful. She say I must not give any answer now, we wait and see, maybe he lose interest and go. But every day this man he come to the shop. He will sit and his friends will take a few things and not pay, cigarette and biscuit and Coca-Cola, small things, and I will smile and smile, and he will remind me that he wants to marry my daughter. He begin to call me his father-in-law, just like that. One day he say, "Why you don't want me to marry your daughter, you think I am not good enough? Are people from where you come better than us Somalis?"

'And now I know. It is not only about my daughter, Aisha. He wants to destroy me because my father is not originally from Somalia. That day, we have a family meeting, my wife's two brothers, Mustafa and Abu-Bakr, and my wife and her mother and father. I can see in their eyes that they have no hope for me. My father-in-law, he say, "We will go to Abdel-

Latif's father, I know him very well, he is my namesake, Muhammad. We grew up together, if his son will listen to anyone, he will listen to his father." It is our only hope. The only other choice is to run away to another town far away, but even that is not hundred per cent safe, because these people they can have friends and family in different towns and they can get you. That night we go to see his father, Muhammad, who is namesake of my father-in-law. He is an important man, he live in a big house and there are many people all waiting to see him. Many cars are parked outside the house. It is in the evening, after the Maghrib prayer. We sit on a mat in the outside room, four of us, me and my father-in-law and Mustafa and Abu-Bakr, my wife brothers. Soon he come in and people greeted him. Though others are there before us, the moment he see my father-in-law he invite him forward. "Muhammad," he say, "what a surprise, what a pleasure to see you here in my home." They go aside and they talked. When they come back, I can see there isn't much hope on my in-law's face. But we don't leave immediately, food is brought in by two young girls, their head covered in hijab. Plenty food, because he is an important man. Rice and chicken. We eat together, from the same bowl using our fingers. Then we left.

'"He'll talk to his son," my father-in-law say. "He'll reason with him."

'That night, I go to sleep full of hope. Since the whole thing start, I cannot sleep very well, both me and my wife. The country has changed. People shooting guns every day on the streets. People go about in fear. Women are punished for very small reasons, like not covering their heads, or not marrying the person the mullahs say they must marry. Well, we

wait to see what will happen after the promise from Muhammad. Our answer come two days later. Latif and his friends
came to my shop. My shop is not big, just a small room in
front of the house, facing the road in a quiet part of town.
Suddenly we hear gunfire, ta-ta-ta, they fire gun on the door
of my shop. I thought I was dead. Bullet everywhere. My
eldest boy, Fadel, he is just seven years, he always stay with me
in the shop, he run into the house, me I lay on the floor waiting for them to come in and kill me. They come in, three of
them, Latif is leading. They stand over me where I am lying
on the ground. "Stand up," he say to me. I stand up, and as I
look into his eyes I know it is going to be my last day. It is not
the eyes of a normal man. His senses have been turned by the
terrible plant they eat, kwat. You know kwat? It is like drug.
They eat it from morning to night and is very bad. It make
you go crazy. He is chewing like this, in handfuls.

'He look at me and he say, "So you think my father can
save you from me?" My hand and my leg start shaking, and
all I can do is to pray in my mind that they kill me quickly
and that they don't touch my wife and children. He tell me to
go into the house and to bring my daughter and her mother.
He say he want to hear from their mouth that they have no
objection to this marriage propose.'

'Proposal,' I said.

'Yes, proposal. So, I go in, but the house is empty. My wife
when she hear the gun, and she see Fadel running inside, she
take the children and they run to her father house. I come back
and tell him that they have heard the gun and they are afraid,
they run and I don't know where they are. I am sorry. "Okay,"
he say. "Just prepare your daughter for the wedding. It take

place next Friday, five days from today." This talk is happening on a Sunday, I remember everything as if is today. I tell him I have no problem with that. I only have one request. More time, please. One month maybe, so I can buy my daughter new clothes and pots and other things for the marriage, I am poor man and I need time to get the money together. "Two weeks," he say, and they left. I sit there, too afraid to go out. I can't believe I am still alive. When I see the gun I think my last day has come. As soon as my legs become strong to walk, I go to my in-laws' house and tell them what happened. We have another meeting.

'My father-in-law, he say, "You have two choice here. You can stay and let him marry your daughter, or you can leave town. You decide." "No," my wife said. All these time she have been quiet and left all the decision to me, but now she speak, very strong. "That man will never marry my daughter. What son-in-law is this? He is crazy man and one day he will kill my daughter. My daughter will never sleep in the same room with that man. Never."

'And that is how we leave our country Somalia. First my wife and children leave for Hargeisa to stay with her aunt, my mother-in-law's sister. I stay behind and continue to open the shop, to pretend everything is okay and normal. Latif and his boys sometimes stop in front of the shop to ask me if I am getting ready for the wedding, and I always say, Yes, insha Allah, when they ask me where is Aisha I make excuse, I tell them she have gone to school, or she have gone to the market with her mother. They will take a few cigarette and small small things from the shop and they will go. I wait, and one day before the wedding, I leave town. I follow my wife to

Hargeisa. I leave everything we own, everything, including the goods in my shop. I tell my in-laws to sell everything they can sell and send us the money after. This is the beginning of our life on the road.'

'What year was this?' I asked.

'2002, is twelve years now. I feel sad to leave Mogadishu. I feel in my heart as if I will never see Mogadishu again. I feel sad for my family also. I have three children at the time, Aisha, who is only ten, and Fadel who is seven, and this one, Mahmoud, who is only four when we leave, and his mother was pregnant that time. Now Mahmoud is fifteen, almost sixteen. I leave Mogadishu with three children, now I have five children. Two were born on the road.'

The boy, Mahmoud, who had been quiet all this while, his face glued to the window, gazing at the small towns and countryside and farms outside, now turned and whispered to his father, the father nodded. The boy stood up and headed for the toilet at the end of the carriage. He had a limp, perhaps even worse than it appeared because he walked self-consciously, trying to minimize the limp with a stylish roll of his body. Karim saw me staring after the boy and he said, 'He is a good boy. He speaks four languages, and all he learn on his own. His brother speak five language. I speak three.'

'What happened to his leg, was he born like that?'

'No, no, he wasn't born like this. He get accident. It happen in Yemen. I tell you my story, I tell you everything. It is a sad story, but still, we thank God we are alive together and we are healthy. I have seen people who suffer more than me. I have seen people die in the forest, trying to cross the border. Once, me and my boys, when we are leaving Turkey through forest, we saw a woman and her daughter in the bush. They are looking around, and I ask her can I help you, are you in trouble? She say she was looking for her husband grave. He died when they tried to cross into Bulgaria with human smugglers. He just fall down and died. The smugglers help her quickly bury him in the sand. That was many days ago, but she came back because she kept thinking of him. "You come back to do what?" I ask her. She say she come to say *du'a* for him, to pray for his dead body, she and her son, the son is maybe five, maybe six years old, she say only if she pray for her dead husband can she be able to go forward. Now they look for the grave and she can't find it, it was over a week since they buried him and everything look different. She go from one little place that look like grave, then she begin to pray, then she go to another pile of sand, about four times I see her go from one sand to another. Sometimes while praying she forget what she is doing and she begin to fall asleep because she is so tired and she didn't sleep for many days, then she will start again, then she will forget the words and she will start to cry. We leave her there, she and her son. I tell you, I have seen so many suffering. My story also is sad, but I have seen more sad stories in my travelling. My boy, he broke his leg in Yemen. And you know all his dream is he wants to be a football player. He wants to grow up and play for the Turkish club, Galatasaray.'

'How did it happen?' I asked.

Now we were in Cologne. The noise made by passengers coming in and going out, the sound of their laughter and their German words formed the background to our talk. The boy was back from the toilet. He looked glum, too serious for a kid. His father turned to him and said something in Turkish and the boy looked at me, then he turned back to the window. After a while he stood up and took some money from his father to go to the canteen. At the table to our left a German family was staring pointedly at us, their faces impassive, making no attempt to disguise their curiosity.

'Life in Yemen was not easy at first. But good thing is that we are safe and we are together as a family, this is the most important blessing. We register with the United Nation refugee service, and they give us small money every month, not much, about fifty dollars each. That is not enough for food and house, but things cheap in Yemen. And soon my in-law was able to send us small money from what they sell of my property back in Somalia. We rent a small place, just two rooms and a little kitchen. The children in one room, me and my wife in another room. Sana'a, the capital of Yemen, is a small city. The buildings is not much different from Mogadishu. Large families live in large compounds, with many children and the women wearing their veil and people walking on the narrow streets, just like Mogadishu. There isn't much work to do, but soon I meet some Somalis and one of them, Othman, he invite me to work with them. We buy cigarette and small small things we can buy cheap in Yemen and we take it to Somalia and make some profit, not much, but enough to survive.'

'Was it dangerous?'

Karim laughed and shrugged. 'Well, what we are doing is smuggling, you know. I don't ask too much question. My partner is young Othman. There are many Somalis like him in Yemen, they live in the refugee camps, with no wives or children. I don't even think they are real refugees, just businesspeople. He sometimes talk that his brothers are Somali pirates and they kidnap big ships on the sea and make big money, but something happen and his brother die and they stop doing pirate work. He doesn't say more than that. Now they smuggle people from Somalia to Yemen and other countries. And then they take back cigarette and other small things to sell in Somalia. Me, I did not join in smuggling people, but I join in buying and selling cigarette. Still, my wife, she was not happy. She said I can't do this kind of business. But I tell her, What can I do? We can't live on fifty dollars every month. We will die.

'Well, everything is good for a time. Everything go fine. We are happy. My children start going to school and we can eat good. My wife give birth and we move to a bigger house, not too bigger than the last one, but with three rooms. This is our first year in Yemen. The Somali community is very small then, but soon things start to change. More people start to come, then Othman start doing more people smuggling, and he want me to join him. I will not lie to you, I did join him for a time, and the money was good. Then my wife become unhappy, she say, "Why you do this? Are we not managing okay, what if you get arrested, what if you die, then what will happen to us? Now we are in this strange land, you can't break any law." I say I will think about it. And that day, as I go to meet Othman to tell him I can't do people smuggling any more, they tell me Othman is dead. He died in a boat on the sea. His people were sitting in the room and they are crying and I quietly left them. That same day my son fell from the veranda. Because we are on the fifth floor, in our new house, it is cheaper to rent the fifth floor, the ground floor is more expensive because no elevator or anything and everybody want ground floor, and there is a little garden in the yard. Well, my son was playing with his brother, Fadel, and he is leaning on the rail and it broke, he fell and thank God he survived without any major broken bone, but he broke something in his kneecap and from that day he was limping like this. At first we didn't know that his kneecap broke. But after a while we see that as he grow, his left leg is not growing like the right leg.'

'Did you take him to the hospital?'

'Yes, but in Yemen, there is nothing they can do. Yemen is small country, and poor. They tell me the only place you can get help is in Europe, Germany, or France. I look at my son who all his life wants to play football and I promise myself that I will bring him to Germany or France as long as I am alive.'

They were three years in Yemen, from there they moved to Syria. The family continued to grow. There were five children now, three girls and two boys. They got to Syria in 2005. In Damascus their life improved almost immediately. There they'd spend the best seven years of their lives since they left home. The economy was good, Karim was able to get a job with no difficulty, as a kitchen assistant in a hotel he described as the best hotel in all of Syria. His face lit up as he remembered. 'Food is not a problem. I get plenty food from the hotel. Food they want to throw away, good food, the best food in the world because this is a very big hotel. I tell them no, I will take it. That way I didn't have to spend my money on food. No more fighting with the wife, and the kids all go back to school. My oldest son, Fadel, he is now ten, and my daughter Aisha is almost fourteen; she was only ten when we left Mogadishu. My wife have not seen her mother or her father for over three years.

'In Damascus we decide we will not get in touch with the Somali community. The last experience with Othman was not good. But we are able to keep in touch with our family back home. They tell us things in Somalia are getting worse every day. Every day Shabaab is growing bigger, now there are bombs on the street. Some of my wife people and my uncles have now moved to refugee camps in Kenya. We hear that Abdel-Latif, the evil young man who caused us to leave home, is now one of the most powerful men in all the country. Seven years in Syria, and we would have stayed even longer but for two reasons, one is my son's leg, we have to get to Europe, and second reason, every day Syria is becoming like Somalia. War has started everywhere and even the Syrians are running away from the cities to the countryside, some are leaving the country. And so my wife said, "We have to go, we are not safe here with our children." We left Syria in 2012, we follow a group that is leaving for Istanbul in Turkey.'

Karim fell quiet, and before he turned to the window I saw his eyes fill up with tears. The boy was asleep, his head resting against his father's shoulder. Outside, night had leaped onto the landscape, and we could be anywhere, Turkey, Syria, Yemen, Germany, it didn't matter. What mattered was to hear what happened next. I wanted to know what happened in Turkey, why was it only him and the boy on the train, where was the rest of the family, Fadel, the girls, the mother . . . ?

'In Turkey things very difficult. My wife almost left me. We have only one room and a parlour for me, my wife, and the children. We are always fighting and the children couldn't even go to school. When we live in Syria my wife and daughter are able to get work, sometimes cleaning, sometimes cooking, and in the hotel there was always food, leftovers, chicken, rice, fish, and we were never hungry, we eat rich-people food. But in Turkey, all the foreigners are treated bad. I only get the worst job, in a furniture company, we carry furniture to people houses, sometimes we repair furniture, and as you finish one job, another one is coming. You have to work many hours, for very little money, they just force you to work overtime with no pay, whether you like or not. If you complain, they say okay, go, other people want your job. You work like slave. My wife say, We can't continue like this. If we continue like this, we will die. We have to decide. We have to go to Europe now.

'Every day I worry: how we get money to travel, where do we stay in Europe? I was afraid, I was tired, I miss my home and I miss Mogadishu and my shop and my simple life selling little things with my family. I know if I enter Europe, I may never come back to my country for ever. So, me and my wife, we agree, I say, I will take the three older children with me, she will stay with the two young ones. I go first, if everything work out fine, she will come after me. But my wife, she say, No, take the two boys, I stay with the girls, Aisha who is nineteen and Fatima who is eight and the youngest, Khadija, who is only three. She say girls must stay with their mother because they are women and they need their mother. I agree.

'The next big problem is, how to go to Europe? My son, this one, he say, "Baba, can we not take our hundred euro that we get from the refugee service people and fly to Europe?" We laugh. It is not so easy. Our two choice to travel is to go through Greece, and directly to Western Europe, but if we go through Greece we have to fly and we have to have papers and do registration and fingerprint and so many things, the other one is to go from Istanbul, which is near the border, then we walk across the border into Bulgaria, which is East Europe, but it is still Europe because Bulgaria just join the EU. Finally, we decide we will go by foot to Bulgaria.

'So, we say goodbye to my wife and my daughters. That night we did not sleep. All of us, we cry all night. I didn't know if I will see my little girls again, and my wife. But we have to go, there is no choice. In Istanbul we meet the people who will help us across the border to Bulgaria. Ten hours we walk with my two boys, in night, from nine p.m. to seven a.m., always hiding. Ten hours and we have to hurry all the time because of danger and we have to stay with the other people in the group and the smugglers who are guiding us. My boy, this one, with his leg, he get tired and he cannot walk any more, and he start to cry. I tell him we are doing this so we can get medicine for his leg. He said no, he doesn't want it any more, he say he only want to go back home. He is tired. Me and his older brother we carry him, under the arm, like this. That is when we saw the woman and her son who are looking for the grave of her husband to say the *du'a* for his soul. It is long time ago, but I feel sad and scared every time when I think about it. That woman alone in the forest with her son, not knowing whether to go forward to Europe or to go back, because her husband died. What can she do, where can she go?

'As we got to the Bulgarian border the border police come out and arrest us. We are happy to be arrest, I tell you. As they put us in line, one lady come, she is not Bulgarian, she come from France or Belgium, I think, she say to me, "Are you together with these boys?" I say, "Yes, they are my children." She say, "In that case you are lucky, because we treat family different. We will keep you together and you will get a better room and food and everything will be fine. Just always remember to join the family line." We very happy, me and my children. We think, this is the end of our journey, our suffering is over. But we don't know this was just the beginning of our bad luck.'

I said, 'What do you mean? You had made it to Europe at last, with your kids, and the nice lady had promised to assist.'

Karim shook his head. 'Ah, she is nice, but the Bulgarians are different. They are not like real Europeans, I tell you, they are more like Asians, and they just join the EU, they are not very friendly.'

'What do you mean?'

'I'll tell you. They bring truck to take us to town, and because of what the lady said, I take my boys and join the family line, but a man come and say to me, "Hey, you can't join this line, this is only for women and girls, are you a woman?" I say, "No, but I am with my children. The lady say I am to stay with family because I am together with my young children." The man say, "Where is your wife?" I say, "My wife is not here, only me and the boys." The man say, "Okay, join the men."

'I want to argue more, but I can see they are getting angry. They say to me, "Hey, we don't care who you are." This is after I show them my refugee protection paper from UNHCR in Yemen, they say as far as we are concerned, you have no right here. You enter this country illegal and you are a criminal. So just shut up. Now I see my boys are beginning to cry and people are staring at us. Everybody is tired and I don't want trouble, so I join the men in the line and we enter big truck, like military truck. We drive far and we can't see outside because we are sitting on the floor inside this truck and there are many men, many from Morocco, Algeria, Eritrea, Nigeria, Ghana, Mali, Afghanistan, Syria . . . everyone speaking different language. When we get to the home, which is actually a prison . . .'

'What do you mean prison?' I interrupted.

'This place used to be an actual prison, but now is empty so they use it for refugee but it is really prison. Very big stone building with iron bars and many floors, with women and family on one side and the rest for men, all packed into small tiny rooms. As we are coming down from the truck to be registered, we see the woman again and I quickly run to her. "You," she say. "Where did you go? Why are you not with the families?" I told her what happened. She turned and talk angrily to the man who say I cannot join the family. They argue, then she say to me, "Don't worry, from now on, I talk directly to his boss. You will be fine. Just finish registering and I will see you inside." She was angry. We register and we go inside and all the time I keep looking for her, but I didn't see her again. They begin to take us to the rooms, and I tell you this is a bad bad prison. As we go to our rooms the refugees who are there already, they stand by the door and shout at us and spit at us. My children they are crying now. "Where are we, Baba?" they ask me. They have never seen anything like this before. I tell the official, "But you can't do this, you can't put my small children in the same place with all these men. It is not right. Look at my youngest boy, he only seven, how he stay in the same room with all these men?" I touch his hand when I talk and now he is angry. He push me away and call me illegal alien. He say, "If you don't like our accommodation, you can go back to your country." Still I try. I say, "But I am a United Nation protected refugee, see my paper here. You can't do this to us." He say he does not care about any rights and protection, and I can wait when I go Western Europe. Here is Eastern Europe, they don't care about this. Still, we are a bit lucky, they put us not in the long big room with dozens of men, but in a smaller room with four other people, with my children we are seven in the room. There are bunk beds, and my boys are able to get the top bunk bed, one on top of my bed, the other on the next bed. We stay in that place for one year. It is a bad place, a prison. There are guards everywhere, these guards they work with prisoners before, so they still treat us like prisoners. The food also was bad. We all have to eat in the cafeteria, and even if you are not hungry you cannot take your food to your room, not even bread. It was hard for the young boy because we eat at five p.m. and by eight to nine before we sleep he is hungry again and he will be crying.'

He was quiet for a while, looking out of the window. The boy was still sleeping. The father gently ran his hand on the boy's head, his eyes faraway. The memories of that grim place, the prison as he so bitterly called it, had darkened his face, and yet, when he looked at the boy, his eyes softened and he sighed and turned back to me.

'It was not all bad, you know. We are lucky to be in that little room away from others. It is only seven of us in our room, in the other rooms there are twenty, thirty people. And most rooms are doing segregation, the people stay together in one corner according to their country or colour or religion. The Algerians and Pakistanis and Syrians, they stay together. Our room is black people, African. But I tell you, after a few days, the Algerians and Moroccans, these people who didn't want to stay with us, they run away from their room and come to our room because they say, Hey we African too. They say the other rooms are too much fanatics. Too much argument and fighting over religion and Arab Spring and little little things. Our room is called TV room because everybody like to come and watch TV in our room, even though they also have TV in their room. Any chance they get, they come to our room. The TV room is more fun. If you see any refugee who was in Bulgaria, ask them about TV room and they tell you. It was popular place. People everywhere, some playing cards, some eating, some listen to music, some fighting!'

Was that nostalgia in his voice? Did he perhaps in some little corner of that recollected room etch his name in the wall: 'Karim Was Here'? Why do people do that only in places of bitterness and suffering and sweat: prisons, locker rooms, grimy toilets; but never in fancy hotels or restaurants or churches? Is it to affirm their existence in those places that try to diminish the human in them, a cry against extinction? Karim sighed and went on, 'And sometimes they call my children to interpret for them. Sometimes when there is argument and two people can't talk to one another, because one speak English and the other is only speak Arabic and maybe the other Turkish and even Bulgarian, it is my children who help them talk. This is a good thing for us, because everybody in the prison now know Fadel and Mahmoud. One day, the big overall prison guard, his name is Bogdan, but everybody call him Boss Bogdan, he come to the TV room. He stand by the door like this and say, "Who is Fadel?" At first I fear, I think, what has my son done now? Is he in trouble? But my boy he stand up and he say, "I am Fadel." The officer enter the room and he speak to Fadel in Bulgarian, but Fadel his Bulgarian is not very good yet. Boss Bogdan speak in English, now they talk, and they laugh. Then Bogdan switch to Turkish. The younger one, Mahmoud, he jump in, because his Turkish is a bit better, and the officer turn to me and he say, "Interesting family." Boss Bogdan he say, "Okay, come quick quick, we go to my office." A lawyer is having meeting with one refugee in his office, and the lawyer speak only Bulgarian and English, the refugee he speak only Arabic. Many of the refugee they only speak Arabic and nothing else. Fadel he go and he translate for them. Boss Bogdan is very impress. And suddenly he become friends with my boys. Sometimes he ask them to come to his office and read a letter for him, or just to talk and to watch TV, like his own children. When he go on inspection around the prison, they go with him. They walk with him from floor to floor, talking to the prisoners, my boys they translating for him what the prisoners are saying. He give them extra food and little little present. From that day, many refugees who want to talk to their lawyer, they come to look for Fadel and Mahmoud. Many of them want to leave Bulgaria immediately and they need lawyer so my children have to interpret for them all the time. If Fadel is busy, then Mahmoud will translate. For that they respect us and they always tell me, These children are very smart, you must take them to school. And even though they say it as a praise for me, I still feel sad because of the life we are living. I always think, what if we are back in Somalia, and everything is okay, and we are living in our small house with our shop. My daughter, Aisha, who is almost nineteen now, she would have been married, and maybe I will be a grandfather. Fadel would have started taking over my little business by now, and maybe we will have another shop by now. But here we are in this place and we don't know what will happen to us today or tomorrow.

'One day, Boss Bogdan he call me and say, "These boys, they are very intelligent, they should be in school, not in a prison like this. We will see what we can do for you." I tell my boys and they dance and jump. I look at them and I begin to cry. Fadel who was big and strong in Syria, he is now so thin his eyes are big in his head. And Mahmoud, he doesn't like the prison food and he has been having stomach problem since we came here, his back is all covered with rashes and we have no doctor, no health workers. People die in their rooms from sickness and there is nothing anyone can do for them. Every day they take out dead bodies. Mahmoud, as he is growing taller the limp in his leg is becoming bigger. Whenever we talk to the mother she ask, "Are you really in Europe, how soon can we come and join you? The girls are getting bigger every day, and they miss their brothers. The youngest one is always asking for you, because you used to play and carry her, now she cries and ask for Baba."

'One day a woman, her name is Sonia, she come and say Boss Bogdan send her and she is going to help us. She belong to a charity that work with refugees. She say she have find us a place to stay, but it is outside town, not too far, but it is cheap. It is a little house in a big bloc of houses, they all look the same, with one room and one living room and a kitchen, but for us it is like a palace. We can cook and take shower and have a little privacy. Sonia, she pay the first rent, and she say after this I have to find work and continue to pay my own rent.

'So finally we leave that prison. We leave TV room and everybody is sad. But it is not easy to get work. Me I have no training, I am a shopkeeper, and also, Bulgaria is not a rich country. Even the people of Bulgaria they can't find work, they want to leave Bulgaria and move to France and Germany, just like me. But I keep trying, every day I take the bus and I go to town to look for work, I go from hotel to hotel from shop to shop, anything I can find, and sometimes I don't come back home till night. Sonia keep coming every day. She try to help. But nothing. Soon however a bigger problem begin. Every day the Jehovah people come to our house to preach to us.'

'You mean the Jehovah's Witnesses?' I asked. He pronounced it *Yehova*.

A family of five in the seats behind ours, mother, father, girls and boy, were talking at the top of their voices, one of the girls kept trying to sing in a shrill voice. Karim had to raise his voice to be heard. 'Yes, these people are not good people. They are like the Al-Qaeda.' There was so much anger in his voice.

'Why do you say that?'

'I tell you why. When they come first time, I tell them, me I am not Christian, I am not even a very good Muslim, all I want is to take care of my children and for my family to be safe, just leave us alone. Please, please, don't come again. Leave us alone. Then one day, I come home from looking for work, and Fadel is not around. I ask his brother, "Where is Fadel?" He say to me, "Fadel he go out with the Jehovah people." I say, "When did this thing start?" He say, "For many days now. One day the Jehovah people come when you are not around and they become friends with Fadel. They come every day and talk to him and he begin to follow them."

'When Fadel come back I just look at him and I can't speak. I ask him, "Why you do this, Fadel? What you want with these people?" He stand there, he say nothing, just looking at me. I look at him, and I see that my boy has grown up. He is already a man. He has a little moustache already. Some beard is already on his chin. I tell him, "Look, I don't care what religion you follow, you can be Catholic or Protestant Christian, but not this people. They will break our family. They are like cult." He say nothing, and I know it is too late already. I search his room and I find a Bible that the Jehovah people give him. The next day I did not go to look for work. I stay at home to watch him. They did not come that day, but in the night, Fadel he ran away from home to stay with these people. They have plan it long time. Now, I don't know what to do. I go look for Sonia to ask her to help me, but when I see her, she tell me, the social service people they want to speak with me. Fadel has told them that his father, me, Karim Al-Bashir, is a religious fanatic, and I am forcing him not to be Christian. I go with her in her small car to the office. Fadel is waiting for me with the Jehovah people, three of them. Two men and one woman. That day, I cry. I stand there in the office and I look at my boy, sitting with these people, the Jehovah people, and me sitting there, and I don't know what to say. I wanted to go away and let him do what he want. But then I think of his mother, I think of him when he was a little boy, when he was playing with Mahmoud and he fell from the balcony and how he was crying and saying sorry, it is his fault, and how he didn't eat food for two days because of his sadness for his brother. I say no, I will not give up my first son so easy. I will fight these people.

'Sonia say the only thing I can do is talk to the Muslim Council of Bulgaria. I didn't even know there is a Muslim Council. She tell me, Yes, there is Muslim Council in Bulgaria, they are mostly from Turkey, but they have been in Bulgaria many years and they are very strong, they even have like thirty per cent in parliament. Maybe they can help and talk to the government and government can help me get my boy back. So, I go to these people. I meet one of them in mosque, during evening prayer, and after he take me to his house. I tell him everything that happen with my son. Well, he is angry when he hear everything, he say it is not right to break family because of religion, and he say he will help me. We try to meet Fadel, but he will not meet with us. We only meet the Jehovah people and they say Fadel doesn't want to see us. Every time we try to set up meeting, he will not come. His brother say they sometimes see him walking with the Jehovah people, dressed like them in black jacket, and they go from house to house to preach. The Muslim Council, they get a lawyer and the lawyer say I must say that the boy is young, and he has to stay with me. So, we have another meeting at the social office, and they say he say I am religious fanatic and he is afraid to stay with me. But I say he is my son and he too young . . . and he is . . .'

'Underage.'

'Yes, he is underage, so they can't take him from me. But the social people say okay, they will keep him and when he is eighteen he can decide what he want. In a few months, he will be eighteen. Now, I don't know what to do. Finally, I begin to give up. What can I do? I am a poor man, this is not even my country. I say to the Muslim people, I give up. I have to leave here, I can't stay here any more, we have to go to Germany. Because I think of all we have come through, from Somalia to Yemen to Syria and Turkey and Bulgaria, and I say, Well, we are lucky we are still alive. I think of that woman and her son in the forest trying to pray on her husband grave. And I say to myself, I don't want to lose my other son. They say no, you must stay, we will put Mahmoud in Islamic school and he can become good Muslim and we will keep fighting for the other one. But I don't want to be trap in religion and fighting over religion. I am tired, and I still have no job, and life in Bulgaria is too hard. If Fadel want to see me one day, he know we are going to be in Germany. So, we put together all our money and we get some help from the Muslim Council and we come to Munich.'

'How has it been in Munich?' I asked.

His face looked drawn in the poor light of the train carriage. The family of five had finally quieted down and we didn't have to shout. He shrugged. 'Sonia, she connect us with another charity in Munich, a church. They give us place to stay, me and Mahmoud. I have a lawyer, he help me apply for asylum and I have document to stay in Germany for five years. He say we will fight my case and we will win. We will get paper for my wife and my daughters to join us. He say the German government care very much about family and education, and they will not send us back to Somalia because no school there for the children, and maybe my son will soon have his operation. I am happy for that.'

'What of your wife, have you been in touch?' I asked.

He lowered his head. 'I talk to my wife. I say soon maybe now she can join us, because the lawyer say it is now possible to get them to come. I have not seen my daughters in almost three years and I don't know how they look now. You know women grow fast and their face change. My wife say Aisha now has a boyfriend, and he want to marry her, but Aisha say no. She say she will not leave her mother alone.' He looked at me, his expression an alloy of sadness and pride and despair. He said, 'Why God give me such good daughter and such bad son? Why? When I tell my wife about Fadel she get angry. She start to cry, all the time on the phone. She say I lost her son. She say is my fault. She say she will never join me in Germany if I don't find Fadel. So, every day I call Bulgaria, I ask Sonia if she hear about Fadel and she say she hear he has move to Switzerland, to another Jehovah people. Switzerland, how possible? Well, I go to Basel in Switzerland, two days ago. We stay with friends Sonia introduce to us, and we ask everywhere, all the Jehovah people, but no Fadel. We can't find him. I don't know what to do. Maybe I go back to Bulgaria. Maybe I wait. Maybe my wife will change her mind.'

His eyes searched mine in the gloomy carriage, and I saw

the hunger on his face. He was hungry for hope, hungry for
a break. He shouldn't feel down, I told him. He had come a
long way from Somalia. His boy would be fine. I patted the
sleeping boy gently on the head before leaving them. We were
in Frankfurt and I had to change for my connection to Berlin.
I waved goodbye to them, my mind already moving on to the
next thing. I had an hour to kill, and it wasn't till I sat down
in the empty food court with a cup of coffee before me that
I realized I had left my bag on the train. The bag in my hand
was Karim's – it was similar to mine, a black leather valise,
but a bit older, more tattered. I jumped up and ran down to
the platform, foolishly hoping the train would still be there,
but the platform was empty, and was this the right platform to
begin with, it was a big station, and the platforms all looked
the same, with the German signs incomprehensible to my
fatigued eyes. I stopped the first uniformed person I saw. He
shrugged. He couldn't help. He looked at my ticket and spoke
into his phone, he pointed up, I had to go to the information
office upstairs, maybe they could help. But, as I dragged my
feet toward the escalator, an ominous feeling descended over
me, I felt I had dreamt this scenario before and I knew how
it was going to unfold. Everything was in that bag, including
my passport and my green card.

At the office I stood in line, lost in thought.

'*Nächste*,' the lady behind the counter barked at me. When
I didn't move she snapped louder, '*Nächste, bitte!*' her German sense of order ruffled. The man behind me gave me
an impatient nudge, muttering angrily in German, and still
I hesitated. What would I tell the woman, even now my
bag was flying away in the night, would Karim get down

at the next station and report the bag? He didn't have my address or number, and would he even notice he had the wrong bag before he got to his destination? I could follow him to Munich and try to locate him, but he said he might soon be leaving for Bulgaria. I needed to keep calm, I was tired, sleep-deprived, I decided to go on to Berlin, to think things through on the train. I had my ticket at least. I left and went back to the platform.

I saw the same officer, standing on the platform. He looked at me suspiciously when I asked him for the train to Berlin. 'You find your bag?' he asked. Just then a train pulled into the station, and I saw a face at the window, it was Karim – he was back, looking for me. I ran toward the train. The officer called after me, trying to tell me something, but I was already entering the train. Through a window I saw the officer waving urgently at me, but I made my way down the aisle, toward that face at the window, and why was the train so dark, it felt like a continuation of the darkness that had settled over me since I discovered my bag was missing. The train jerked forward, almost throwing me into the lap of the person sleeping in the aisle seat next to me. I groped my way to an empty seat at the back, one row next to Karim, who even as I sat down I realized was not Karim, and flopped down by the window, looking at the receding platform dotted with sleepy passengers holding their tickets in one hand and their bags in the other.

I sat, tense and alert – I'd get off at the next station and catch any train to Berlin. But the next station came and passed, and the next one, and still the train didn't slow down. I fought to keep my eyes open, I couldn't work up the strength to turn to not-Karim, to ask what train this was. The sense of doom settled more firmly over me like a blanket. Soon the lights and buildings gave way to monotonous open country. I jumped to my feet and rushed up the aisle looking for an official to ask when the next stop was. I passed through the carriages, eyes glowed at me from the seats, faint reflection of the light outside rose from dark faces; there were no officials to see. I dropped into a seat, exhausted, and immediately fell into a deep stupor. A baby was crying in my sleep and when I woke up it was still crying. Perhaps it was the crying that woke me up. We were pulling into a station, and I got up, trying to see the name of the station, definitely not Berlin Hauptbahnhof, my destination.

More people were coming on, there was a commotion by the door, curses and shouts, a man fell and then stood up again. There were guards, holding guns, forcing more people onto the train. Now I noticed the people being forced on were mostly women and children. Mostly Asian and African.

'What train is this? Where are we?' I asked the man next to me.

He shrugged. 'We are at the border.'

'What border?'

'Italy. That guard was speaking Italian. I speak the language.' He said the last with pride.

The train started to move again.

'Italy?' I asked, flummoxed. Perhaps I hadn't heard right. 'I am going to Berlin.'

'You are on the wrong train, my friend,' he said, and started to laugh. Another man joined in the laughter. I looked around the dark train. 'What train is this?'

'We are being deported, don't you know?' the man asked.

His words were gentle, chiding almost, as if he were talking to a slow child. The exhaustion redoubled heavily on my shoulders. The train grew darker, the way the light fades as day ends abruptly in winter. I stood up. If only the baby would stop crying. I wanted to go and talk to the mother, to tell her to feed him, to do anything to shut him up, but suddenly my willpower left me and I sat down again, my brain simply shutting down, and I couldn't keep my eyes open. When I woke up we were being led off the train to buses waiting by the kerb outside the station. It was a small station, with a single track passing through it and a single exit on either side of the track. I hurried over to the soldier.

'There's a terrible mistake. I got on the wrong train.'

I showed him my ticket to Berlin. He called to another soldier and they conversed for a while, the other soldier shrugged and turned away. I felt my heart sink.

'I cannot help you here. You make complaint when you get to camp,' the soldier said, gently turning the barrel of his gun toward me. The weak morning sun splashed itself over the trees and concrete buildings as we came out of the station and into the buses. I couldn't read the signs, they were in Italian, probably. We followed the direction of the sun, meandering and climbing through sleepy villages and hamlets and endless olive farms.

The bus was worse than the train. At least in the train there was more space and more air. In the bus the press of bodies and the cries of babies and the cursing of men intensified. The crying baby was in the same bus, and the mother's cooing continued, trying to calm it down, until suddenly it stopped. I could understand how it must have lost its will to cry any more, the same way the energy had drained out of me earlier. I waited for the cry to resume, but it didn't. We were in some countryside, and suddenly we could smell it, the sea. The smell was unmistakable, salty, minerally, and then we could hear the distant rush of water against the coastline. Somehow I wanted the baby to cry again, to articulate the feeling inside me, a deep, confused cry.

Book 5

THE SEA

As he drove down the sloping road to the camp he caught a glimpse of the sea below. The southern Italian sun was gleaming on the waves and for a moment it all came back, the woman lying half-covered in the foaming waves on the beach, and he running toward her. At first he thought she was dead. The camp sat on the slope of a hill by the sea. Today the sea was restless, roiling and snapping at the foot of the hill, spouting foam like an enraged leviathan. This hilly landscape, which in his childhood had looked postcard-idyllic with its view of the endless blue Mediterranean below, was now ruined by the slapdash red-brick structures and white tents covering it, and the smell, the unbearable smell.

His late uncle, who had been in a prisoner-of-war camp in
WWII, said the smell was unmistakable, it was more than
human effluence and trash, it was the smell of misery and
despair. The tents were more recent; the brick structures
had been there since the 1920s as offices and temporary staff
accommodations when the hill was mined for copper, when
the copper veins ran out in the 1940s the mine was turned
into a military camp, and when the war ended the site was
abandoned to wild goats and rodents, and for decades its
brick structures and iron roofs rusted away in the humid,
acidic sea air. When, a decade ago, the refugees started coming and the small island started running out of space to keep
them, the town council voted to salvage the rotting structures and turn the place into a refugee centre. The migrants
were brought here as soon as they arrived in their boats, to
be examined by the doctors, to be deloused, to be registered,
and officially welcomed to Europe. As Matteo drove past
the sign that said *Welcome Centre*, he couldn't help grinning
at the lack of irony by whoever had proposed the name.
A bored-looking guard nodded at him and he parked his
motorbike under a tree and climbed the four concrete steps
to the camp director's office. He wondered why the man
had sent for him. They had been together last week – a body
had washed up on the beach in front of his house, and he
had called the director to come pick it up. It was not the
first time. Twice, a leaky boat with shivering, terrified and
surprised-to-be-alive families had beached on his property
and he had driven them in his truck to the refugee centre.
All except the woman and the child.

North, they all want to go north, the director shouted into

the phone as Matteo entered the tiny office. The man caught his eye and nodded.

Yes, Germany, France, England. This is not a prison, you understand, they are free to go if they want. He put down the phone and stood up and shook Matteo's hand. American reporter. He wants to know if this is some sort of detention centre. Whatever gave him that idea.

Perhaps he wants to borrow my truck, Matteo thought. The refugee centre was badly underfunded, and the director was often asking for help, which Matteo was always willing to offer. Most of the town's inhabitants, men women children, had at one time or another volunteered at the camp.

Come, the director said, I have something to show you.

They descended the steps and followed the path leading to yet another gate which opened into the camp proper. The ground underneath was hard and pebbly; this stark, ugly landscape was somehow offset by the sea, white foam turning to soft aquamarine. Between the hill and the sea was the camp. A central structure dominated the entire camp – rectangular and unremittingly utilitarian, its aluminium roof arched over the concrete building, square windows cut into the concrete at precise, regular intervals. This was the medical centre where all newcomers were examined by doctors, nurses and other volunteers. Matteo had volunteered here before, more than once. On busy days it looked like a marketplace, men and women and children dehydrated from their long ordeal on the sea were stretched out on cots and hooked to drips for rehydration – it was never a pretty sight: some had feet rotting in their wet shoes, some had shit and vomit caked to their skin and hair, some were delirious with fright from being trapped between dead bodies for days in the boat – pregnant women had to be checked to see if the baby was still alive, or not, in which case emergency caesarean sections were performed right there on the floor, more serious emergencies were flown out by helicopter to bigger and better-equipped facilities in Palermo and nearby cities.

Matteo hadn't been to the centre in over a month, but nothing had changed, it was overcrowded as usual, it was meant to hold five hundred people, but it always had over two thousand migrants, some just arriving and waiting to be processed, some leaving. Toilets had been converted into sleeping spaces, it was either that or leave women and children exposed to the weather. As they descended further into the camp he saw them coming from all directions, men and women and children, in their hands were bowls they presented at a table where two men stood behind three huge aluminium basins from which they ladled out food, which the inmates began to wolf down immediately without waiting to sit.

The director, still not explaining where they were going, said, There are more in those tents. Some are too sick to come out.

They came to a tall fence facing the sea. Matteo was about to ask what exactly they were looking for when he noticed the line of bodies standing or sitting, men and women and children, all facing the sea, their faces pressed against the fence. They were not talking, just facing the sea, away from the kitchen and the diners. Nearby a woman sat on the hard pebbly ground, moaning softly, all the time knocking her head against the fence. They did not turn when Matteo and the director approached.

What are they doing here? he asked.

The director pointed at the woman and whispered, They say she sits here every day to listen to the voices of her children who drowned.

Matteo imagined the voices rising from the impassive depths, woven into the wind and waves, faint and then dying, snuffed by the wet air, but since they say sound never really dies, the voices must continue, diminished, inaudible to ordinary ears, but still detectable with the right listening device, like a mother's ears. The director came to a stop abruptly. His voice still at a confidential pitch, he said, A week ago a man hanged himself in one of the bathrooms. Another woman went crazy and started screaming for no reason around the camp, she was subdued, but that night she stabbed herself to death. Another man managed to scale this fence and threw himself into the waves, he drowned immediately.

In the distance a fishing boat, or a ferry, rose and dipped, leaving a contrail of churning sea behind it. Coast guards, most likely, on patrol. In the sky a Frontex helicopter circled in long and widening loops as it searched the inscrutable waters.

I don't understand . . . Matteo tried to hide his impatience. The director raised a hand, urging him toward a man standing alone by the fence, also staring into the water, quiet and motionless. The day was dying and soon the mild Mediterranean sun would dip into the sea, its last rays slanting over the water and the coastline, turning the skyline and the white sands and the rooftops russet, and the aquamarine water black.

Who is he? Matteo found himself whispering, not sure why.

He has been here for a month now. He has been passed

from camp to camp. He is very sick and I fear he cannot last much longer.

Now Matteo noticed how frail the man looked, with the wind flapping his baggy shirt and pants, threatening to sweep him over the fence and into the sea. He was of average height, his clothes hung on his gaunt frame and a beard covered his chin. The director was staring at the man with a regretful look on his face. Matteo wondered why the man was important, why his case differed from the other hundreds around him.

The director turned to him. He was brought here with a bunch of others, deported from the north. This has been happening more and more often, migrants rounded up and dumped into trains and sent back to their first European country of entry, usually Italy or Greece. They want to send them back to their countries, or at least to Libya or Egypt, but the government often forgets about them. After a while most of them simply walk out and return to the north. This one, he came to my office two weeks ago. He was not a refugee, he said. His documents went missing and he ended up on the train by accident. I didn't believe him of course. You get such stories every day. Once, a woman from Togo told me she was a queen in her hometown, she had been chased out by rivals and should therefore be given automatic Italian citizenship, not even asylum, citizenship. She demanded to be taken to the king of Italy.

What did you tell her?

I told her we had no king. I get all kinds of stories here. But this guy, he persisted, and I agreed to take him to the US consulate in Palermo. We went and he placed his complaint, but they said there was nothing they could do about his green card. They said they'd flag it if it ever appears anywhere and let him know. He can apply for a replacement only in America or in his home country, Nigeria, meanwhile, he can apply for a visitor's visa, but he needs his Nigerian passport to do even that. They gave him some forms to fill out.

If he is not a refugee, then he shouldn't be here, Matteo said.

Yes, I told him the same thing. But it appears he has nowhere to go, or nowhere he wants to go. I also suspect he doesn't have the means to go anywhere . . . but most important, he doesn't appear to want to go anywhere.

Doesn't he have family, a wife?

He mentioned a wife, but I got the feeling he doesn't want to call her. The director sighed and with a last look at the man turned and started uphill back to his office.

You believe him? Matteo called after him. The man hadn't once looked at them.

I retire next week. This is my last week here. I can't sleep at night. I see dead babies and drowning mothers. The director's face was gaunt as he stared at Matteo, his eyes hollow with sleeplessness. I don't want to leave any loose ends, you understand.

How does that involve me? Matteo asked, even though he was beginning to suspect just how. Giuseppe, the director, was a childhood friend. They had grown up in cottages next to each other, their fathers, fishermen, and sons to fishermen, and grandchildren to fishermen, co-owned a fishing boat, till Giuseppe's father died five years ago, drowned on a fishing expedition off the Tunisian coast. Unlike Matteo, who had never left the island, Giuseppe had studied at the university in Palermo before returning to the island. He had been the camp director for three years now.

This man will die if I don't get him help.

Suicide?

No, he doesn't look suicidal. But he seems to have lost all will to live. I have seen it happen before. When I told him that he was free to go, that this was not a prison, you know what he told me? He said he was thinking about it. About his next move. Go back to Germany, I told him, get in touch with your friends. But he said no, not Germany.

Maybe he wants to go to his country, Nigeria, Matteo suggested.

Maybe, but he has been here over one month now. He is ill. You see how he looks. I have seen people like that. They grow apathetic, they withdraw, they neglect their health, and they die.

And why do you believe I can help him if even he doesn't want to help himself? That's why you called me, isn't it?

Well, he came from Berlin. He has lived there for over a year. I thought that might interest you.

•

I stand by the fence till the sun sets. This is the best spot to watch the water change colour with the dying sun. I don't want to go back inside. Last night the man, boy really, on the bed next to mine was screaming in his sleep, and this morning he refused to get up, he lay there, staring at the ceiling. He is not more than twenty, and usually he is very chatty, always talking about his journey across the desert and his prospects

in Europe. England is his ultimate destination, he and everyone else. If not, he would settle for Germany. And should we
travel together, do I have any money, and how long have I
been in this camp. Then the lapse yesterday. I have seen many
like him, the high spirits alternating with depressed silences.
This is my third camp. The first was Lampedusa, then Greece,
then this island. Every camp is different, and yet the same.

I spend my time staring at the water. If you stare at it long
enough you notice the gradations of colour, the minute shift-
ing spectrum between green and blue and indigo. Once, the
director came and stood next to me, this was a day after we had
gone to the American consulate in Palermo, he asked me what
I looked for in the water. Nothing, I told him. I have always
been fascinated by water. I was born in a landlocked town,
with no rivers or lakes, the streams were seasonal, formed by
flash floods of the rainy season. As kids, after it rained, we
stood on the banks to watch the moving mix of water and
mud and tree limbs and dead birds and the occasional goat
or dog and marvel at the power of water. Rainfalls were the
most spectacular events, magical, and anything seemed possible, giants could fall from the sky, trees could be uprooted and
tossed about like twigs, humans could wash up by the roadside,
sometimes chunks of ice fell, making holes in the roof and
shattering car windshields and windowpanes. Hail. After the
rains, vultures sat for hours on baobab trees, their cinereous
wings soaked and useless, waiting for the sun to come out. It
was the most pathetic sight, these huge ungainly creatures, yet
still birds, still built for flight, and yet, for this moment, before
they dry out, stuck on tree branches, wingless.

Try to get out of here, the director urged, if you stay here, you will die. I have seen too many die here. Healthy, normal people. The next day they fall ill and the next day they are dead. I listened. I nodded. I thought, Who is to say if I am not dead already, the people around me could be shadows, wraiths, like me. If I am alive, then I am barely alive. Barely walking, mostly standing and staring at the water.

I feel his gaze, he and the other man, a new face, a reporter, perhaps, but he has no notebook, no bag for his recorder, and he doesn't have that hungry, vulpine look reporters have. Just another islander, a church member perhaps, another attempt to save me, to get me out of this camp. He was quitting, he told me. He seems desperate to save me. No man can save his brother, or pay his brother's debt – or something to that effect. Some poet said that. I pretend not to see them, and finally they turn and they leave. I am thinking, I wanted to tell him. I have all the time in the world. I have nothing to do but stare at the water and think. I am trying to decide if I want to go out there, to live, or to wait here and embrace whatever comes. No, I am not a fatalist, I am not reckless, but I feel if I wait here long enough, presently something would be revealed to me, someone would step up to me, a familiar face, or a total stranger, a child, a man, a woman, and they would say, Listen. And they would tell me a story, a fable, a secret, something so pithy, so profound, that it is worth the wait. Listen, they would say, listen carefully.

•

The next day the man comes back alone and offers to take me into town, if I have time. Time. He is mocking me, perhaps. Time is all I have. He introduces himself, Matteo. A friend to the director, and perhaps like the director he also suffers from a saviour complex. But I indulge him. All I have is time, after all. I have been here one month, and I have never been into the village. We go in his small car, up the hill, past a line of trees, and we are in the town centre. It is a small town, its narrow stone-cobbled streets meandering between white-painted houses and a central church facing a square with a water fountain with the statue of a lion rampant in its middle.

We park by the fountain and walk around the quiet town. Sleepy old men and women sit in front of cafés under umbrellas and awnings, drinking coffee in the hot afternoon sun. We come upon a busy street leading away from the fountain, a street market is in session; we pass a butcher's stand displaying haunches and sides of sheep hanging on hooks.

I grew up here, Matteo says, waving at a familiar face. I know literally everyone in this town.

After the market is a line of stores selling clothes and ladies' bags and shoes. The clothes on display make me self-conscious about my own tattered clothes; I have been wearing the same thing for weeks now and I must look like a scarecrow. More and more I notice in front of hotels and pensions African and Asian men sitting in little groups on steps and on benches, talking in whispers. Their faces have a speculative, haunted look, as if weighing how long they could stay in this small town before wearing out their welcome.

Come, let's have coffee, Matteo says.

We sit outside one of the cafés and order coffee. From here the sea is visible in the distance. There are a few men and women sitting at nearby tables, most of them stare curiously at me as we sit down. A group of young men at the next café stare pointedly at me and whisper among themselves. The waitress refuses to look at me and addresses herself all the time to Matteo. I order tea. When she comes back she slaps the tea-cup in front of me and stands there waiting for payment. Matteo says something sharply to her and hands her some money. She gives him change and walks away.

I am sorry, he says. There is anger in this town. Half of the population has left.

Why? I ask.

The economy is bad. People blame that on the refugees. In the last five years the refugee population has almost surpassed the population of the locals, and so more and more locals leave. As he speaks an African woman drifts into view, she is wearing a colourful print dress and leading a child by the arm. She walks slowly, meditatively, and she could be in her hometown, going on a visit to the neighbours'. More brown faces pass as we sit, Indians, Arabs, Africans. I drink my tea. The bell at the church tolls the hour. From where we sit the church steeple is visible, pointing forlornly into the glaucous air. Matteo says in the Middle Ages anyone who broke the law would be hoisted up in a cage in front of the church and left exposed to the elements till they died. It was useful as a crime deterrent.

The director told me you used to live in Berlin.

Yes, I reply. I want to thank you for the coffee, and for this. I wave my hand.

We can do this again tomorrow if you like, he says.

He has something to tell me, or to ask me, I can tell, but he is waiting, sizing me up. We go back to the camp as the sun is going down. He comes again the next day, at the same time, and we go back to the same café. The same waitress brings me my tea, with croissants, avoiding my eyes as she places down the tray. I watch the Africans pass, and in the distance the blustery sea is bluer today.

I'll tell you a story, Matteo says. He sips his espresso and lights a cigarette. He has an angular face, his skin is sunburnt. He is a housepainter, he tells me, he used to be a fisherman, like most men in the town. His hands are covered with streaks of green paint. It is about a woman, he says. Think of it as a fairy tale.

•

Once upon a time a man came upon a woman lying on the seashore, half-covered by the foaming waves. A mermaid, he thought. Her lower body was in the water, her wet hair falling over her face, her clothes wave-torn. He stood over her, the waves crashed and receded and crashed back again, she appeared dead. Then he saw the child some distance away from her, struggling to rise, tied to a life buoy with a piece of red cloth. He ran over and scooped up the child. It was a boy, about one year old, with seaweed tangled in his hair and water pouring out of his mouth and nostrils. The woman was moving, raising a hand toward him, trying to speak, her voice weak. He ran back to her and brought his ear close to her. Help, she croaked, pointing at the boy. Please. He tried not to panic, he looked around, seeking help, but the beach was empty. Only the waves washed against the sand and rocks of the narrow bay. He pulled the woman away from the waves. He took off his shirt and covered her naked chest.

Can you stand?

She tried to stand but her legs kept giving out under her. He put an arm under her shoulder and, the child in one hand, he led her to his house not too far away from the beach. He lived with his old father, Pietro, in a house that had once been full of the voices of his brothers, but his brothers had all left for the city, and three years ago his mother had died. Only he and his seventy-year-old father lived in the big house, which was now crumbling as houses tend to do in this weather.

For two days mother and child slept, side by side, on the queen bed in one of the bedrooms. The man sat on a chair and watched them, scared they might be slowly dying from some secret injury, an internal haemorrhage or infection contracted in the water. He watched the woman turn and kick and roil in her sleep, re-creating the motions of the sea that had recently disgorged her. The child whimpered and held on tightly to the arm of the woman. All night long he watched, sleepless and anxious, sometimes raising his hands as if to still the restless motions of the sleeping pair, then retracting them. Fancying the couple were too still, he placed a hand on the woman's chest to feel the heaving, up down, up down, of her breathing, then he placed a moist finger under the child's nostrils to feel the draught of its breath.

Come, his father, Pietro, said, go and rest. There is nothing you can do. I'll watch over them and I'll call you as soon as she wakes up.

The woman woke up that night. She stared at the old man dozing in a chair by the window and she looked neither surprised nor alarmed. Her first action was to reach over and cradle the sleeping boy in her arms. The old man brought her a bowl of soup and watched her as she drank.

•

They say I collapsed while standing by the fence, watching the water as I always do. I have no recollection. I wake up and a doctor in white is crouching over me, shining a flashlight into my eyes. I am in the medical centre.

Can you hear me? the doctor asks.

I close my eyes and turn away from the light.

How do you feel, any headaches? he asks.

No, I reply, well, a little bit.

I try to sit up but the doctor pushes me back to the cot. I have seen the doctor before, there are two of them, him and a woman, they take turns, each dropping in about twice a week. He is not up to forty, about my age, with a receding hairline and a permanent frown of worry on his face. He sits on a chair by the cot, the frown deepening.

You are dehydrated and malnourished. We are going to keep you here for a few days and give you saline solution.

In the morning the director comes, and he sits down on the same chair the doctor sat in and shakes my hand, as if congratulating me on something I have achieved. You are leaving, he says. It is all settled. The man, your friend, Matteo, he is taking you with him. You can stay with him till you get better.

I want to protest that Matteo is not really my friend. I hardly know him, or when and how this was all settled, but I don't want to sound ungrateful. Matteo looks harmless, polite, ready to listen, I am sure I will get along with him. Still, I don't want to be in someone's house, I don't want to be obligated to anyone. But I am too tired to argue. Back in my corner, I get my things together. I don't have much. A toothbrush given to us by the camp, a comb, a change of underwear, a sock, my slippers – I put them all in a polythene bag and I sit to wait for Matteo.

The room is empty. The bunk next to mine has a new

occupant. The young man has left a few days back. He wanted me to go with him, he said we'd make a good team. He was from a small town in Nigeria, he told me, not mentioning the town or the state. He was poor and felt he stood no chance in his hometown of ever achieving the good life, so his mother sold their land and gave him the money to pay his way across the Mediterranean. I imagine him on a train, or in the back of a truck, or walking on a bush trail, going north. I admire his optimism, which, inevitably, will get shattered, it is impossible that it won't, but still I admire it. In a corner of the tent I hear a radio, BBC, the announcer's voice interrupted by static. I used to listen to BBC a lot as a child. Another voice is on the phone, always on the phone, the ubiquitous cell phone, the only link to the world left behind.

I am in Italy. Everything is good. Everything is working fine. Soon I go to Germany. Yes, insha Allah.

I think of Karim and his son Mahmoud, and how he chose the wilderness of exile over home. I remember the pain in his voice when he said he knew he might never see Somalia again. Once upon a time, to be away from the known world was exile, and exile was death. Through the tent entrance I see a group of young men, about four of them, they always gather there, by the hillock, talking earnestly, they keep to themselves, sometimes it appears they are arguing. They make phone calls. They are planning their route, their forward path. They talk bravely, boldly turning their back on all they know, embracing change and chaos, and yet, sometimes I catch the nervous note in a laugh, I imagine them back in their tents, on their cots, pining for home. I hear their voices heading toward the gate, going into town, to try to earn some money, or to make connections, to hustle. Endlessly hustle.

•

The first day she was able to stand up, she followed a door, which led into a larger room, and then into another room. Some of the windows were broken; the walls had cracks in them. An air of decay and forgetfulness pervaded the entire house, and even in her semi-somnambulistic state she could tell there was no woman's touch anywhere, and that, for some reason, made her sad. She stood in a room between a kitchen and another room, a dining room perhaps, and looked around, lost. It was some sort of storeroom; there were boxes under wooden shelves, and cans of paint piled on top of each other, there were brushes on a table, the paint dry on the bristles, some of the paint had run down on the table, making lines, now dry and multicoloured. Then the old man entered.

My son is not here, he has gone to work. Do you want something?

I want to go outside. Please.

He looked closely at her for a while, then he nodded. He led her by the hand through a side door, then down a flight of half a dozen lichened stone steps, down a vine-hedged path, and they were in a garden. This used to be a beautiful park and people would come from the village just to sit here and look at the roses, he said. As they approached a fountain, the smell of dead leaves in the water rose in the air. Nearby a nymph held a cracked vase, in her abdomen and shoulders were what looked like bullet holes. He led her to a bench facing the sea.

This is where my son found you, Pietro said, pointing. And suddenly she was agitated again. He reached out and took her hand, she looked at him without recognition. The children, she cried. She wrung her hands. Where are the children? He took her back inside, and they passed through the many doorways until they came to the bedroom. The boy was there, sleeping. The worry and panic left her face, she sat on the bed and folded the boy in her arms, burying her face in his chest, all the time whispering to him.

She looked up and the old man had gone, in his place the younger man was standing there. How much time had passed, she had lost track.

What is his name? he asked.

Omar.

What is your name?

She shook her head. At night she dreamt of fire and loud explosions in the sky. There was a man, and a girl. And there was water, so much water, and she was swimming in it, kept afloat by the orange life buoy around her middle, she and the child. She dreamt the same dream in a loop, over and over, and the dream always ended with the man standing over her, telling her it was all right, she was safe.

He whispered again, What is your name?

She shook her head, desperately now.

Come.

He led her to the bathroom and stood her before the mirror. Toothbrushes with flat, chewed bristles stood in a cup over the sink. The mirror was stained by soap suds and dirt, there were cracks in it, a long diagonal crack ran from bottom to top, cutting her face in two. Her hand flew up to her face, as if in reaction to the cut in the mirror. She ran her fingers through her hair; she touched her cheeks and her lips and her eyelids, as if touching the face of another.

I am sorry. I don't know.

Behind her in the mirror he smiled in encouragement. He said, It will all come back to you. Take a bath, then rest. He left. Alone in the bathroom the woman looked at her face in the mirror, she saw the grime, the sand and sea salt in her hair, and try hard as she might, she couldn't remember who she was or where she came from. All she could remember was the sea. She undressed and ran her hand slowly over the caesarean scar on her abdomen.

•

This is my house. It is not much, but here you are safe, the man said gently.

She looked up at him, the word 'safe' registering in her sea-muddled mind. Her eyes at first questioned him, then they trusted him, and could that be the moment that he fell for her, for her eyes, so huge, so beautiful. He fell and it was a long and bottomless fall.

She was scared of the dark, she told him. She slept with the lights on, and sometimes he heard her screaming in her sleep. At those times he'd sit on the chair till she slept, sometimes he knew she only pretended to be sleeping, like a child, her eyes closed, listening to him breathe and move in the chair, but he knew she found his presence reassuring. Once she woke up when the lights were off. She raised a hand and pointed to the window. Light, she said. Please. She remembered the dark boat; all she wanted as they rode the waves up and down was a ray of light to touch her skin. Please, she repeated.

Once she had overcome her fear of waking up in this strange place, she loved to take walks in the mornings, while the boy still slept, to walk in the park and sit on the bench and stare at the water in the distance. The man watched her from the house, through the kitchen window. A week ago she wasn't here, a week ago he didn't know her, now here she was and all he could think about was her. She was a mother, a wife, perhaps greatly loved by a husband who was now probably dead in the water, his corpse beached and half-buried on some European shore. Of course he might not be dead, he might be somewhere, ahead, or behind, sitting with his cell phone in hand, waiting for a word from her. The man was surprised by the quick jealousy he felt at the thought of a husband waiting for her.

She could stay here, he said to his father.

Why not. She had no memory of a past, or a destination; sending her to the camp would be cruel. With a child. This would be a new beginning for her, for them. He could give her that. He would give her that. But he had to take it slow. He didn't want to scare her.

•

We used to be fishermen, Matteo told him, but not any more.

Why did you stop fishing? the man asked.

Fishing became too painful, Matteo said, and he did not elaborate. He went on, I taught myself how to paint. The painter left the island, so I am in some demand at the moment.

He had been a week in the house now, and already the memory of the camp was fading from his mind. He remembered the woman who sat by the fence and said she could hear her children's voices from the depths of the sea. And the camp director, Giuseppe, who must have retired by now. Every morning he took a walk on the beach, for about thirty minutes. The doctor ordered it.

It is up to you if you want to recover or not. You are young, nothing is really wrong with you. Your malaise is really in your mind. Of course your body is weak, due to poor diet and other minor infections. But it is in your power to get better. Eat well, exercise. It is the best medicine I can prescribe for you, the doctor told him.

The doctor was an old man, a childhood friend to Pietro. He had sat on the chair next to the bed, the very bed the mermaid must have lain in, and he wondered if the doctor had also attended to her when she lay here, lost and sick with fear. He was wearing a white doctor's coat, as if he were in a hospital making his rounds, his doctor's bag by his side.

Tell me, the doctor asked, are you married?

Yes, he nodded.

Don't you miss your wife, don't you want to be with her?

Did he miss Gina? He thought of home before he met Gina. He had two sisters whom he hadn't seen in over ten years. They were much older, married with grown-up children, and when he was a child they never really had time for him, and apart from the occasional phone call, they hardly met. His father was a retired government contractor and he had been born when his father was in his fifties, too old and too tired to take much interest in him after the initial joy of having the much-desired male child. Once, during his early months in America, he missed his mother so much he felt embarrassed by how much he missed her, but after a while he got over that. Gina had replaced his family, and he was not lonely any more. He missed Gina, he missed her so much it felt like there was a hole in his chest, but he knew with time her memory would get blurry and it would be like a dream, recollected vaguely at unexpected moments. He felt scared when he thought of that. He didn't want to forget her. He wanted to call her a thousand times every day, but for what purpose? He had avoided calling her so far, he felt ashamed at the way they parted. Time would fill up the void in their hearts left by the other, fill it up like an empty well gradually filled up with household junk till people have forgotten that it was once a well. Those who dug it would die, those who knew it was a well and even drank from it would move on, and its time as a well would be forgotten.

Twice the doctor came back to see him, and he always stayed for dinner. Meat, and vegetables, and pasta, but never fish. They sat, the three of them, eating and watching the sea through the window, in the distance a boat circled the water. Pietro's dog lay in the corner, its eyes closed. Coast guards, Matteo said; no, that is the *carabinieri*, the police, the doctor argued; wrong, Pietro said, squinting his old eyes, it is a private boat, one of the rescue volunteers.

Matteo told him the doctor's story: he had left the village to go to Rome to study medicine, he had married there, making a good living, but he missed home, he missed the sea, and when in 2013 he saw in the news, with the rest of the world, the bodies of over three hundred migrants fished out of the Mediterranean in the nearby island of Lampedusa, he had gone there to volunteer, and he had never returned to Rome since then. He moved back to the island and opened his own practice. He volunteered at the refugee camp, and old as he was, he went out with the rescue boats daily to search for capsized migrant boats.

Before leaving, the doctor ordered him to rest, he still wasn't as strong as he thought he was, it would take time for his body to recover. He tried to read after his walks. There were books in the house, on bookshelves in the living room, all in Italian, except for one in English, translated from the Italian, *The Leopard*, by di Lampedusa. Matteo asked him if he wanted to go out on the boat with them, they were going round the island, he and Pietro – the island was so small you could go round it a dozen times in a day – and at first he said no, but once they were on the water he liked it, until he grew seasick and started to vomit and had to be helped out of the boat to his room when they got back.

•

He said, You have been here six months now. Tell me, what do you remember?

She said to the man: Omar is my son, I know that, instinctively, but I don't remember his birth date, or his favorite colour. I know I am a good mother. I will do anything for him, I will give my life for him, willingly.

But there was more she was not saying, recently she had started to dream of other faces, a man, a girl, and when she woke up her head ached from trying to follow those images. All day the headaches persisted, a dull blunt pain at her temples. Other images came up unbidden, street names, faces, she remembered a car number. 1980. She saw herself walking down a street and into a white house with a date palm tree in front of it, with two children holding on to her hands. A boy and a girl. It was a happy place, but she couldn't get past the doorway, she always stood by the door, and when she opened the door everything was blank.

She said, There's a man. There is a house, white. We live there, I am sure. It is burning. There are gunshots and buildings are crumbling about us. That is all I can see, the man, the house.

He said gently, sadly, Don't think about the past. You are safe here. I'll take care of you both.

•

We are in the kitchen. I stand in the corner watching Matteo cook. He throws a slab of red, bloody meat on a skillet. Next to it long stems of asparagus are steaming in an open pot. He cooks well, self-sufficiently, waving me away with a napkin whenever I offer to help. I stand by the open window, feeling inadequate. From somewhere in the house a radio is playing, a woman's voice singing a sad opera tune. I pass him the salt, I clear the table of onion skin, and when I run out of things to do, I engage him in small talk: why does he live alone with his father in this big house, where's the rest of his family? It is hard to tell if he is young or old, his face is indeterminate, sometimes when he sits facing me in the room, bent forward in his chair, he looks old and wise and tired. He must have witnessed a lot of things thrown up by the waves in front of his door. I have seen some myself since I have been here, pieces of clothing, children's toys, a shoe, a cell phone case, when walking on the beach.

We have settled into a routine, I wake up, I walk on the beach, when I get back I wash the dishes if there are any to be washed, then the rest of the day I sit in the park facing the water. Sometimes staring at the beach, I see the old man appear out of the distance, with his dog, and then I'll join him and we'll walk together quietly, the waves lapping at our feet, the distant roar rising and falling, soothing, and at such moments I almost forget how malevolent and predatory the sea can be. I feel indolent, and for the first time in a long while I have started thinking about what to do, where to go. But, when I bring this up with Matteo at dinner, he shakes his head. You are not fit. You think you are, but you are not. The doctor said you need at least a month before you can even think of travelling.

And to take my mind off my restless thoughts he takes me for a walk into the town. We go past the water fountain, past the church, past the café. He points, There is the telecommunication store. It does more business than all the other stores in town.

There is a line of dark-skinned men in front of the store, they are buying SIM cards and call credit, they will call home and let their family know they are alive, they have made it to Europe. As we pass them some of them turn and stare at us curiously, I look back trying to see if I can recognize a face from the camp. I wonder, are they disappointed yet, is this what they expected, these empty, cold and wet cobbled streets, the deserted hotels, the crumbling aged houses? Behind the square is the museum – Matteo says it used to be a fortress, long ago, in the time of Garibaldi, and in front of it is a statue of a soldier on a horse, wielding a sword. The fortress juts out of the rocky ground and over the water, defiantly facing the African shore in the distance. It is surrounded by a wall bearing gun towers at intervals, each tower has a rusty cannon facing outward, ready for the enemy to emerge, spectral, from the sea mist.

We go from room to room in the museum, starting from the ground floor – the entire museum is dedicated to military history. The artefacts are curated to start from the earliest and most rudimentary weapons, spears, lances, bayonets, with drawings of ancient knights dressed in chain-link body armour, on foot and on horses, charging into the fray, and then progressing to rooms showing more sophisticated and contemporary weapons, guns, pistols, muskets, rifles, cannons and machine guns. There are pouches of gunpowder, grenades, rockets. Here is a history of a militarized Europe, of war and conquest and devastation.

Back in my room, I stare out into the park, the dying

light has thrown dappled shadows of the tree leaves onto the flowers. Somewhere behind the house Matteo has shown me a tilled patch of ground where the mermaid in his story had tried to make a small garden last spring before she left. It isn't big, just a practical, workable portion, which she tried to bring alive, pulling out the weeds, crushing the hard lumpy clay with a shovel and soaking it with buckets of water, transferring some of the living roses from the flower beds in the park and planting them in a row. It was tough making plants grow in the acidic, saturated sea air, yet she persisted, daily, doggedly, and at a point he realized she was not really convinced she could make anything grow, really, she was just killing time. She was sowing her fears, her doubts into the ground – who was she, where was this place, who were these people she was staying with? – and hoping some answers would sprout, magically, out of the soil. Matteo would watch from the window, and he saw how she sometimes forgot where she was, squatting and staring at the soil absently for minutes, muttering to herself. Then she caught herself, she looked around guiltily, she sat on one of the iron benches, her head bowed, and he knew the tears were running down her face as she stared out to sea. He came out, casually, as if he were just passing by, taking a walk on the beach, he sat next to her, pretending he didn't notice her covertly wiping her eyes, and he talked disconnectedly, trying to take her mind off her troubles. When she appeared exhausted, when he saw her attention wavering, her eyes turning to the water, he stopped talking and led her back to the house. He'd sit and watch her sing to the child a nursery song in a strange language.

•

She was conscious of him staring at her from the house. Soon he would come out and ask her, anxiously, if she remembered anything at all. They would sit for hours, hardly talking. Once, he pointed at the tall stone building near the water and said it used to be a fortress before it was converted to a museum. A fortress with moats and drawbridge – the moat was now dry, the drawbridge broken. Then he turned to her and whispered suddenly, Sophia.

Sophia? she asked.

You don't remember?

She repeated the name over and over in her mind, trying to see if it resonated, if it struck a chord. Should I know the name? she asked, her face beginning to look confused.

It is your name, he said.

The words came of their own will. He hadn't planned it, but as he spoke it all made sense. At first he thought with time she'd forget who or what she was looking for, where she was going, and settle down. This would be home. She'd get used to the sea, and the house, and him, show him some love. But she had been here for months now and he couldn't wait any longer. And now that he had started talking he couldn't stop. And as he spoke he also believed what he was saying. Every word rang true. Because he wished them to be true.

We were lovers, many years ago. I visited your country. We met. We fell in love.

She turned to him. She ran a nervous hand through her hair. Then what happened, did we break up?

No. We couldn't get married because your parents . . . well, they had another man they wanted you to marry. And I left. I had to come back home. I was heartbroken.

Then what happened?

You promised you would never forget me. You promised you would come find me someday, no matter how long it took.

And you, you waited for me?

Yes, I promised I would never leave my island, I'd wait for you. Time passed, I had almost given up. Then there you were, in the water. You came like you promised.

She wanted to believe him, she wanted her days to have meaning, she wanted the headaches to stop. She believed him. She said, *I am sorry. You must have suffered, waiting for me.* She took his hand. He leaned forward and kissed her on the lips.

You came, that is all that matters.

That night she tried to make up for the pain she had cost him as she lay under him, her arms and legs locked around him. In the other room the child slept alone for the first time.

•

Carefully they dressed up in the new clothes he had bought for them. She wore white, and over that a red spring jacket. The child wore a blue jacket and khaki pants. The man wore a black suit, a white shirt and a blue tie. They drove in the tiny car to the town centre, the boy sat with his face pressed to the window, following the backward swirl of the lampposts and the narrow streets that receded and convoluted and rose and fell. They got down at the square. The boy watched a family, a man, a woman and their daughter, throw bread crumbs to dun-coloured pigeons that fluttered and settled and fluttered again as people passed. They sat on a bench before the fountain, the man and the woman. They watched the boy join a group of children dipping their hands in the fountain. The town hall was a few metres from the fountain, and the registrar was waiting for them. The registrar asked if *the woman wanted to freshen up in the restroom before the ceremony, she said no.*

Good, he said. Please, come this way.

Afterward, the family of three had lunch in a Greek restaurant, then they entered the car and drove back home.

•

In the evenings he took her on a drive around the town. It became their routine. Far from the town centre, on the road that followed the coastline, with a clear view of the water, half-circling the town. He drove fast, trying to outrun something behind, some memory, some history that doggedly followed in their wake. They drove, his eyes on the strip of empty road ahead, her eyes on the ineffable view of the sea and sand. They came upon a ghostly housing development of villas and apartments, grand and untenanted. They passed courtyards and gardens that had started to run to seed, over roads eaten away by neglect and weather. The waves' whoosh was a lover's lament of loneliness. They drove round and round, through some developer's failed dream of sand and sea that came up against harsh economic reality, and not a single human being was in sight. The streets between the villas and apartments were named after famous cities, Naples, Paris, Milan, Barcelona, Berlin, Frankfurt, Athens, Florence, Vienna, each one deserted.

•

And then one day she woke up suddenly, it was midnight, but the moon was shining into the room, and she could see everything, clear as day. He sensed her movement and asked, Is everything all right?

She turned to him, and he saw that something had changed in her eyes. She said, My name is not Sophia.

What did you say? He sat up and moved to the opposite side of the bed. She was looking out into the garden, the light on her face, her back to him.

My name is not Sophia. She turned to the man. Calm.

Well, what is your name?

She shook her head, overwhelmed by the memories racing into her head, a flash flood carrying so many things in its stream. He waited, his breath coming out with difficulty. He had seen this before. Soon would come the panic, the tears. He waited.

I have a husband.

I am your husband.

She raised a hand, and in the movement there was a sadness he had never seen before. *Please, don't say that. I remember everything.*

She looked at him, her eyes bitter.

Well, what is your name?

Basma, she said, and repeated the name slowly, savouring it, like the name of a newborn, uttered for the first time, *Basma. I have two children, Omar and his sister, Rachida.*

The man stood up. He was naked. He quickly put on his clothes and sat with his head in his hands, saying nothing, not looking at her. That day she moved out of his bedroom and into the guest room with her son. She didn't come out all day, and all day the man stayed in his room, and she could hear him through the wall, pacing up and down, she could hear his father knocking on his door, but he didn't open it. At night she lay awake, and her mind was like a churning sea, throwing out to shore bits and pieces of floating memory.

As he paced his room he asked himself why he was surprised, surely he knew this day would come, his father had cautioned him about it. He loved her, he loved her like he had never loved anything before. He felt like dying.

Be brave, his father said through the door, maybe she loves you too. But she has a child, and a husband. Let her decide what she wants to do.

When she finally came out, she was dressed to leave. She had a little plastic bag with a single change of clothing in it, the boy was dressed in his blue suit. Father and son were seated at the dining table, she went to them and sat, and they could have been a family at dinner, except there was no food in front of them. Finally, he said, Please don't go.

How she had changed. Already he could see the resolute, confident woman she must have been. Where was Sophia, the woman who had flailed about, plucking at plants in the garden, singing soft lullabies to the boy?

She said, her eyes staring neither at him nor at the old man, We were the last to get out. We made our way to the coast and paid five thousand American dollars each to get on a boat. I was scared, I didn't want all four of us on the same boat. What if something went wrong? I told him, go on ahead, find a place and come back for us later. But he wouldn't hear of it. Without you and the children, I die, he said. So we left, all of us. They shot at our boat as we left the coast. I don't know what happened, or why. There was confusion, the screams began and never stopped. Have you ever been on a refugee boat? Pray you never do. Pray your country never breaks up into civil strife and war, that you are never chased out of your home. The boat was really nothing but a death trap, an old, rickety fishing trawler that should have been retired a long time ago. Because we paid five thousand each we got to sit on the upper deck where we could get a bit of fresh air. Some, who were down below in the hold, stacked on top of each other, died within hours of our departure – the children and the pregnant women died first. We saw them bring up the bodies and throw them in the water. Our engine was on fire, the captain wanted to turn back, but we begged him to go on. We would rather die in the water than go back. There was nothing to go back to. My husband tried to save us as the boat sank. He is a great swimmer. He held me and the boy and I held the girl and for an hour we floated, clinging to a raft. A helicopter appeared overhead, and we thought finally we were safe, but after circling for a few minutes it left. I told my husband to let me go, to save the children, but he wouldn't. We decided that he would take the girl, and I would take the boy because he was smaller. He gave us the life jacket. We drifted. I tied the boy to my back. Something, a log, rose out of the water and hit me in the head, and I must have fainted. When I woke up you were standing over me, and I couldn't remember a thing. I guess my mind didn't want to remember. After a while I stopped trying to remember, it was easier to listen to your stories. Sophia. How badly I must have wanted to believe I was Sophia, and that this place is my home and I have not lost a husband, or a child.

He stood up and went over to her. Is there no way I can convince you to stay? You are making a mistake.

Was there really a Sophia?

He went back and sat next to his father, he stared out the window. The sky was low and darkening; it was setting to rain. Seagulls flew over the water in cycles, making weak and shallow dives. He lowered his head, his elbows rested on the table.

Yes, there was a Sophia, but that was a long time ago. Someone I knew as a kid.

She stood up and took the boy's hand. He stood up and followed them to the door. You don't have to go today.

She turned and looked at him. I have to go. I thank you for saving my life. But I am angry at you for lying to me. I have a husband and another child, I belong to them.

You don't know if they are alive. You don't know where to find them. Stay. I can help you find out where he is.

I know where he will be. In Berlin. We agreed, if we ever got separated, to wait there. In Berlin. He has a friend there. Every Sunday we promised to go to a spot and wait, Checkpoint Charlie.

The man followed her out of the house, down the lichened stone steps. She stopped briefly in the garden and looked at the roses that had started to sprout, now wilting in the autumn chill. He took them in the small car to the ferry depot to catch a ferry to the mainland, the first stop in their uncertain journey. As she got out of the car he handed her an envelope.

Take this, he said. Our marriage certificate, you will need it. You can't travel without some form of documentation. You'll also need money. Here. Please take it.

She began to shake her head, opening her mouth to utter no, but he pressed the papers into her hand. You can destroy it as soon as you get to your destination. He stood by the car and watched her and the boy join the line of passengers waiting to get onto the ferry.

•

Finally, the story has come to an end. We are in the park, sitting on the bench on which he and the woman must have sat so many times before, nearby is the patch of ground where she attempted to start a garden.

Basma, I say. Is that why you helped me, why you brought me to your house, in the hope that I might have some knowledge, some information about her?

He shrugs. His eyes are dark, hooded, and for the first time I see how withered and tired he looks.

He says, I am like a man drowning, and I must grasp at

every straw. Have you ever been in love? Surely your wife, or another?

I think of Gina, and I wonder where she might be now. In America, probably, right now she'd be in a studio, in her overalls, painting, trying to capture on canvas something elusive, something even she can't put a name to. Our story is over, the ink has dried, each of us must move on now and it will be as if we had never met, never loved, and never dreamt together.

Maybe not your wife, Matteo says shrewdly, reading my face. Maybe another.

I think of Portia, and I feel light and breathless with longing. I would like to see her again. You are right, I say to Matteo, there is someone else, but I doubt I will ever see her again.

Why did you let her go?

I didn't let her go. Circumstances got in the way.

Far away we can see old Pietro staring at the water, next to him the dog chases seagulls as they skip and flutter over the waves. He looks like he belongs here, megalithic, one with the rocks and sand and waves that throw themselves at his feet like supplicants. The dog yelps, then retreats and returns in a playful dance with the waves and the gulls.

Did you go after her, Basma? Did you try to find her, to convince her to come back?

He says, I went to Berlin, twice, but I just sat in my hotel room and watched the streets through the window all day, then I came back. Twice. I didn't have the will to go into the streets looking for her. I thought, what if I saw her with her husband, her children, and what if they were happy together? I couldn't bear it. So I took the train and I came back. I promised myself to forget her, but then, when the director told me you were from Germany, from Berlin, and since you have been among the refugees, I thought, perhaps you might know something, anything.

I say, What of her husband, what of her children?

He says, What of me? What of love? His voice is at once pleading and also defiant. I can't sleep. I think of her all the time. I want to know if she is okay, and the boy.

So I tell him of Manu, the doctor turned bouncer, who sat for Gina, who went every Sunday to Checkpoint Charlie hoping to see his wife and son there. As I tell him I see his countenance fall and his eyes grow more hooded. He is a good man, even if a little unusual, and I owe my life to him. We continue to sit as the sun goes down, turning the water and the sand purple and pink. The iodine smell of the sea is in the air. In the distance the old man appears, heading for the house, the dog by his side, in the sea a rescue boat rises and dips on the water, searching for distressed migrant boats.

That evening we leave in the boat as if we were going fishing, then we head south and keep going. I watch the coast recede and shrink – somewhere out there is the refugee welcome camp on its hilly perch, and I imagine the inmates seated against the fence watching the water and the distant African coast hidden in the mist. I imagine the Syrian woman, knocking her head against the fence and moaning the name of her vanished children, and of her destroyed hometown over and over, Aleppo.

We will be a few hours, Matteo says, you should go down and get some rest.

Earlier, before we set out, he asked me if this was what I wanted, if I wasn't better off staying on in Europe, going back to Berlin, or even staying on the island with him and the old man. I lie on the bunk downstairs, using the tiny backpack Matteo gave me for a pillow. All my worldly possessions are in there, a pair of pants, some underwear, the book *The Leopard* by Tomasi di Lampedusa. I close my eyes but I can't sleep, under the engine sound I hear the susurration of the wind on the water, and soon I am on the deck, standing by the rail watching the water. It is dark, the fog lies thickly over the water and there is nothing to be seen but the inky black. I feel as if there is no deck under me – I am standing over the water, and when I bend down I see my reflection glowing up at me, my forehead glistens with sweat. I am . . . I look terrified. A restless, writhing motion fills the water. Fish. A school of them in a feeding frenzy, but when I bend closer, my face almost touching the water, I see they are not fish, they are human. Bodies floating face-up, limbs thrashing, tiny hands reaching up to me. Hundreds of tiny hands, thousands of faces, until the surface of the water is filled with silent ghostly eyes like lamps shining at me, and arms reaching up to be grasped; they float amidst a debris of personal belongings, toys, shoes, shirts, and family pictures all slowly sinking into a bottomless Mediterranean. I drift past, and they drift past, and God drifts past, paring His nails. I pull back, tears on my face. *I had not thought death had undone so many.* I repeat the line over and over, rolling it over my tongue like a prayer, till my whisper turns to a scream. A hand on my shoulder is shaking me.

Wake up, Matteo says, we are here.

I sit up and grab my bag, discombobulated from my vivid dream, and follow him up to the deck. At first I don't see anything, then gradually over the bow a finger of light appears. Then more lights. Faint, wavering needlepoints of light.

Tunisia, he says, we can't get any closer than this, I am afraid.

We drop the tiny, inflatable dinghy into the water and using a small rope ladder I lower myself into it. I look up at the face looking down at me anxiously. The dinghy wobbles and rises and falls with the waves, then I begin to paddle. I feel like a man treading water, then I begin to pull away, carried by the flood tide, and soon the coastline is rushing at me. With a mighty heave the water spews me onto land and I am on all fours, my eyes and ears and mouth filled with briny seawater, but underneath me is the firm African soil. I grasp a handful and feel the emotions overwhelm me. I stagger to my feet and look back to sea, but there is nothing to see, only mist and black rushing water.

Book 6

HUNGER

When I got her email saying she'd be in London in July, and if I happened to be in the neighbourhood she'd love to see me, I packed my bag and got ready to travel. The invitation came at a good time – I had completed my dissertation defence back in Virginia and I was contemplating whether to return to Nigeria or to stay on in the US. Her father's English mistress, who was also his translator, had died and her son had discovered a box full of her father's things, including unpublished manuscripts, and she was going to London to pick it up. The flat was in a high-rise on Boswell Street, a narrow back road tucked away in the warren of roads behind Russell Square. There were similar buildings on both sides of the road housing boutique hotels and one or two art galleries, others were council flats with balconies littered with satellite dishes and children's toys – plastic cars and bikes too big to store indoors and too new to throw away, blocking the space between the doors and the stairs, a veritable fire hazard. Not too far away was a park, a rectangle of green enclosed in a chain-link fence, where workers from nearby offices sat during their lunch break to catch half an hour of air and sunshine. The offices were mostly hospitals and labs that seemed to be concentrated in the neighbourhood, over three hospitals within a radius of a few blocks, there were also pubs and cafés. The park soon became our favourite spot, and in the first week we spent hours there every day, mostly in the late afternoon when the workers had left, watching the pedestrians pass, sometimes staying till the lazy summer sun finally dimmed at around 8 p.m.

I had never been to London so she sent me a careful description: *Take the Piccadilly Line and you don't get off till you get to Russell Square station, I will be in a red shirt holding a 'Welcome to London' sign.* As promised, she was standing at the station entrance, unaffected by the stream of passengers coming in and going out through the turnstile, the wind pulling at her long skirt and red button-down shirt, and as promised she had a *Welcome to London* sign which she held stiffly in front of her with both hands. She actually had a sign.

I waited for her with my bag next to a phone booth as she dashed into the Tesco opposite the station to grab a packet of tea and sugar and a bottle of wine. Later, she confessed she hadn't recognized me at the station till I stood in front of her and whispered, –Hi Portia.

In the bathroom I stared at my reflection in the mirror: my hair had thinned and turned white at the sides. Friends in Nigeria and in the US had looked at me once, twice, sometimes thrice before uttering my name, with a question mark, unsure if it was really me. My bones showed at the collar, my cheeks were sunken, but I liked to think the fire still blazed in my eyes.

–What happened? she asked.

–I am fine, I said.

The flat was small, large enough for two, an end unit on the third floor with a single bedroom, a living room and a kitchenette. From the stairwells and behind doorways came voices of children and mothers trying to be heard over the drone of the TV. May, the late owner of the flat, was a lecturer at SOAS, she had lived here with Portia's father before he finally moved back to Zambia. She retired four years ago, the year he moved to Zambia, and she died a year ago, three years after him. She was a pretty woman, even in old age: her picture next to the TV showed a steady kindly gaze, with deep laugh lines around the mouth and eyes. She had married once, early in life, and had a son from that marriage, he now lived in Australia, an accountant with a tidy bookkeeper's mind, and it was he who wrote to Portia's mother about the box belonging to her late husband; he said Portia could stay in the empty apartment while she was in London, the flat was paid for till autumn when he'd come and clear away whatever was left before turning over the flat to the landlord. Here the two aged lovers, the exiled writer and the retired lecturer, had spent their days and nights, alone save for occasional outings to readings and theatres and perhaps dinner with old friends:

retired teachers, editors, writers – some of them exiles living anonymous exilic lives in the big, grey city.

We did not sleep early that first night – it had been two years since we last met, and then for less than a week. I had thought I would never see Portia again, and to have heard from her, and now to actually be with her, left me speechless. I tried to tell her how I felt, but lacking words I simply held her and kissed her slowly on her lips and all over her face before leading her to the bed. Afterward we opened the bottle of wine and sat staring at each other, smiling wordlessly. What were we to one another, lovers, friends, strangers? We sat by the window and talked till the weak, watery sun inched its way over the trees and the morning birds began to chirp. I hadn't talked to anyone like this in a long time. It felt good. I told her about my time at the refugee camp, and about Matteo and his father. When I finished the tears ran down her face.

–I am so sorry, she said.

–Why, sorry for what? I tried to sound cheerful, lighthearted.

Later, when we crawled back into bed, she showed me a picture on her phone. Me and her, standing in the courtyard of the cathedral in Basel, overlooking the Rhine.

–Do you remember? she asked.

It seemed a lifetime ago. I looked different then. I said, –I feel like the guy in the John Donne poem.

–Which poem?

–I don't remember the title, but it is about a lover who left on a long trip. Before leaving he hands his girlfriend his picture so she would remember how he looked in case he returns all worn out and changed by time.

—I know the poem, she said. You really haven't changed that much.

She put her head on my shoulder, running her hand over my chest. —You are the same inside. And that's what matters.

•

When I woke up Portia was hunched over a rugged, much-travelled red Echolac suitcase with combination locks, taking out binders and notebooks, one item at a time. She took out a moleskin diary and flipped through the pages. I went to the kitchen and filled the kettle with water to make tea. My mornings never came into focus till I had a cup of tea in my hand. I made two cups and placed one on the table beside her.

—Thanks, she said.

—What's that? I asked.

—My father's notebooks. There are at least five of these. I am not sure what to do with them.

—What's in them? I asked, taking it from her.

—All sorts of things. Poems, diaries, essays, articles.

She held her tea mug in both hands. She looked around the room. She had been here four days before my arrival.

—Do you think they were happy here? she asked, staring at May's picture, almost glaring at it. There was an unuttered subtext to her question. Was he happier with this woman than he had been with my mother? she was asking.

—Who can tell? Remember, he left her and went back to Malawi to be with your mother. That says lot.

Portia too had changed. Physically she was the same, a bit softer around the eyes, a little fuller around the hips, but the quick clever girl had turned into a quieter, more patient woman. I liked her this way. She was now a mother, she said, almost casually. She showed me a picture on her phone. A curly-haired, twinkle-eyed boy, with a smile like his mother's. She had married the German in whose apartment I first met her in Berlin, couch-surfing. He had turned up in Lusaka three years ago, and he needed a couch to sleep on. That was how it started. He had broken up with his girlfriend, Ina. He was on an assignment, a film company was making a documentary on the 1884–1915 German genocides on the Herero in neighbouring Namibia, and he was writing the script. He didn't need to be in Zambia, actually, but he remembered she lived there and he wanted to see her. He stayed for two weeks, and every night he took her and her mother out, to dinner, to dance, to the cinema, and on the final day before he left he told her he loved her, he wanted to marry her. Her mother liked him, she thought he was a gentleman.

–By then, Portia said, I had given up hope of ever seeing you again. When we parted in Basel, you were supposed to get in touch. I gave you my email, I didn't have yours. When you didn't write I guessed it was because you didn't want to.

She didn't give Hans an answer right away, she held out for six months, till one day her mother said to her, –What do you want, my child? Does this person – this Nigerian – even know you are waiting for him?

And so she called Hans in Germany and said yes. He flew back and they got married in a small church in Lusaka and they moved back to Berlin, back to that same apartment where we first met, and every time she passed my door, where she first saw me standing on a ladder, she'd linger, hoping the door would open and I would step out and say, –Hi, can I help? Finally, she couldn't bear it any more, she told Hans she couldn't live in that house, she told him it was because of the pregnancy, she didn't like climbing the stairs daily, she wanted to live near a park. They moved, out of the city toward Wannsee, but even then she felt Berlin closing in on her, daily, slowly. She fell ill constantly, she was sick for home, sick for something she didn't know. She stayed indoors and cried all day. Hans thought it was the pregnancy, the hormones, and he said yes when she decided to move back to Zambia, ostensibly to give birth at home, to be with her mother.

—I felt myself descending into depression, I was losing track of time, of my mind, and I feared I'd harm myself, she said. Hans didn't come to Zambia with her, he sensed that something had ended. The marriage had lasted less than a year.

—What's the baby's name? I asked.

—David, she said, we named him after my brother. My mother did.

Hans came to visit after the baby was born, twice, he tried to convince her to return to Berlin, but she said no. Her stay in Berlin was over, and going back wouldn't be fair to him. She didn't know how to tell him it had been a mistake. She told him she wanted to raise her child in Africa, surrounded by family. Some days she woke up in the night to scour Facebook, trying to find me. Several times, she called my Berlin number and listened to the German voice telling her the subscriber didn't exist. That was when she decided to write to Gina to ask for my email.

—It was the only way I knew how to contact you. I remember you mentioned she was a Zimmer fellow, so I wrote to them asking for her contact details, I told them it was about a painting. They were helpful. I wrote to her and she wrote back.

–Yes, Gina forwarded the email to me.

•

Of the three of us, Gina had perhaps changed the most. Since Berlin she had become something of a world traveller, when I arrived in Virginia a year ago to complete my PhD she was just returning from a six-month stint in Paris, and was on her way to Venice for the Biennale. She had visited Germany again, many times, had been back to Berlin, and once she spent a month in Dresden. We met in a restaurant in Chantilly not too far away from Dulles Airport, she had an hour to spare before her flight to Rome. I was staying in a drab hotel off Highway 66 in Manassas, and each morning I'd pick up the phone to call her, then put it back again, and when I finally called she told me it was fortunate I called that day, she was on her way to the airport. She sounded happy to hear from me. She looked different, she had a red scarf around her neck, its colour reflected against her skin, making her cheeks and her eyes glow.

–You look great, I said when I sat down.

–You don't look well. What happened? Why didn't you call? How long have you been in the States? Why are you staying in a hotel?

–Which question do you want me to answer first? I asked, raising my hand.

–All of them.

So I told her of Italy, of the refugee camps, of the two months I spent in Tunisia trying to convince the Nigerian embassy I was Nigerian. Finally, they put me on a plane with over a hundred deportees and dumped us at the airport in Lagos.

–Where is your American wife? my mother asked me when I got home. I explained to her that we were separated, but each time people came to see me, she would tell them, 'He came back alone, but his American wife is coming soon to join him.' I could hear the shame in her voice, her son who had gone to America had returned poorer and thinner than he had left. I left as soon as I recovered my health. My father cleared his bank account and gave it all to me; he wanted me gone to spare my mother the pain of having me there, of having to explain to people why my American wife still hadn't arrived.

Our tiny apartment was still there if I needed it, Gina said. She wasn't staying there. It felt too big for her alone so she had moved in with her parents and used it only occasionally to paint. The light there was always good in the afternoon.

–It belongs to you as much as it does to me. How long are you here for?

–I don't know. I am meeting my supervisor tomorrow. I'll leave as soon as I defend my dissertation, maybe six months, maybe a year.

–I'll be away for over a year, she said.

The waiter was standing over us, a smile on his face, his pencil poised. Gina ordered a salad, I ordered the sea bass with asparagus.

–You look weird with your hair all white, she said. She

reached over and touched my hair, as if to confirm the white was real.

—Tell me about your travels, I said.

She told me about Dresden. She had spent a winter month there, painting, and sightseeing. Their guide told them Dresden was the most bombarded city in the Second World War, if not in all of history, 3,900 tons of bombs dropped by Allied bombers, destroying up to 90 per cent of the town, and then, after the war, when the town had a chance to rebuild, they decided to re-create most of the buildings exactly as they had been before the bombardment. Their guide took them to the Altstadt to see the rebuilt cathedral, the Frauenkirche, which took almost ten years to reconstruct, with architects using 3-D computer technology to analyse old photographs and every piece of rubble that had been kept.

—They had the choice to do something new, make a clean break from the past, but they decided to rebuild the city like it was.

—Nostalgia, I said, they were homesick for their past.

She looked disapproving. —Not all of us have that luxury, of a past. My history doesn't offer me much in that respect. Once I go past Martin Luther King and Rosa Parks, there is nothing else but the plantation and after that the insurmountable Atlantic. So, I have learned to look forward, to embrace the new and to shape my future. I find it weird, this clinging to the past.

Gina, I realized, was saying goodbye to me. I felt sad, and proud all at once: I liked what she had become. I was a part of her past, therefore I had contributed to her present. I reached across the table and took her hand. And we sat like that, holding hands, not talking, till at last she looked at her watch and said, –Time to go.

–Have a safe flight. And . . . take care of yourself.

•

–Did you see her when you went to the US? Portia asked.

–Yes, I said.

She was sitting with her head bowed, doing her nails. Her voice sounded remote, almost cold.

–Did you stay with her?

Portia had these dark moments. This morning I woke up and found her crying into her pillow, when I asked her what was wrong she told me about a girl she saw when we were in Basel.

–I didn't tell you at the time, but I saw this girl, a school-girl, a black girl, about six or seven years old. Her hair was nicely braided. The whole class was going somewhere, walking in a neat file, their teachers walking beside them. The black girl was alone at the back of the line. All the other kids were chatting and laughing, except the black girl. I saw her nice braids, and her little red barrette, and I thought of her poor mother, she'd be anxious all day think-ing of her little daughter, the only black girl in the class in that strange, cold country.

•

I told her about my stay in the US – I stayed for exactly one year, and I never saw Gina again after that goodbye in the res-taurant. It was strange being by myself in our small apartment overlooking the empty parking lot, in the evenings I almost expected the door to open and for Gina to walk in, back from work. In the closet she had neatly stacked my clothes and books and binders in a corner.

Our photos still hung on the walls and on the stand next to the TV. In the wedding picture I looked so young and happy, in a black suit, Gina was smiling into my face in her white wedding gown, a bouquet of flowers in one arm, and around us were the faces of her family and our friends. Some of the faces I now couldn't put names to.

The year passed by quickly. I worked on my thesis at night, in the day I walked around the city, I rode the train to the end of the line, I went to the National Mall and walked with the polyglot crowd at the Cherry Blossom Festival. I stood under the Washington Monument and watched parents and children pulling and running after kites, I passed the Tidal Basin to the new Martin Luther King monument and read the wise quotations on the wall. Once, I went to the public library near the apartment and walked between the aisles, running my hand on the book spines. I sat and read the papers, hoping someone would recognize me – this was where I used to teach ESL classes and had formed a nodding acquaintance with most of the staff – but no one did. I passed in front of the information desk, the lady manning the desk was called Jill, and I had often stood there and exchanged small talk with her, but now she smiled vacantly at me and asked if I needed help finding a book.

Gina called me on Thanksgiving Eve from Venice, Italy, and asked if I had any plans for Thanksgiving. I didn't. She said she hoped I was not planning to sit in the apartment alone. She had told her parents I was around and they were expecting me for dinner. The next day I dressed carefully and bought a bottle of wine and got into a taxi to go to her parents' in Takoma Park. Her whole family would be there, cousins, nephews and nieces, uncles and aunts – I was particularly fond of Uncle Keith. On my first Thanksgiving with them before we got married, before dinner the whole family had gone to a nearby park to play football. It was something of a family tradition, Gina told me. I knew nothing about football, but I was conscious they were all sizing me up, trying to see what kind of in-law I'd make. I gamely chased the ball with them, I endured being knocked down multiple times by Gina's six-foot-four, two-hundred-pound knucklehead cousin, Ruben, who was playing football at college. Finally, when I could do so without loss of face, I left the players and joined the old folk cheering from the sidelines. I stood next to Gina's father, who nodded at me encouragingly, and Uncle Keith, who looked at me and said, –That was an awful performance. Clearly you know nothing about football.

I nodded, trying not to appear miffed. My knees were scraped, my ribs were sore from collisions. I thought I had handled myself well under the circumstances.

–Yes. I am more of a soccer person, I admitted.

Uncle Keith, it turned out, was a former football player, now a coach. He walked with a limp, which he got when he broke his leg playing. –Listen, all sports are essentially the same. Decisive victory is the aim of every game, just as it is in war, because all competitive games are descended from warfare. Remember that.

Now my taxi was in Takoma Park and almost at the house. Suddenly I knew I couldn't face them. I couldn't imagine myself seated there, trying to appear cheerful, trying not to have to explain to the whole assembly why my marriage to their daughter, niece, sister, cousin, was no more. I couldn't. I told the driver to stop. I paid him and told him to keep the wine. I got down and went into a restaurant and ate by myself, then I returned to the apartment and sat in front of the TV till I fell asleep.

On my last day in the apartment, before leaving for the airport, I signed the divorce papers which Gina's lawyer had sent over by courier. I sat in front of the computer and tried to compose a short, sincere email to her: *Thanks for the past we shared, and good luck with the future*, but it felt inadequate. I deleted it, turned off the computer, and left.

–No. I didn't stay with her. She was out of the country. It is over between me and her. I signed the divorce papers.

–Well, what next? You have your PhD. Are you going back to the US, to become an American, or back to Nigeria?

–I haven't decided.

She went back to her nails. After a long while she said, –Come with me?

–Where? Basel? Again?

She laughed and shook her head. The dark cloud had lifted. –No, not Basel. To Lusaka. If you want. And, I can offer you a job. My mother is retiring, so I will be running the school. You can work with me.

–I have never been to Zambia. I don't know what to expect.

–Oh, you will love it. She put down the nail polish. Her

face lit up, her voice became eager, joyful. The kids are great, you will love them. And, it is quiet, peaceful. You will have time to think while you decide what to do next. You can expect to stay with me and my mom. Plus . . .

She held my gaze, a wicked smile on her lips.

—Plus what?

—All of these. She stood up and gestured at her body, shaking her full, braless breasts and her curvy hips. —Think about it.

•

Portia and I sometimes walked from Boswell Street all the way to the British Library. She used to live not far from the library when she was at SOAS, she said. She pointed out a Pret a Manger. She said she and her roommate used to have lunch there every day for a whole term, the roommate's boyfriend worked there.

—This roommate of yours, was her name Portia? I teased.

—You are jealous. Some emotion, at last.

—What do you mean? I can be emotional. I am emotional.

Sometimes we took the opposite route, toward Holborn station and on to the British Museum, or to Covent Garden to mingle with the tourists watching the painted jugglers and magicians. Once we stumbled on a pop-up street market selling food from every corner of the globe. We joined a line at a Thai stand, then we sat and ate in the open air, tears running down our eyes from the spice. It was getting dark when we came back. A crowd was standing in front of our building, some of them holding placards.

—A protest, Portia said.

There were actually two protests, the one in front of our building entrance, and another one across the road, on both sides men and women held up signs, the two groups appeared to be in opposition to one another. Two police cars were parked by the kerb at a distance, their lights flashing.

—What is happening? Portia asked a lady next to her. The lady was wearing a tracksuit, as if out for a jog, except she was pushing a child in a stroller – the child looked contented, swaddled in blankets and sucking its thumb. It appeared a man was hiding in our building, the lady told us breathlessly, an asylum seeker, being sheltered by a humanitarian organization. She pointed vaguely to a window, —Up there.

At that moment a bus cruised by, and as it passed the crowd before our entrance gave a loud cheer. I looked at the bus puzzled, till I saw what they were cheering. On the side of the bus, in huge black letters were the words: *Foreigners Out!* The other group shouted jeers and threw water bottles at the bus. The bus disappeared at the end of the street, and as we stood there it came back again from the direction where it first appeared, eliciting the same response from the two groups as before. I wondered how long it had been circling the block, round and round, slowly, like a shark circling a drowning swimmer.

—He is Nigerian. His name is Juma. We were back in the room and Portia was on her laptop. I went over and sat next to her. An organization, calling itself 'The Guardians', appeared to have been hiding the escaped asylum seeker for weeks now, moving him from one safe house to another, evading the police and immigration officials. His asylum application had failed and he was about to be deported when he escaped with the help of the group, who claimed the deportation order was illegal since they had an appeal pending. Nativists had finally traced him to our building, and what we saw downstairs was a standoff between them and the anti-nativists.

–It says here he has been on hunger strike for months, and he swears he'd rather die than be deported.

Juma appeared to be quite popular, there were dozens of articles and opinion pieces about him in the papers, some supporting him, others calling for his arrest and deportation. The home secretary had vowed to deport him. There was a photo of him under one of the articles, a gaunt, pensive, yet defiant face, staring unblinking at the camera.

The next morning, I woke up and went to the window almost expecting to see the demonstrators still there, and the bus with its ominous sign circling the block. Had there really been a large red bus circling the block, or was it all a dream? And the police car by the kerb, and the woman with her child in a pram, breathlessly describing to Portia what was going on. The wind blew dead leaves and pieces of paper down the deserted street. Only plastic water bottles trapped by the kerb and a few discarded placards on the grass bore testament to last night's protest. It was only 6 a.m. on a Sunday, the streets were empty, the city was still asleep, recovering from the weekend's endless parties and drinking, getting ready for Monday.

As I sat on the windowsill, looking out, enjoying the quiet, waiting for Portia to wake up, I became aware of voices coming from the hallway outside. The voices had been there for a while, quietly buzzing, and now they seemed to be coming from right outside the door, arguing in lowered tones, as if afraid of being heard, or of disturbing the still-sleeping neighbours. I opened the door and poked out my head. A door down the hall near the stairs stood half-open, the voices were coming from there. I put on my shoes and went over to the door and knocked, the voices stopped, when no one came to the door I stepped in, not sure what I was doing, or what I was going to say. A young man, dressed casually in tracksuit top and jeans, was standing in the middle of the room, alone, and didn't appear surprised to see me. Where was the other voice?

—I'll be with you in a moment, he said, and he went back to his phone, furiously typing a message with his thumbs. Behind him was a table loaded with cartons stuffed with folders from which pieces of paper were falling out. The room was sparsely furnished, a table by the wall, a couch in a corner. I wandered over to a window which opened to the street and looked out at the same view as the one from my room. Now I could hear movement from another room, the sound of things being dismantled, books taken off shelves and put into boxes – that must be the other voice. A windowpane behind the table was broken where a brick had sailed through it last night. I had no doubt this was where Juma was being kept. But where was he? I waited for the young man to look up from his phone, but he kept fiddling with it, sending out texts and staring at the screen, waiting for the ding of the answer. Just then the owner of the second voice came out from the inner room, carrying a carton filled with books.

—You look like you are moving out, I said.

He stopped, carton in hand, and looked from me to the phone-obsessed young man, not sure what to make of me. He ran his hand in his hair and looked around the empty room. He must have been in his twenties.

—The landlord wants us out by the end of the week. You saw the damn fascists throwing rocks at us yesterday. Who are you?

I said, —I live down the hall. I heard the commotion yesterday, and I wonder if everything is okay?

The other young man finally looked away from his phone and said, —You are not from the *Metro*? I thought you were from the *Metro*.

—The *Metro*? I said blankly.

—They were sending a reporter for an interview . . . forget it. What do you want? Now he looked suspicious, turning to the open door as if expecting more people to come in. He went and closed the door.

—I am your neighbour. I heard all the noise last night. And, I am Nigerian, like Juma. If I can be of help . . .

He ran his fingers through his hair, a thoughtful look on his face, weighing me. The other young man dropped the box on the table and stretched out his hand to me. —I am Josh, this is Liam.

We shook hands. Liam appeared to relax.

—Well, Josh said, I have to head out. Nice to have met you.

He left and now it was just me and Liam in the half-empty room.

—Listen, I began, I hope I am not disturbing you or . . .

—Come, Liam interrupted, let me show you something.

I followed him to another room that looked like a study, with bookshelves against one wall. He stood in the middle, staring at me. This was where they must have kept Juma. It looked like a monk's cell, with a narrow cot in a corner, a bare redwood table with a single book on it, a chair; a naked lightbulb hanging from the ceiling threw a dull yellow spray of light on everything. I picked up the book. It was *Hunger*, by Knut Hamsun.

–He read that over and over, as if he was preparing for some exam, Liam said. His voice was low, almost reverential. I opened the pages idly. I could understand why a starving man would read a book about food, but not why he'd read a book about a starving writer. It seemed masochistic.

–Is it true, I asked, that he has fasted for seventy days?

He started to answer but we heard a knock on the door and he hurried out. The reporter, most likely. I put down the book and followed him. A man in a shabby rain jacket and a backpack slung over one shoulder was talking to Liam. I nodded to the newcomer and headed for the door.

–Well, good talking to you . . .

Liam stepped toward me, almost blocking my path, and said, –Listen . . . I was wondering . . . you are Nigerian, right?

–Yes. I am Nigerian.

He lowered his voice. –Can he call you? It'd be lovely for him to have someone to talk to, someone from home.

–Where is he?

He glanced at the reporter, who had gone over to the table and was taking out a notebook from his backpack. –Well, we don't know.

–You don't know?

–Last night, when those fascists started gathering outside, we smuggled him out, through the back entrance. Molly took him to a café near the square to wait out the protest. He gave her the slip. He went to the bathroom and he never came back.

—Who is Molly?

—My colleague, one of the volunteers.

I said, —I am in flat number 20 down the hall. If there is anything I can do . . .

On impulse, which I would soon after regret, I gave him my number. Perhaps I felt the unfairness of it, the crowd with their placards, like a lynch mob, and the bus like a shark circling the block, while the gaunt, terrified Juma lurked in his room, unsure what his fate was going to be. I couldn't help but be in solidarity with him; I had known so many like him along the way, I had been one of them.

Portia noticed me checking my phone.

—You are not listening to me, she said. She was telling me about a cousin in South London. Her mother had called and wanted her to go see him.

—I am sorry, I said, and told her of my meeting with Liam, of the tiny, empty room a few doors down the hallway.

—And they don't know where he is? The Guardians don't sound very professional to me. Who are they?

—Well, I met only two of them, both are young. And there is a third, a lady, but she wasn't with them.

When the phone rang it was almost 10 p.m. The voice was low and apologetic, they were outside and could they come in for a few minutes? We were already in bed. Portia, tired of poring over her father's notebooks, was watching another episode of *Doctor Who* on her laptop, she watched the show addictively, sometimes I watched with her — a Dalek had the doctor trapped, and this time it looked like there would be no intergalactic escape through the trusty phone booth.

–They want to come here? Right now? Portia asked, tearing her eyes away from the screen. It is late.

–They are at the door.

–Bloody hell, she muttered. I changed and went to the living room. Portia cleared the empty teacups from the table while I removed the wine bottle and opener from the windowsill. The doorbell rang. I went and opened the door. There were two of them: Liam, still wearing the track-top and the jeans, followed by a tall, sturdy young lady. She was strikingly tall with a ponytail severely twisted at the back of her head – she looked capable, ready to take charge. Like a nurse, I thought.

–I am Molly, she said. Her grip was firm, and she was a nurse, as it turned out.

I pointed to the couch. –Sit, please.

Liam began to apologize for the unexpected visit, and for the late hour, but I told him it was fine.

–We couldn't come earlier because they are out there again.

We had seen them through the window, arrayed in the same formation as yesterday, including the big red bus.

–Have you found him yet?

–No, Liam said. The worry lines were pronounced on his face. Molly, on the other hand looked calm, unflappable.

–He is fine, I am sure, she said.

–How can you be so sure? Liam snapped.

–If he had been found, if something had happened to him, it would be on the news by now.

Liam and Molly had met Juma at the hospital where Molly worked. He had been brought there from the detention centre after he had started his hunger strike and his health

was failing. The officials wanted to force-feed him, pushing tubes down his throat. Molly was the nurse assigned to
him, and she was horrified by what she saw. When she was
alone with him she asked him about himself and gradually
he opened up to her. Liam, her boyfriend, had also been following Juma's story in the news, and together they decided
to intervene. One day, Juma tried to escape. Molly met him
in the hallway, he was barefooted, his bedsheet wrapped
over his hospital gown, he looked confused, searching for
the exit. She led him, protesting, back to his room and told
him she could help. —You can't make it this way, she told
him. I have a plan.

The next day she brought a pair of sturdy boots, a jacket
with a hood, sunglasses and a pair of jeans. She hid them in
the men's toilet and as soon as the guard was out of the way
she led Juma to the toilet where he changed, and then to her
car in the underground garage. It was easy, easier than she had
hoped. She took him to her one-bedroom apartment, which
she shared with Liam. That was how it began.

—Why? I asked. You could lose your job, or go to jail.

—I have lost my job already, she said calmly, and I don't
care if I go to jail. I just couldn't sit and watch them try to
force-feed him with those tubes, it is horrible, inhumane. It
is illegal.

—So, who else is in your organization? I asked.

—Well, we are a small organization, Liam said, looking at
Molly.

—How small? You must need a lot of logistics to keep ahead
of the immigration officials.

—Well, there are only three of us. Me and Molly and Josh.

–Just three of you? Portia asked, giving voice to my surprise.

–Well, we have done well so far, Liam said defensively.

Liam was a postgraduate student at the University of East Anglia, Josh was a schoolteacher, both were passionate advocates for migrants' rights. Molly was passionate about health care and justice in general. They had made up the name, The Guardians, to make themselves look professional, but there were only three of them. How did they manage it? It hadn't been easy, and as they spoke I could hear the stress reflected in their voices. The organization was born when Juma stayed in their little flat, sleeping on the floor in the living room, then, when they got a tip-off that officials were coming, they moved out. In the past few months they had moved Juma to five different locations, mostly the houses of friends, some of whom didn't even know who Juma was or what exactly was going on. Others knew and were willing to help on principle. All the time they had kept the media involved, sending detailed information about Juma's hunger strike, about the government's efforts to arrest him even though his case was under appeal. They were excited when Josh told them they could bring Juma to this place – the flat belonged to his uncle, a banker who had been posted to Spain and left the flat in Josh's care. I tried to hide my disappointment. The whole plan sounded shockingly rickety, and it was just a matter of time before everything came crashing around their heads. I was not so sure I wanted to be involved in it, that would be foolhardy.

–Well . . . I began, turning to Portia.

–You will need help, she said to Molly, leaning forward. How can we assist?

–Yes, how can we help? I echoed, reluctantly.

But, as it turned out, their request was pretty modest. They wanted me to inquire discreetly among the Nigerian community if anyone knew Juma's whereabouts, if some Nigerian family or organization was hiding him. They felt bad that they had lost him. I didn't know any Nigerian groups in London and I doubted if he'd go to any of them for help, but to cheer them up I promised to ask around.

•

Last night, unable to sleep after our visitors had left, Portia had gone back to her father's diaries and had discovered a forgotten picture tucked in the pages of one of the notebooks. It was her, at age one, the picture was turning yellow at the edges, but the likeness was unmistakably her. She was standing outside in a park or in a yard, it was a spring day, behind her a field of green followed by a row of fir trees overlooking a lake. She was facing the camera, striking a pose, her hand on her hip, laughing.

–I have no recollection of this, she said. She sounded perplexed.

On the back of the picture was a date, and a place. *April 1992, Leeds.*

–My mother never mentioned a visit to Leeds when I was one.

–It is definitely you, I said. The same nose, the same mouth, the eyes confident and beautiful even at that age. On

the back of the picture there was a poem, handwritten, dedicated to her. She read it out, slowly.

SPRING
(for Portia)

It is spring, child
Feel the juices, only last month frozen –
Like the lake outside this window –
Let the juices flow

Stand, totter, fall, then stand again
See, the rabbits are out again
And the leaves on the larch

The colours are here again –
Blue daffodils, yellow dandelions,
And green, evergreen for you.

Rejoice with the vine and the poplar,
Shout viva! for the winter was long,
And the sun is here again!

–It is a beautiful poem, I said.
–He wrote it for me. In Leeds. There was wonder in
her voice. She called her mother, who confirmed that yes,
they had been to Leeds when she was just one, it was a brief
visit, they stayed only one month, March to April. It was her
father's last year at Leeds, the next year he moved to Norway

and they never saw him again till Portia was ten. She read the poem to her mom down the phone.

—I am not sure what to do with the diaries, she said later. So far she had located over twenty poems in the five diaries she had found, not all the poems were complete, some were only fragments, about the weather, the sea. Several were dedicated to May, his mistress. One, titled 'Home Songs', was more complete than the others. In it he talked about his childhood and the first day he left home to go to boarding school. There was, in all, about twenty years' worth of writing, all unpublished. The diary entries were sporadic, going entire years without any entries, but toward the end of his life, from 2009 to 2011, he kept a constant flow of notes with several pages for every single day.

—You should get in touch with his publisher.

—They are all retired by now, or dead.

•

We took the National Rail at Charing Cross. It was after the morning rush hour, and the crush of bodies began to thin out as we went further southward, till there were only about six of us in the carriage. A man seated across the aisle was cackling loudly to himself, his long narrow beard shook and wriggled as he laughed. He looked tired, his eyes were red and he kept sipping at his coffee in between laughs, long noisy sips. Portia glared at him, then turned away to look at the passing scenery outside. Balconies with laundry hanging from the rails, brick walls with unreadable graffiti on them. Next to the laughing man was a young woman trying her best to ignore him. She couldn't be older than fifteen, one hand held on to a stroller with a child in it, the other hand held a phone to her ear. She was dressed in pink sweatpants and a flimsy T-shirt against which her tiny breasts strained.

I watched her hand, the long nails painted red, tapping on the phone with its diamanté-encrusted case, its red colours matching the colours on her nails. The words flew faster now, her fingers tapping a beat on the phone as she emphasized each word in a mash of accents, Caribbean, West African and South London. It was a slow train, stopping at every station on the way. The laughing man stopped at Gillingham. At Crayford the young woman stood up to exit. Then came Abbey Wood. We got down.

That morning, Portia's mother had called to remind her to go see her cousin, who hadn't been back to Zambia since he left to study in England. She had handed the phone to me and said, −My mother, and when I looked at her blankly she had nodded encouragingly. −She wants to say hi, she mouthed.

−Hi, I mumbled. I had never spoken to her mother before, I didn't know how her voice sounded. She asked about the London weather, and whether we had been to Piccadilly Circus. I answered 'yes' and 'no' to the strong, clear voice on the other side. Finally, she asked me to make sure Portia went to visit her cousin, Jonah, because his mother was sick and was worried about him.

−I am sorry, Portia said afterward, I took you unawares.

−It's okay, I replied. I was surprised, and impressed, that the mother was fine with the idea that her daughter was here with me, alone, in London. But then, Portia had always made it clear how close she and her mother were. I wondered what she had told her mother about me. Did the mother worry if I was a responsible person, if I was taking care of her daughter? Of course, she must, what mother wouldn't.

I thought of my mother. When I came back from Italy she had pretended I was not home when friends came to see me, or she'd say I was asleep. One day my father said to me, –Your mother had built so much hope on you. She used to tell her friends one day she'd go visit you in America, to meet your wife and play with your children.

My father looked tired, he sat there, not looking directly at me. –Listen, I don't know what happened to you. I just hope you did nothing illegal. I hope you can go back someday and set your affairs in order.

We exited the station and followed the line of litter by the sidewalk, papers, beer cans, cigarette packets, marking the path like signposts. We passed a Waitrose, a curry shop, a laundromat, Portia taking seemingly random turns as guided by her cousin's voice on the phone, and finally we were facing a cluster of council houses behind tall birch and elm trees somewhere off Abbey Road. The houses looked identical: semi-detached, each with a picket-fenced garden at the back and green plastic trash containers at the front. A line of square flagstones led to the front door. Portia rang the doorbell and the door opened. A man in his thirties stood there, still holding the phone to his ear, dressed in Arsenal FC jersey and shorts, and soccer boots, looking like he was about to step out to the training field. He hugged Portia and shook my hand.

–Come in. You guys are just in time. The match has just started. Ten minutes in.

We followed him into a narrow hallway, stepping over a pile of mail covering the doormat, and into a dark and poky living room illuminated by the light from the big TV screen dominating one wall.

–Sit down, Jonah said, his eyes on the screen.

Now I noticed two kids, a boy and a girl, seated on the floor directly facing the TV, they were also wearing Arsenal jerseys. One said Thierry Henry on the back, the other said Pires, the father was Patrick Vieira.

–Hey, Tom, Sheila, say hi to your auntie Portia. The last time she was here was when? He turned to Portia.

–Four years ago? I was at SOAS then, so about four, five years now.

–Wow, Jonah said. Tom was only four then, and Sheila was two. Look at them now.

Tom and Sheila turned briefly and shouted, –Hi Auntie Portia, in unison, their faces dull and expressionless, then they turned back to the screen. Arsenal was playing Tottenham Hotspur. Jonah sat on the edge of his seat, wrapped up in the game, following every strike, every save, groaning or cheering. Often he'd lean forward and clap his son on the back. The kids were as animated as their father.

–Did you see that, did you see that, Dad? the boy shouted. He ran to the kitchen and we could hear him telling his mom what had just happened. The mother had only briefly stepped into the living room to welcome us and then returned to the kitchen, a small woman with a pinched, fierce face. At half-time Jonah stood up and stretched. He looked hopeful – the game was tied at 1–1. He went to the kitchen and came back with three cans of beer, he handed one to me, one to Portia, and opened one for himself. –To Arsenal, he said, raising his can. I have a good feeling about this one.

His wife came in and sat on the arm of his seat, draping one arm over his shoulder, and it looked to me as if she was restraining him. Jonah waved his beer at her in a salute. She had a half-smile on her face, she refused to meet my eye, or Portia's, she kept her eyes fixed to the TV, but it was obvious she wasn't watching the game. The halftime break was over, the players were coming out of the tunnel, making the sign of the cross as their legs touched the field, some bending down to touch the grass, finding their way to their positions. Things took a downward turn for Arsenal in the first ten minutes, and by the end of the match they were down 3–1.

Jonah crushed his empty beer can and flung it against the wall. He jumped up and rushed to the kitchen, his wife threw an apologetic look at us before she followed him, and soon we heard the sound of a scuffle. I stood up, but Portia shook her head. I sat down. The children were still seated, staring at the screen where the pundits were analysing the just-concluded match. They looked as if they were waiting for the players to come back from the locker room, and the game to restart, and their team to reassert its invincibility.

Jonah came back, a bottle of Smirnoff vodka in his hand. He flopped into his seat with a loud sigh and slapped the bottle on the table, he didn't glance at us, not even once. We watched as he filled a glass to the brim and drained it in one go, and repeated the same twice. Half the bottle was gone in a few minutes. I heard the steps of the wife slowly climbing the stairs, each step squeezing out a loud creak, and then the sound of a door closing and it was like a light switch turned off. The children continued to watch the screen. Portia was looking at her cousin, a sad look on her face. He sat slumped in his seat, his face buried in his hands, shaking his head violently, and soon a muffled cry came out between his fingers. −Goddamn you, Gunners! he sobbed, why, Arsenal, why?

After a while the wife came down, she stood at the door, looking at him.

−We will be going now, Portia said, standing up.

She walked us to the door, her back straight, her head high. −He lost his job, you know, she said, looking directly at Portia, the half-smile on her lips. He had a good job at the factory, then the drinking started. He can't keep a job. Security, deliveryman, waiter, taxi driver, he has tried everything. Now he has stopped trying. He watches football and he drinks.

•

The protesters were gathered again, about a dozen persons on both sides of the road, as usual the nativists were closer to the entrance, bunched together, holding up their placards and shaking them in the air. They jostled us as we passed through them, calling out: 'Go back!' and 'Where is he?' and 'Fucking illegals!' Portia calmly opened the front door while I stood behind her, positioning my back against hurled missiles or words. I pushed the door shut behind me and held her before the stairs where she stood, shaking and unable to climb. I felt the shivers traversing her body and I held her tighter till they ceased. For the first time I began to contemplate the possibility of our moving out to a hotel, we might not be safe here. The hallway leading to our door was dark, and so at first I didn't see the two figures standing in front of a door next to ours, huddled in the dark, dressed in long coats, the taller figure was checking in her bag as if for a key, but as we got closer she looked up and I recognized the face: Molly. At the same time she said, −It is me, Molly.

−Hi Molly, I said.

The other lady remained a step behind Molly, her face in the shadows. Now I saw she was black, and her head was covered in a head scarf that fell to her shoulders like a veil. They followed us inside and sat on the couch and now, in the brighter light of the living room, the second lady's face looked vaguely familiar. I had seen those eyes somewhere. Portia went into the kitchen to make tea, I followed her.

−I wonder what they want, I whispered, and the other lady looks familiar, doesn't she?

−It is not a lady, Portia said, it is a guy, it is *him*. Didn't you see his shoes, and the hands?

Of course. She was right. I returned to the living room, and yes, it was him, the head scarf was off, now lying in a pile next to his feet, next to the muddy, broken, laced-up dress shoes. He sat hunched forward, hands clasped between his knees, his eyes looking out at me, waiting, unsure of his welcome. It was a face used to being turned away, kicked out, a pariah dog. I sat, facing them, waiting for Molly to speak.

−We found him, she said.

Juma had wandered back by himself, disguised in a head scarf. Molly looked sheepish, like she was about to make a request she knew was outrageous, one she shouldn't be making. I steeled myself for it.

−Where is Liam? I asked.

She looked at her phone. −I am expecting his call. He has

gone to meet a pastor at St Luke's. He is one of our supporters, he has promised to put Juma up for a while. It is not safe for him here any more.

I turned to Juma and smiled. –Hello.

He shook my hand, then laid his palm over his heart. The gesture took me by surprise, it was a common part of greeting back home, to put the right palm over the heart after a handshake, but I hadn't seen it done in a long time, and I certainly wasn't expecting to see it here.

–Hello, he said. His voice was hoarse, whistling out of his mouth, the long hunger strike had drained him. He accepted the cup of tea from Portia.

–Thank you. I can drink tea and water only, he said. He seemed careful to explain how scrupulously he was observing the rules of his hunger strike.

Molly said, –I am sorry to surprise you like this. But Liam said you are from the same place as Juma, that you are willing to help.

When I said nothing, she looked at Juma, then at Portia. She lowered her head. –We have nowhere else to go.

Another brick had been thrown into the window last night, and the landlord was threatening to call the police, he wanted them out immediately. Tomorrow, if things worked out with the pastor, they'd move to the church, but tonight they needed a place for Juma to stay. They feared either the police or the nativists outside would come banging on the door at any minute. They couldn't even slip Juma out through the back, the protesters had discovered the back entrance and some of them were stationed there. Molly and Juma had been hiding in the stairwell and in the hallways, waiting for us, since 2 p.m. We had not headed home directly after leaving Portia's cousin's house, we had wandered aimlessly for a while, then we went to the British Museum to view the Egyptian collection, we stopped at a Caribbean restaurant for dinner, and from there, instead of taking the train back, we walked about for almost an hour, then we sat in the park for a while, and all that time they were waiting for us, skulking by the doorway, going up and down the stairs, careful not to be recognized by residents who passed them in the hallway or on the stairs.

–Listen, I began, we don't own this place, like you we are sort of caretakers . . .

–It is okay, Portia said from the kitchen. I smiled and shrugged at Molly. –He can stay. For a night.

After Molly had left, I asked Juma if there was anything he needed. He needed the bathroom. He said he hadn't showered in two days. I showed him the bathroom, and the extra towels in the closet. He took off his broken shoes and walked to the bathroom in the flip-flops I gave him. Portia stood looking at the shoes, the heels were so eaten away I wondered how he was able to walk in them, the socks, stuck into the shoes, were patched and grimy. –These socks need to be aired, she said, they stink.

We debated what to do with them: throw them in the trash and get him new ones tomorrow, or take them to the laundry, which might not be worth the trouble, they were practically coming apart in threads. We decided to take the shoes with the socks out and place them by the door – he would find that least offensive, it was customary back home to leave shoes out by the doormat. And then there was the matter of food: what if we wanted to cook, Portia liked to make omelettes in the morning, would that interfere with his hunger strike? It would be extremely cruel to cook while he struggled with hunger. Fine, we would skip breakfast tomorrow, and if he was still here at lunchtime, we would eat out – it wouldn't kill us to alter our routine for one day. Hopefully Liam would be here to get him before the end of day. Portia hung his boxy jacket in the closet, the scarf she also hung carefully next to the jacket.

He sat in front of the TV, his eyes glued to the news. I wondered if he was waiting for news about himself. I asked him,
–Where did you go to yesterday? They were searching for you.
–I took the bus, he said.
–The bus?
He nodded. –Yes. It is really safe on the bus.
He explained that when he first came to England he used to take the bus at night, in winter it was the warmest and safest place he could be. He'd take the bus plying the longest routes, his favourite was the one going to the airport, and he'd stay on for hours, sometimes as long as three hours on one bus, back and forth, only getting down to look for something to eat.
–I was new in the country, I had only my bag, a very small one, containing just my toothbrush and one change of clothes and a book or two. I was afraid to go anywhere or do anything. The bus seemed the safest place to me.
–And the drivers, didn't they complain?

–No. Sometimes I'd hang around at the airport. I didn't stick out, so many faces coming and going. And there is good food there, in the bins outside. I did that for months before they caught me.

–Who?

–The immigration. A driver must have reported me. He stopped talking abruptly, his eyes glued to the TV. Portia nudged me and whispered, –He needs rest.

She gave him a blanket and asked if he needed anything before we turned in. No, he didn't.

In the bedroom I said, –What if Molly and Liam don't turn up tomorrow?

She seemed less worried than I was. –They will come.

After we turned off the light I stood briefly by the window. The protesters were still out there, standing with their signs, some sitting by the kerb smoking, in the corner the police car waited idly.

He was still sleeping when we woke up. We decided to let him sleep and we went out for a walk. We ate in a little place just opening, the owner looked sleepy as she went from table to table, arranging chairs and laying down the cutlery. When we finished we stopped by a fruit stand and Portia bought a crate of apples. He was awake when we returned, watching TV. Portia first put the apples in a bowl by the window, then, with a guilty look at Juma, she moved the bowl to the kitchen. He noticed and said to her, –You really mustn't worry about me. And, as if to further put her at ease, he broke into a story about fruits. He seemed to have a story for every occasion – it was his way of communicating, with stories of all he had been through. Or perhaps it was his way of trying to forget his hunger, and he did it with unexpected stamina, his hoarse voice droning with no inflection. His English was adequate; the English of a non-native speaker, learned mostly from books, making up his own pronunciations of words he had never heard spoken.

–Once, he said, in Greece, two years after I had left home, a friend and I were attacked by skinheads. They trapped us in a building for two days, with no food.

–How did that happen? I asked.

He looked at me and then at Portia, straight in the eyes as he spoke, pinning us down, making sure we paid attention.

–Well, my friend and I had been picking strawberries for over a month for a farmer who then refused to pay us, and when we complained, he had sent these youths after us. We were passing through Greece, trying to make our way to France and then to London. We never planned to stay long in Greece, we arrived at the harvest season, and my friend, Hassan, I met him in a camp in Italy, he is an Afghan, he said it would make sense to arrive in France with some money to pay the people smugglers, or guides as they preferred to be called, who'd get us to England, and so we worked. Five euros a day, plus food. We worked, and at first the farmer was paying us regularly, he'd send his manager in the evening each day with his little bag of money and we'd line up and he'd hand out our money. And then the pay stopped coming. The first day we thought it was a mistake, we went to work the next day, and the next day, now he was owing us for a few days, and when a whole week passed with no word from him, we went

to his office in a group to protest. But he had been expecting
us. The police were there, he must have had them on standby,
like he had done this before. They told us to leave the farm,
and we did, peacefully. We went back to our tents. We were
camped in a park outside of town. Early the next morning the
skinheads came in their black shirts. They started breaking
our tents and beating us with baseball bats. There were many
of us, a few hundred, including women and children, but we
were no match for this dozen or so young men. They were
full of fury, and now, looking back, I wonder why they were
so angry, they were clubbing children and women, kicking
them, screaming. Well, we ran away in different directions,
my friend and I entered an abandoned building and we were
trapped in this building for two days. The skinheads knew we
were in there, but they didn't come in to get us, they waited
outside, it was a game for them, they wanted to starve us into
submission. Two days, with no food, only a little water in a
bottle, and no heating. They waited in a bar across the road,
taking turns to watch us, and when the bar closed they waited
in the street, they knew we wouldn't be able to slip out, there
was only the front exit. We could see them, occasionally coming out to look up at the building, in their black shirts and
boots. My friend Hassan almost gave up. I told him to hold
on, he was crying and begging me to allow him to surrender,
then miraculously we found a can of preserved apples in a
closet in the kitchen. We opened it and drank the juice, then
we ate. We were able to last a day longer on that can, and that
day the skinheads gave up, they just left, and we were able to
get out. When we opened that can and I took out a piece of
apple, the smell of it brought tears to my eyes. I remembered

all the fruits I ever ate growing up, the mangoes, the bananas, the melons, the pineapples. I wanted to go home. The longing for home was so strong I could feel it in my stomach. It was a moment of weakness I never allow myself to indulge in any more. Hunger is a tool. It is power. By refusing to eat, you are telling your enemy, There is nothing you can do to me any more. If I am willing to starve myself to death to prove a point, what else is there to fear?

–Why did you leave Nigeria? I asked him.

The stories kept coming, discursively, randomly. He sat on the couch, the blanket draped over his lap covering his knobby knees and shrunken calves. The sentences tumbled out and it was nothing short of fascinating that so many words could be coming out of this small frame. In the refugee camp in Calais, he had met a woman who used to be rich back in her country, she had a restaurant and a big house, cars and servants, and then she had to leave to save her life. In the camp, bereft of everything she once possessed, she would put on airs, she would refuse to eat, wouldn't take a bath, she would lie in her tent, on a mattress, calling out the names of her maids, now back in her country, to come and clean up the place, to draw her a bath, she would get angry when she got no response and she would storm out of her tent and stalk the little space before the tent, throwing out curses, waving her hands at the children gathered to watch her tantrums. It was sad to see. He didn't know what happened to her afterward. He was there for just two days, but it was the bleakest place he had ever been, the Jungle, they called it, worse than Niger, or Greece, or Germany. In Germany, he had witnessed a demonstration in Berlin, at the Oranienplatz. A man had stayed up in a tree for three days, defying the police who had come to break up the refugee tents. Juma's voice was full of admiration. The police were flummoxed, they didn't know how to handle the man. He stayed there, in the cold European winter, hugging a tree branch, in the falling rain, shitting and pissing on himself, with no food, and only rainwater to drink, but not coming down.

They came and took him away in the afternoon. The landlord, it appeared, had relented after a call from Josh's uncle, he had given them two more days, and then they had to move out.

—Will he be okay? I asked Liam.

I realized Juma might not be all there, mentally. His travails had taken a toll on his mind and often he appeared to be lost, drifting and sometimes hardly aware of where he was or what he was doing. Liam shrugged. —We have no idea. Our greatest fear now is the authorities. Our contacts told us to expect a raid at any moment. We are trying to mobilize the media, to build up some public pressure to stop them.

The demonstrations began early that afternoon. From our room we could hear the chants, swelling and ebbing, they sounded like soccer fans in a stadium, without the density, without the mass, but there was no mistaking the passion. I kept my ears cocked, expecting to hear the sound of boots marching to door number 12, for a call for them to open up, or for a battering ram breaking down the door. But nothing happened. There was a brief mention of Juma on the news, on Channel 4. The shadow immigration minister was condemning the

Home Office's cruel and inhumane immigration policy, and the promise to create a hostile environment for immigrants. Migrants' rights groups were urging their members to go on hunger strike in solidarity with Juma. Inmates in detention centres all over the country were refusing to eat.

–Something is going on down there.

Portia was by the window, looking out at the demonstrators. I joined her. Today the anti-nativist group was larger, some had Juma's name boldly printed on their placards.

–Well, it seems our friend is winning hearts and minds, I said. I feared that this newfound support might work against him. The government wouldn't like to lose face, and might feel compelled to act quickly. My fears were justified, as it turned out.

The next day the police came. Early in the morning, when the street was still asleep, and the sidewalk was still littered with picket signs and water bottles and cigarette butts from last night's protests, we heard loud banging on a door down the hall and I jumped up and rushed to our door. There were five of them, dressed in riot gear and helmets. The door opened and they walked in. Now Portia had joined me at the door. She slipped her hand into mine and held tight.

–What is happening? she asked. But she knew what was happening. After a while they walked out again, two hefty men holding him by his thin, twig-like arms, his skinny, shoeless legs barely touching the ground. Behind them came Molly, also being led by the arm, and then Liam and Josh, and all the way down the stairs Molly's combative voice rang out clearly, –You can't do this. It is not right. You have no right.

Then the footsteps ceased, and the front door closed. We

rushed to the window and caught a sight of the top of the police van pulling away.

—What should we do? Portia asked. She was close to tears. —Is there nothing we can do?

I watched her face crumble, like a child's sand castle on the beach dissolving before the waves.

—I am sorry, I said, holding her.

—It is not fair, she said, echoing Molly, it is not right.

When I was in secondary school I had witnessed a public execution, when such things were still happening in Nigeria. Three robbers had been brought to the soccer field on the outskirts of town and we had come to watch, children, men, women, some with infants tied to their backs. The robbers, their hands tied behind them, were led out of the military pickup and lashed to sand-filled oil drums. I was surprised at how young they looked, like teenagers, their faces sleepy, dazed. We watched the soldiers line up in front of them, and after a barked order from a captain the soldiers opened fire. It was quick, and brutal, and in a minute the men, who a while ago had been alive and young and maybe even hopeful, were now dead, their heads lolling on their necks, and their lifeless bodies being untied and dumped into the pickup. Later, my friends told me that I kept screaming as the shots rang out, over and over: It is not fair! It is not fair!

—I know, I said, hugging Portia tightly, my cheek against hers, feeling the tears streaming down, and I wasn't sure if they were all her tears or mine, I am so sorry.

It was the last time we ever saw Juma, in the flesh. But his images kept popping up everywhere. The news was a brush-fire roaring the name of Juma. There were debates and hurried justifications for what happened. On every TV channel the red-faced home secretary faced a battery of microphones and tried to give plausible explanations why the government found it necessary to spend all that money to deport the Nigerian, and bungle the whole thing in the process.

That morning, they had taken him straight to Luton Airport and bundled him into a specially chartered plane to fly him straight to Nigeria. I imagined the scared Juma huddled in his seat in the plane, empty but for the two security officials sitting on either side of him, too weak and confused to protest or resist, the night outside the window taxiing past, and then the uplift into the clouds. In Abuja the Nigerian government refused to grant the plane permission to land and it had to turn back to London, with its perplexed passenger, after a brief stop in Malta to refuel.

.

It felt strange to come out of our building and not be met by the protesters, with their placards upraised, faces snarling, and shouting obscenities. Molly and Liam were waiting for us by the entrance, and I remembered how they had waited on the stairs that day, two weeks ago, Molly and Juma, like two undercover characters in a B movie. When Liam called and said he had a letter for us from Juma, we had invited them over, but they said they'd rather meet elsewhere, in a pub nearby, and I didn't blame them, the building must hold unpleasant memories for them.

It had rained overnight and there was still a chill in the air, rooks in a nearby rookery called valiantly to each other, lending some cheer to the dull, damp day. We sat in a crowded café behind a bus stop, there was a match on TV and the excited crowd vociferously cheered and jeered the progress of the match. We sat in the back, away from the screen, and ordered a beer each.

–Where is he kept? Portia asked.

In reply Liam handed me the letter.

–His lawyer gave me this. For you both.

Portia and I opened the letter as soon as Molly and Liam left. As Portia read it out aloud, Juma's voice jumped off the page, and it felt like he was there with us, his impossibly sonorous voice coming out of his scrawny, diminished frame, continuing his narrative thread where he had stopped two weeks ago:

You must have heard on the news by now, or from Liam, how my deportation didn't work, and how I am now back in the UK. Let me just say I never thought I was coming off that plane alive. But I don't want to talk about that ordeal, it is too painful. Instead, I want to tell you why I left home. Remember, you asked me, and I never got a chance to tell you. Well, to answer your question, I have to tell you my whole story. But then, some of it I have already told you, and some you have experienced yourself in the course of your travels. This will be a long letter, but I have time here at the detention centre. I spend the days reading books sent to me by kind charities. Today I am reading The Lonely Londoners. *It is about immigrants from the West Indies. Their English is sometimes hard to understand, but I empathize with their situation. 'Are the streets of London paved with gold?' a reporter asks one of them. Very funny. I guess most of them didn't come for gold, they came for a better life, for a better chance. I imagine their lives in the Bayswater, how they negotiate the streets filled with signs and graffiti telling them, 'Keep the Water White!' Nothing has changed. As I write, I remember that bus with its warning sign driving round and round the block. But to go back to my story, I'll take you to the night I left home. It will take me a few days to finish writing, so you will have to forgive me if in places it feels disjointed or if I become repetitive.*

The school where I taught had been attacked by religious extremists. One of their aims is to stamp out Western education. We had been hearing of them for weeks before they came, how they go from town to town, attacking police stations and taking away guns, and attacking local banks and taking away money, every day we see a steady stream of people fleeing from the killers, they pass through our town in increasing numbers. Some have been walking for two or even three days, mostly women and children. I remember one woman, she must have been over seven months pregnant, and when we advised her to stop in our village and rest, she refused. She wanted to put as much distance as she could between her and the killers. We didn't ask her where her husband and the rest of her family was.

That night our village was attacked. The school where I taught was attacked first. It was located a little outside of town, and from our house we saw the flames rising in the night sky. They went to the principal's house and killed him and his wife and three children. They drove through the town in their pickups, firing into the air and shouting religious slogans. I tell you, I have never known fear like that. Each shot was so loud, imagine someone knocking on your door with a rock in the middle of the night, the sound cutting through your dreams. My old father came to my room and told me to run. He handed me a little package, in it was all his life savings. He is over seventy, he and my mother, and they said they were not run-

ning, they'd stay there and face whatever fate had in store for them. 'The worst they can do to an old man like me,' my father said, 'is to put me against the wall and shoot me. As for your mother, they don't kill women. But you, if you stay they will take you and turn you into a killer.'

My father was trying to make me feel better about going away, and I knew he was right, but it was hard to turn away from them and leave, knowing I might never see them again in this life. Well, that is how I left home, with only the clothes on my back.

Why did I leave my country? Well, I didn't even know I was leaving my country. We ran all night long, we crossed a stream, and in the morning they told us we were in another country, Cameroon. We camped in an open field at a school, sleeping on the grass, men and women and children, still too dazed to know what was happening. But our ordeal was not over yet, in fact, it was just beginning. Two days later the terrorists crossed the stream and attacked that schoolyard, killing over half of the people as they slept in the open, the rest of us, the lucky ones, we had to run again. We ran for a whole day and when we finally stopped, they told us we were in another country, the Federal Republic of Niger. I was a refugee. I had no family, no home, no friends, the people running with me were my new family.

I was in Niger for over six months. We were kept in an open field, over ten thousand of us. There was no town or village around us for miles, in the distance there were nothing but baobab trees and scrublands and a few nomadic settlements. I don't want to bore you with the details, I don't want to say how much I suffered, or what kind of suffering I witnessed, but imagine this: over ten thousand people living in a place the size of a secondary school, how much food would be enough to feed them, how many emergency toilets would be enough to serve them, and just imagine the darkness at night because there was no electricity, and the mosquitoes were everywhere because it was the rainy season and sometimes the tents we were in would be swept away by the storm and we had to sit like that, huddled under the falling rain till morning came. And every day people died like flies. You would see a child today, playing in the dirt, tomorrow they'll tell you he died in the night. Often I'd look around me and ask myself, Where am I? Who am I? How did I get here? I saw how others had already become used to this lifestyle. Strange how life goes on. There were people actually giving birth, and getting married and children going to school, all in our ever-burgeoning camp. But my eyes were always turned toward home, I dreamt every day of my father and my mother, and I wondered what had happened to them that day I left.

Every once in a while, officials from the Nigerian government would visit to assure us things were getting better at home, the war was being won, and that soon we would go back home. Six months. The same story. But instead of shrinking, the camp grew daily with new arrivals. And one day I said to myself, You are never going back home. At night we listened to the radio, mostly BBC and the German Africa radio, and from there we learned that the war was only growing, the killers were taking more towns and villages, and they had already established what they called a caliphate, and soon they would be attacking villages here in Niger. Twice our camp was moved, away from the border region. And that was when I finally accepted that I might not be going back home, not so soon anyway. To stay in the camp would be to die, no doubt about that. I decided to leave. Others had left already, mostly the young and strong and healthy. Every day men came from Libya and Algeria and Morocco to tempt us to leave with them. I gave them the money my father gave me, we left, there were ten of us, three men and four women and three children, two boys and a girl. I will not bore you with how we sat huddled in the truck, hot and baking in the merciless heat, or how the truck broke down somewhere in the middle of the Sahara Desert, near the town of Agades, and how we joined other groups of travellers to walk the rest of the way, with no food, and little water, and how we refused to look back when those walking alongside us suddenly slumped and fell into the burning sand, never to stand up again. I made it to Libya, only to be arrested by border police. I was in prison for many days, weeks, or even months, who knows? We were kept in a dark room and forgotten, in that room I heard different stories from those who had been there for days and weeks and months: they said we were being kept there to be sold to people who would harvest our kidneys and hearts and other organs. Others said no, we would be sold to rich households to work for ever as slaves. I will not tell you how, to survive, we had to drink our own urine, or that only about six out of the twenty men locked up in that room eventually made it out. I had sworn to myself I was going to make it. I had already started training for hunger. One day we heard the sound of gunfire, and then our door was thrown open by men carrying guns and they told us we were free to go, just like that.

I was in that hell in Libya for a year.

I worked, when I was able to, I won't tell you what manner of work I did, but I was able to save up a thousand dollars after a year. Why did I leave? How do I know? I knew that to stay alive I had to keep moving. I found myself in a group getting ready to cross the Mediterranean for Europe. They gathered us at gunpoint in a little harbour in the middle of the night, hundreds of us, men and women and children, families mostly. It was a sad sight to stand there with that group, knowing that each one of them had a similar or even a more sad story than mine. I saw a man and his wife and two children, dressed in expensive coats and shoes, the wife was carrying a very fine handbag, as if she was in an airport waiting to fly for a holiday.

Later I discovered why our guides had us at gunpoint. You were not allowed to protest where you were assigned in the boat, regardless of how much money you paid for the crossing. It was tight. It was noisy. Next to me a group of women was singing, Hallelujah! They kept singing. It was like a church revival. I was positioned down below deck, next to the portable toilet that served the over three hundred people in that rickety vessel, and which soon overran with urine and faeces. I will spare you the details.

The boat sank of course, less than an hour after we set out. I don't know what happened, I was down there, next to the toilet. Some said we were shot at by a militia boat, some said it was the same traffickers who wanted to take us back and make us pay all over again, I don't know, and right now it is not that important how or why it happened. All that matters as our boat sank into the water was that I couldn't swim, and that people were clawing their way up to the deck, kicking and screaming and holding on to their children's hands. Most of them, like me, didn't have life jackets and couldn't swim. I was saved by that stinking toilet. One moment I was down there below deck, next moment I was underwater, and then I came up, and in front of me was the blue plastic portable toilet. Some pocket of gas, or maybe all that decomposing shit, was making it float. I held on. I wouldn't float for long, I knew. All around were people struggling, floating, screaming. Children floated past, and their mothers, belly-up before sinking, plastic slippers, bowls, books briefly floated, and soon there wasn't anything at all. There was nothing, no heaven, no earth, no boat, only water and the sound of wind over water. It didn't take too long for the toilet to sink, luckily for me at that moment a dinghy came by, and they pulled me in. In the dinghy were two rescuers and a father and his daughter.

The father was the most heartbroken, wretched man I have ever seen. His wife and his son were out there in the water, and he was here in the flimsy craft with his daughter. He pulled at his hair, he strained his eyes looking into the horizon, hoping to catch a glimpse of them. He was a good swimmer and he jumped into the water and swam around, searching, and then his daughter, about ten years old, began to cry and call after him and he quickly came back. He sat, torn and helpless, and me and the other men held him, scared he was going to do harm to himself. I said, remembering what my father said to me the night I left home, 'If it is God's will, you will see them again.' But he kept looking around, standing up, screaming into the wind till night fell, till his voice grew hoarse, and then he sat down and held his daughter in his arm and together they cried and none of us could console them. Often I wonder what happened to them, father and daughter, if they ever reunited with their family. Later, I learned, that of the over three hundred of us who left Libya that morning, only me, the man and the girl, and five other people survived.

Why did I survive? I often wonder. I am not a very religious man, but you can't go through the things I went through without realizing there is a God, somewhere, in the affairs of men. But sometimes, also you wonder if there is a God, why does He allow such things to happen. Why are some people born to suffering and heartbreak, while others from the day they were born till they die know nothing but happiness and pleasure? Is God biased, what did I do to face so much suffering? What did that man and that little girl do to be separated from their family? I mentioned this once to a clergyman I met in Germany. I had spent the night in an empty church, cold

and hungry, in the morning the clergyman woke me up, and with-
out saying a word, offered me food and shelter for that night. We
got talking and I asked him that same question. Is God partial? He
said sometimes our suffering only prepares us for a great destiny. I
laughed in his face. How were the men and women who perished in
that boat being prepared for a great destiny? They are dead. Dead.
Is God having a laugh somewhere in His living room, playing chess,
or watching TV, oh, I see, we are the TV, a reality show about sur-
vival. I get to thinking like that, sometimes, but then I tell myself,
Hey, at least I survived, I made it.

I did mention this was going to be a long letter. But now I am
almost at the end. I have already told you some of the story, how we
were trapped in a building in Greece for two days without food, I and
a friend of mine, Hassan the Afghan. He it was who told me of Eng-
land, and said we must make that our target. But first, we needed
to raise some money, which is why we were working in that farm
picking strawberries. I remember those two days in that abandoned
building, and I remember the sounds of the skinheads' voices at night,
their footfalls as they walked around, waiting for us to come out, I
remember the smell of fear and sweat on our bodies. Sometimes we
would crawl to the window and look into the square at the restaurant
where people sat dining, smell the aroma of food wafting up when the
wind blew in our direction, driving us mad with hunger.

We eventually made it to Calais in France, through Germany.

Hassan had some contacts in Calais, and he said from there to
England was a very short distance. He made it sound so easy, and
so I wasn't prepared for what I met there. They called the place 'the
Jungle', and it was a jungle. The day we got there, at the edge of the
camp, we witnessed a fight. A man was stabbed with a knife. Just
like that. An argument had started when one man accused another

of stealing his bicycle, an Indian man, who said no, he just used it to go to the city to buy some grocery and he was returning it. But they started fighting and the other man, an Eritrean, stabbed the other one in the neck. That was our welcome to Calais Jungle. I remember the smell, and the trash, it was everywhere.

Hassan took us to his friends and they started talking in their language, I noticed one of them looking at me suspiciously. They offered him a cup of tea but they did not offer me anything. It is strange, I thought. I said I was going to go out, to ease myself. Now the younger of the men actually talked to me, in English, he said be careful, it is a jungle. He looked as if he was trying to scare me, but I felt grateful for his warning, after all, he was the first person to even notice me. I thanked him, and I walked out. I wanted to see if I could spot a known face, anything. I saw a man, a black man, and I went up to him and asked him where he was from. Why do you want to know? he asked, he looked angry. He looked mad, his eyes were wild and his mouth was so smelly when he came close to me and put his face next to mine. I turned and left. Hey, he shouted after me, hey. I kept on walking. I felt scared looking at him, and I asked myself, was I also like that? Did I smell like that, did I look crazy and I didn't even know it? It had been a while since I took a bath, or ate properly, or changed my clothes.

We were there for only two nights, but the memory of that place will never leave me. I already told you the story of the woman who was once a rich person in her country, Eritrea. She refused to talk to anyone. She would sit in the tent and call out orders, she would call out the names of her maids: Esther, come here right now. Bring me my meal, it is past mealtime, Esther. Or she would tell them to run her bathwater. There she sat, in the doorway of her tent with everyone looking at her curiously, like an empress, surrounded by all the trash and her clothes torn and smelly and the flies all over her. Those who knew her said she had lost everything to the government of her country when she escaped. Houses, cars, and her husband was arrested.

Anyway, we left after two nights, and I was feeling lucky, and thankful, that we had made it. We were led to the trucks where they were camped for the night, far away from the Jungle. What if we were caught, I asked, but the smugglers assured us it had been arranged with the truckers, all we had to do was secure ourselves under the truck and hold tight, and to get off as soon as the trucks entered the UK. But my friend did not make it. He must have fallen asleep, or something must have gone wrong with his harness, all I heard was the scream as the tyre ran over him, and then a wet, squelching noise.

The night before we had stood on the beach in Calais, looking across the water at the lights on the other side. My friend said, That is Dover Beach. He knew a lot about England. His father had studied there, and he had gone to an English school in Afghanistan, it was as if all his life he had been preparing for this moment. 'England,' he said, and there was awe in his voice. He asked me if I knew the famous poem on Dover Beach, and when I said no, he quoted a line, from memory. He said the writer's name is Matthew Arnold. The writer had stood on the opposite shore from where we stood, looking at the French shore. I don't remember all the lines, but there is something about the 'eternal note of sadness'. I know what that means.

Well, that is my story, my friend. That is how I came to England. That is why I left my country. You know the rest. Now I am here, in this remote detention centre, waiting to find out about my fate. Liam and Molly still come to visit me. I still continue with my hun-

ger strike; I have gone a hundred days now without eating. I have no illusions about how this is going to end. The government thinks I am going to relent and give up, I can't. I am tired, actually, and I know in the end this will not change anything, they will continue to detain people, long after I am gone and forgotten. A doctor came to see me. He warned me that my fasting will cause irreparable damage to my body if I continue. He looked worried. He took my blood pressure and looked into my eyes and my mouth and my ears. He was trying to scare me, to make me give up my hunger strike, to break my will. I told him I am fasting not because I want to any more, all that has lost any meaning to me. The truth is I have lost all desire for food. I even try to put something in my mouth, but I always throw up after eating. I can't eat. My teeth are falling out. I can't find any food to my liking. They gave me everything to tempt me, meat, fruit, vegetable, trying to entice me to eat, but I can't keep anything down. I want the perfect food. I tell them I want manna, or ambrosia, the food of the gods themselves, and they thought I was joking, but I am serious. I want the perfect food, but where can I find it here on earth? I want my mother's food, the one I grew up eating. I want the first food I ever ate in this world. I want my mother's milk, but by now I am sure my mother is dead.

The café had quieted down. The game was over; our stay in London was also over, we had only two days left. Tomorrow Portia was meeting with her father's editor, whom she had been able to track online, to hand over the notebooks to her; I had offered to go with her but she said no, this was something she wanted to do alone.

Now she wanted to know if I was coming to Lusaka with her. She stood up and said, –I am going to freshen up, and when I come back I want you to say yes. She leaned over and placed her lips over mine before heading for the restroom. I watched the men's eyes follow her as she made her way across the room. She looked stunning in a knee-length black dress that hugged her hips and emphasized the slenderness of her waist. I felt proud that she was with me, and often I wondered why she chose me when she could have any man she wanted, and why did I hesitate, why couldn't I say yes?

Soon she was back, she sat facing me, she took my hand.
–Have you decided?

I imagined her home in Lusaka, and it was as if I had been there, she had talked about it so much that I could see the school, the jacaranda trees, the children in their neat school uniform. And she would be there with me, every day. But how would I fit in, and would it matter, as long as we were together? Things would fall into place. I stared at her and I marvelled at how much she had changed from the young impulsive girl I first met in Berlin. How beautiful and restrained she had become. She had suffered too, that was why.

–What if I am not who you think I am, what if something has shifted and broken in me since you last saw me?

–We will start from somewhere. Plus, you must admit, you don't seem to do well by yourself. Last time I left you, you ended up in a refugee camp.

•

I thought of Juma, he'd be in his tiny cell at Harmondsworth Removal Centre, perhaps reading, drifting in and out of sleep, too weak to stay awake for long. Liam and Molly will keep visiting him, daily, dutifully, not knowing any more what drives them. They talk about the weather, how summer is almost over. Juma's voice has grown hoarser and flimsier, and the visitors have to draw nearer to hear him. Liam asks him if he needs some water and he says, Yes. He takes a tiny sip, wetting his chapped, shaking lips. Then the lucidity leaves his eyes and they leave him. The next time they come the officials deny them entry, they say he has been moved to another facility, no one knows exactly where, Liam and Molly will protest, they will talk to the lawyer, but eventually they stop coming, worn out, they stop making inquiries, for even the kindest and most empathetic of us can get emotionally fatigued. Liam returns to Norwich to focus on his studies, Molly goes with him to take up a new job at the N&N hospital. The din in the media quietens. Juma sits in his cell, thirsting for mother's milk, unable to eat anything else, he shrinks, he regresses, back to childhood, curled up in a corner foetus-like, his flesh withers, his bones become as frail as twigs. One day the guards open the door and he is not there, only a pile of twigs on the floor. The cleaner comes and sweeps up the twigs and bags them and throws them into the dumpster.

I stood up and helped Portia with her jacket, then I put on mine. I said, –Yes. Let's go.

END

Helon Habila

WAITING FOR AN ANGEL

Lomba is a young journalist living in Lagos under Nigeria's brutal military regime. His mind is full of soul music and girls and the novel he is writing. Yet when his room-mate goes mad and is beaten up by soldiers, his first love is forced to marry a man she doesn't want, and his neighbours are planning a demo that is bound to lead to a riot, Lomba realizes that he can no longer bury his head in the sand. It's time to write the truth about this reign of terror . . .

'An exciting book. The narrative is astonishing, at once tender and embittered, humorous and unforgiving' *Daily Telegraph*

'The culture of poverty, violence and fear is so skilfully and quietly evoked that it is almost palpable . . . The story is peopled with well-drawn, idiosyncratic characters. Deeply moving and memorable' *The Times*

'A telling insight into life under a modern dictatorship and a moving testimony to trials, tribulations, injustices, imprisonments, loves and deaths' *Time Out*

Helon Habila

MEASURING TIME

'Triumphant' *Guardian*

In the small Nigerian village of Keti live Mamo and LaMamo, twin sons of a domineering father. When one day the boys try and escape the village, only LaMamo succeeds and in time becomes a soldier well-versed in the ways of life and death. Mamo, too sickly to leave, remains in Keti finding solace in the arms of Zara while watching impotently as his detested father grows powerful and corrupt. Unable to wield a weapon, Mamo instead reaches for a pen and soon begins to write the true history of Keti and its people – all the time awaiting the return of his beloved brother, LaMamo . . .

'[Habila's] wit, poignancy and gripping storytelling place this novel among the finest works of Nigerian fiction in recent years' *Sunday Times*

'Haunting . . . *Measuring Time* confirms Habila as an exceptional voice in African literature' *Observer*

'Habila's beautifully (and deceptively) simple style is matched by a story that is strong, clear and richly evocative . . . This novel is so bitter, so sweet, so humbling' Helen Oyeyemi, *New Statesman*

Helon Habila

OIL ON WATER

From the desks of Nigeria's newsrooms, two journalists are recruited to find the kidnapped wife of a British oil engineer. Zaq, an infamous media hack, knows what's in store, but Rufus, a keen young journalist eager to get himself noticed, has no idea what he's let himself in for. Journeying into the oil-rich regions of the Niger Delta, where militants rule and the currency dealt in is the lives of hostages, Rufus soon finds himself acting as intermediary between editor, husband, captive and soldier. As they follow the trail of the missing woman, love for the 'story' becomes about much more than just uncovering her whereabouts, and instead becomes a mission to make sense of their own muddled lives. In a cruel twist of fate, Rufus finds himself taking on Zaq's role much more literally than he ever anticipated, and as the body count rises, and the environment burns, he learns that truth can often be a bitter pill to swallow.

'Powerful . . . Accomplished' *Observer*

'Tautly written . . . A vivid evocation of the embattled, disappearing world of the Niger Delta . . . Intelligent, illuminating' *Sunday Times*

'Habila's writing has that combination of elegance and rattling-good-yarn that we associate with Conrad and Graham Greene . . . Terrific' *The Times*

Helon Habila

THE CHIBOK GIRLS: The Boko Haram Kidnappings & Islamic Militancy in Nigeria

On 14 April 2014, 276 girls disappeared from a secondary school in northern Nigeria, kidnapped by the world's deadliest terror group. A tiny number have escaped back to their families but many remain missing. Reporting from inside the traumatized and blockaded community of Chibok, Helon Habila tracks down the survivors and the bereaved. Two years after the attack, he bears witness to their stories and to their grief. And moving from the personal to the political, he presents a comprehensive indictment of Boko Haram, tracing the circumstances of their ascent and the terrible fallout of their ongoing presence in Nigeria.

'This is a controlled, lucid and deeply felt account of Boko Haram's unconscionable kidnappings. This is essential to understanding the tragedy of the Chibok girls' Dave Eggers

'Helon Habila tells us a heartbreaking story about lives lost in anguish. His book will spread the pain and sorrow of the vanquished Chibok women, not to keep us crying, but to energize us to be part of a path that leads to the rescue' Toyin Falola

'Habila [is] an exceptional voice in African literature. His great skill is to imbue the individual and the local with panoramic, historical significance' *Observer*

He just wanted a decent book to read ...

Not too much to ask, is it? It was in 1935 when Allen Lane, Managing Director of Bodley Head Publishers, stood on a platform at Exeter railway station looking for something good to read on his journey back to London. His choice was limited to popular magazines and poor-quality paperbacks – the same choice faced every day by the vast majority of readers, few of whom could afford hardbacks. Lane's disappointment and subsequent anger at the range of books generally available led him to found a company – and change the world.

'We believed in the existence in this country of a vast reading public for intelligent books at a low price, and staked everything on it'
Sir Allen Lane, 1902–1970, founder of Penguin Books

The quality paperback had arrived – and not just in bookshops. Lane was adamant that his Penguins should appear in chain stores and tobacconists, and should cost no more than a packet of cigarettes.

Reading habits (and cigarette prices) have changed since 1935, but Penguin still believes in publishing the best books for everybody to enjoy. We still believe that good design costs no more than bad design, and we still believe that quality books published passionately and responsibly make the world a better place.

So wherever you see the little bird – whether it's on a piece of prize-winning literary fiction or a celebrity autobiography, political tour de force or historical masterpiece, a serial-killer thriller, reference book, world classic or a piece of pure escapism – you can bet that it represents the very best that the genre has to offer.

Whatever you like to read – trust Penguin.